Chunder Shan, entering his chamber, closed the door and went to his table. There he took the letter he had been writing and tore it to bits. Scarcely had he finished when he heard something drop softly onto the parapet adjacent to the window. He looked up to see a figure loom briefly against the stars, and then a man dropped lightly into his room. The light glinted on a long sheen of silver in his hand.

"Shhh!" he warned. "Don't make a noise, or I'll send the Devil a henchman!" . . .

The invader was a tall man, at once strong and supple. He was dressed like a hillman, but his dark features and blazing blue eyes did not match his garb. Chunder Shan had never seen a man like him . . .

"I climbed a bastion," snarled the intruder. "A guard thrust his head over the battlement in time for me to rap it with my knife-hilt."

"You are Conan?". . .

Chronological order of the CONAN series:

CONAN
CONAN OF CIMMERIA
CONAN THE FREEBOOTER
CONAN THE WANDERER
CONAN THE ADVENTURER
CONAN THE BUCCANEER
CONAN THE WARRIOR
CONAN THE USURPER
CONAN THE CONQUEROR
CONAN THE AVENGER
CONAN OF AQUILONIA
CONAN OF THE ISLES

Illustrated CONAN novels:

CONAN AND THE SORCERER
CONAN: THE FLAME KNIFE
CONAN THE MERCENARY
THE TREASURE OF TRANICOS

Other CONAN novels:

THE BLADE OF CONAN
THE SPELL OF CONAN

CONAN

5

THE ADVENTURER

BY ROBERT E. HOWARD AND L. SPRAGUE DE CAMP

ACE FANTASY BOOKS
NEW YORK

Cover painting by Frank Frazetta . . . with grateful acknowledgement to
Roy Krenkel, advisor

The People of the Black Circle was originally published in *Weird Tales* for
September, October, and November, 1934; copyright 1934 by Popular Fic-
tion Publishing Co. It was reprinted in *The Sword of Conan* by Robert E.
Howard, N.Y. Gnome Press, Inc., 1952.

The Slithering Shadow was originally published in *Weird Tales* for September, 1933; copyright 1933 by Popular Fiction Publishing Co. It was
reprinted in *The Sword of Conan.*

Drums of Tombalku is printed here for the first time. In 1965, Glenn Lord,
literary agent for the Howard estate, discovered, in a batch of Howard's
papers, an outline of this story and a rough draft of the first half of it. L.
Sprague de Camp edited the existing text and completed the story according
to Howard's outline.

The Pool of the Black One was originally published in *Weird Tales* for
October, 1933; copyright 1933 by Popular Fiction Publishing Co. It was
reprinted in *The Sword of Conan.*

The biographical paragraphs between the stories are based upon *A Probable
Outline of Conan's Career,* by P. Schuyler Miller and Dr. John D. Clark,
published in *The Hyborian Age* (1938), and on the expanded version of this
essay, *An Informal Biography of Conan the Cimmerian,* by P. Schuyler Miller,
John D. Clark, and L. Sprague de Camp, published in *Amra,* Vol. 2, No. 4,
copyright © 1959 by G. H. Scithers; used by permission of G. H. Scithers.

CONAN THE ADVENTURER

An Ace Fantasy Book / published by arrangement with
Conan Properties, Inc.

PRINTING HISTORY
Twelfth Ace printing / July 1984

ISBN: 0-441-11464-4

Ace Fantasy Books are published by The Berkley Publishing Group,
200 Madison Avenue, New York, New York 10016.
PRINTED IN THE UNITED STATES OF AMERICA

Contents

Pages 6 and 7: A map of the world of Conan in the Hyborian Age, based upon notes and sketches by Robert E. Howard and upon previous maps by P. Schuyler Miller, John D. Clark, David Kyle, and L. Sprague de Camp, with a map of Europe and adjacent regions superimposed for reference.

Introduction

ROBERT ERVIN HOWARD (1906–36) was born and lived most of his life in Cross Plains, Texas. In his short lifetime he turned out a large volume of general pulp-magazine fiction: sport, detective, western, and Oriental adventure stories, besides his many tales of fantasy. Of Howard's several series of heroic fantasies, the most popular have been the Conan stories. These are laid in Howard's imaginary Hyborian Age, between the sinking of Atlantis and the beginnings of recorded history. Howard was a natural story-teller, whose tales are unsurpassed for vivid, colorful, headlong, gripping action. The Conan stories are the ultimate in tales of swashbuckling adventure with a strong and sinister flavor of the supernatural.

Howard wrote over two dozen Conan stories, ranging in length from 3,000 to 66,000 words. Of these, eighteen were published during his lifetime. Several others, from mere outlines to completed manuscripts, have turned up in Howard's scattered papers during the last twenty years. It has been my good fortune to edit these for publication, to complete those that were only partly written, and to re-write several other unpublished Howard stories to fit them into the Conan saga.

One of the stories in this volume, "Drums of Tombalku," was recently discovered by Glenn Lord, the literary agent for the Howard estate, in the form of an outline and a rough draft of the first half. I have finished the story in accordance with the outline. The other three stories, except for a few very small editorial changes, are in the form in which they appeared in *Weird Tales* in the early 1930's.

As nearly as such things can be calculated, Conan flourished about twelve thousand years ago. In this time (according to Howard) the Western parts of the main continent were occupied by the Hyborian kingdoms. These comprised a galaxy of states set up by northern invaders, the Hyborians, three thousand years before on the ruins of the evil empire of Acheron. South of the Hyborian kingdoms lay the quarreling city-states of Shem. Beyond Shem slumbered the ancient, sinister kingdom of Stygia. Farther south yet, beyond deserts and veldts, were barbarous black kingdoms.

North of the Hyborians lay the barbarian lands of Cimmeria, Hyperborea, Vanaheim, and Asgard. West along the ocean were the fierce Picts. To the east glittered the Hykanian kingdoms, of which the mightiest was Turan.

Conan, a gigantic adventurer from backward Cimmeria, arrived as a youth in the kingdom of Zamora, between the Hyborian lands and Turan. For two or three years he made his living as a thief in Zamora, Corinthia, and Nemedia. Growing tired of this starveling existence, he enlisted as a mercenary in the armies of Turan. For the next two years he traveled widely and refined his knowledge of archery and horsemanship.

As a result of a quarrel with a superior officer, Conan left Turan. After an unsuccessful try at treasure-hunting in Zamora and a brief visit to his Cimmerian homeland, he embarked on the career of a mercenary soldier in the Hyborian kingdoms. Circumstances—violent as usual—made him a pirate along the coasts of Kush, where the natives called him Amra, the Lion. When his partner, the Shemitish she-pirate Bêlit, was slain, he became a chief of one of the black tribes. Then he served as a mercenary in Shem and among the most southerly Hyborian kingdoms.

Later still, Conan appeared as a leader of the *kozaks*, a horde of outlaws who roamed the steppes between the Hyborian lands and Turan. He was captain of a pirate craft on the great inland Sea of Vilayet and a chief among the nomadic Zuagirs of the southeastern deserts. After a spell as a mercenary captain in the army of the king of Iranistan, he arrived in the foothills of the Himelian Mountains, a vast stretch of broken country separating Iranistan, Turan, and the tropical kingdom of Vendhya. At that point, the present volume begins.

—L. Sprague de Camp

CONAN
THE ADVENTURER

The People of the Black Circle

Declining the offer of Kobad Shah's successor, Arshak, to return to the service of Iranistan and defend that kingdom against the incursions of King Yezdigerd of Turan, Conan rides east into the foothills of the Himelian Mountains, on the northwest frontier of Vendhya. Here he next appears as a warchief of the savage Afghuli tribesmen. He is now in his early thirties (about thirty-three, in fact), at the height of his physical powers, and known throughout the civilized and barbarian worlds, from Pictland to Khitai.

1. *Death Strikes a King*

THE KING of Vendhya was dying. Through the hot, stifling night the temple gongs boomed and the conchs roared. Their clamor was a faint echo in the gold-domed chamber where Bhunda Chand struggled on the velvet-cushioned dais. Beads of sweat glistened on his dark skin; his fingers twisted the gold-worked fabric beneath him. He was young; no spear had touched him, no poison lurked in his wine. But his veins stood out like blue cords on his temples, and his eyes dilated with the nearness of death. Trembling slave-girls knelt at the foot of the dais, and leaning down on him, watching him with passionate intensity, was his sister, the Devi Yasmina. With her was the *wazam*, a noble grown old in the royal court.

She threw up her head in a gusty gesture of wrath and

13

despair as the thunder of the distant drums reached her ears.

"The priests and their clamor!" she exclaimed. "They are no wiser than the leeches, who are helpless! Nay, he dies and none can say why. He is dying now—and I stand here helpless, who would burn the whole city and spill the blood of thousands to save him."

"Not a man of Ayodhya but would die in his place, if it might be, Devi," answered the *wazam.* "This poison——"

"I tell you it is not poison!" she cried. "Since his birth he has been guarded so closely that the cleverest poisoners of the East could not reach him. Five skulls bleaching on the Tower of the Kites can testify to attempts which were made—and which failed. As you well know, there are ten men and ten women whose sole duty is to taste his food and wine, and fifty armed warriors guard his chamber as they guard it now. No, it is not poison; it is sorcery—black, ghastly magic——"

She ceased as the king spoke; his livid lips did not move, and there was no recognition in his glassy eyes. But his voice rose in an eery call, indistinct and far away, as if he called to her from beyond vast, wind-blown gulfs.

"Yasmina! Yasmina! My sister, where are you? I can not find you. All is darkness, and the roaring of great winds!"

"Brother!" cried Yasmina, catching his limp hand in a convulsive grasp. "I am here! Do you not know me——"

Her voice died at the utter vacancy of his face. A low, confused moaning waned from his mouth. The slave-girls at the foot of the dais whimpered with fear, and Yasmina beat her breast in her anguish.

In another part of the city, a man stood in a latticed balcony overlooking a long street in which torches tossed luridly, smokily revealing upturned dark faces and the whites of gleaming eyes. A long-drawn wailing rose from the multitude.

The man shrugged his broad shoulders and turned back

14

into the arabesqued chamber. He was a tall man, compactly built and richly clad.

"The king is not yet dead, but the dirge is sounded," he said to another man who sat cross-legged on a mat in a corner. This man was clad in a brown camel-hair robe and sandals, and a green turban was on his head. His expression was tranquil, his gaze impersonal.

"The people know he will never see another dawn," this man answered.

The first speaker favored him with a long, searching stare.

"What I can not understand," he said, "is why I have had to wait so long for your masters to strike. If they have slain the king now, why could they not have slain him months ago?"

"Even the arts you call sorcery are governed by cosmic laws," answered the man in the green turban. "The stars direct these actions, as in other affairs. Not even my masters can alter the stars. Not until the heavens were in the proper order could they perform this necromancy." With a long, stained fingernail he mapped the constellations on the marble-tiled floor. "The slant of the moon presaged evil for the king of Vendhya; the stars are in turmoil, the Serpent in the House of the Elephant. During such juxtaposition, the invisible guardians are removed from the spirit of Bhunda Chand. A path is opened in the unseen realms, and once a point of contact was established, mighty powers were put in play along that path."

"Point of contact?" inquired the other. "Do you mean that lock of Bhunda Chand's hair?"

"Yes. All discarded portions of the human body still remain part of it, attached to it by intangible connections. The priests of Asura have a dim inkling of this truth, and so all nail-trimmings, hair, and other waste products of the persons of the royal family are carefully reduced to ashes and the ashes hidden. But at the urgent entreaty of the princess of Kosala, who loved Bhunda Chand vainly, he gave her a lock of his long black hair as a token of remembrance. When my masters de-

15

cided upon his doom, the lock, in its golden, jewel-crusted case, was stolen from under her pillow while she slept, and another substituted, so like the first that she never knew the difference. Then the genuine lock traveled by camel-caravan up the long, long road to Peshkhauri, thence up the Zhaibar Pass, until it reached the hands of those for whom it was intended."

"Only a lock of hair," murmured the nobleman.

"By which a soul is drawn from its body and across gulfs of echoing space," returned the man on the mat.

The nobleman studied him curiously.

"I do not know if you are a man or a demon, Khemsa," he said at last. "Few of us are what we seem. I, whom the Kshatriyas know as Kerim Shah, a prince from Iranistan, am no greater a masquerader than most men. They are all traitors in the one way or another, and half of them know not whom they serve. There at least I have no doubts; for I serve King Yezdigerd of Turan."

"And I the Black Seers of Yimsha," said Khemsa; "and my masters are greater than yours, for they have accomplished by their arts what Yezdigerd could not with a hundred thousand swords."

Outside, the moan of the tortured thousands shuddered up to the stars which crusted the sweating Vendhyan night, and the conchs bellowed like oxen in pain.

In the gardens of the palace the torches glinted on polished helmets and curved swords and gold-chased corselets. All the noble-born fighting-men of Ayodhya were gathered in the great palace or about it, and at each broad-arched gate and door fifty archers stood on guard, with bows in their hands. But Death stalked through the royal palace and none could stay his ghostly tread.

On the dais under the golden dome the king cried out again, racked by awful paroxysms. Again his voice came faintly and far away, and again the Devi bent to him, trembling with a fear that was darker than the terror of death.

"Yasmina!" Again that far, weirdly dreeing cry, from

16

realms immeasurable. "Aid me! I am far from my mortal house! Wizards have drawn my soul through the wind-blown darkness. They seek to snap the silver cord that binds me to my dying body. They cluster around me; their hands are taloned, their eyes are red like flame burning in darkness. *Aie*, save me, my sister! Their fingers sear me like fire! They would slay my body and damn my soul! What is this they bring before me?—*Aie!*"

At the terror in his hopeless cry Yasmina screamed uncontrollably and threw herself bodily upon him in the abandon of her anguish. He was torn by a terrible convulsion; foam flew from his contorted lips and his writhing fingers left their marks on the girl's shoulders. But the glassy blankness passed from his eyes like smoke blown from a fire, and he looked up at his sister with recognition.

"Brother!" she sobbed. "Brother——"

"Swift!" he gasped, and his weakening voice was rational. "I know now what brings me to the pyre. I have been on a far journey and I understand. I have been ensorceled by the wizards of the Himelians. They drew my soul out of my body and far away, into a stone room. There they strove to break the silver cord of life, and thrust my soul into the body of a foul night-weird their sorcery summoned up from Hell. Ah! I feel their pull upon me now! Your cry and the grip of your fingers brought me back, but I am going fast. My soul clings to my body, but its hold weakens. Quick—kill me, before they can trap my soul for ever!"

"I can not!" she wailed, smiting her naked breasts.

"Swiftly, I command you!" There was the old imperious note in his failing whisper. "You have never disobeyed me—obey my last command! Send my soul clean to Asura! Haste, lest you damn me to spend eternity as a filthy gaunt of darkness. Strike, I command you! *Strike!*"

Sobbing wildly, Yasmina plucked a jeweled dagger from her girdle and plunged it to the hilt in his breast. He stiffened and then went limp, a grim smile curving his dead lips. Yasmina hurled herself face-down on the rush-covered floor, beating the reeds with her clenched hands. Outside, the gongs and conchs brayed and thundered and the priests gashed themselves with copper knives.

2. A Barbarian from the Hills

Chunder Shan, governor of Peshkauri, laid down his golden pen and carefully scanned that which he had written on parchment that bore his official seal. He had ruled Peshkauri so long only because he weighed his every word, spoken or written. Danger breeds caution, and only a wary man lives long in that wild country where the hot Vendhyan plains meet the crags of the Himelians. An hour's ride westward or northward and one crossed the border and was among the Hills where men lived by the law of the knife.

The governor was alone in his chamber, seated at his ornately-carven table of inlaid ebony. Through the wide window, open for the coolness, he could see a square of the blue Himelian night, dotted with great white stars. An adjacent parapet was a shadowy line, and further crenelles and embrasures were barely hinted at in the dim starlight. The governor's fortress was strong, and situated outside the walls of the city it guarded. The breeze that stirred the tapestries on the wall brought faint noises from the streets of Peshkhauri—occasional snatches of wailing song, or the thrum of a cithern.

The governor read what he had written, slowly, with his open hand shading his eyes from the bronze butter-lamp, his lips moving. Absently, as he read, he heard the drum of horses' hoofs outside the barbican, the sharp staccato of the guards' challenge. He did not heed, intent upon his letter. It was addressed to the *wazam* of Vendhya, at the royal court of Ayodhya, and it stated, after the customary salutations:

Let it be known to your Excellency that I have faithfully carried out your Excellency's instructions. The

18

seven tribesmen are well guarded in their prison, and I have repeatedly sent word into the hills that their chief come in person to bargain for their release. But he has made no move, except to send word that unless they are freed he will burn Peshkhauri and cover his saddle with my hide, begging your Excellency's indulgence. This he is quite capable of attempting, and I have tripled the numbers of the lance guards. The man is not a native of Ghulistan. I can not with certainty predict his next move. But since it is the wish of the Devi——

He was out of his ivory chair and on his feet facing the arched door, all in one instant. He snatched at the curved sword lying in its ornate scabbard on the table, and then checked the movement.

It was a woman who had entered unannounced, a woman whose gossamer robes did not conceal the rich garments beneath any more than they concealed the suppleness and beauty of her tall, slender figure. A filmy veil fell below her breasts, supported by a flowing headdress bound about with a triple gold braid and adorned with a golden crescent. Her dark eyes regarded the astonished governor over the veil, and then with an imperious gesture of her white hand, she uncovered her face.

"Devi!" The governor dropped to his knee before her, his surprise and confusion somewhat spoiling the stateliness of his obeisance. With a gesture she motioned him to rise, and he hastened to lead her to the ivory chair, all the while bowing level with his girdle. But his first words were of reproof.

"Your Majesty! This was most unwise! The border is unsettled. Raids from the hills are incessant. You came with a large attendance?"

"An ample retinue followed me to Peshkhauri," she answered. "I lodged my people there and came on to the fort with my maid, Gitara."

Chunder Shan groaned in horror.

"Devi! You do not understand the peril. An hour's ride

19

from this spot, the hills swarm with barbarians who make a profession of murder and rapine. Women have been stolen and men stabbed between the fort and the city. Peshkhauri is not like your southern provinces——"

"But I am here, and unharmed," she interrupted with a trace of impatience. "I showed my signet ring to the guard at the gate, and to the one outside your door, and they admitted me unannounced, not knowing me, but supposing me to be a secret courier from Ayodhya. Let us not now waste time. You have received no word from the chief of the barbarians?"

"None save threats and curses, Devi. He is wary and suspicious. He deems it a trap, and perhaps he is not to be blamed. The Kshatriyas have not always kept their promises to the hill people."

"He must be brought to terms!" broke in Yasmina, the knuckles of her clenched hands showing white.

"I do not understand." The governor shook his head. "When I chanced to capture these seven hillmen, I reported their capture to the *wazam*, as is the custom, and then, before I could hang them, there came an order to hold them and communicate with their chief. This I did, but the man holds aloof, as I have said. These men are of the tribe of Afghulis, but he is a foreigner from the West, and he is called Conan. I have threatened to hang them tomorrow at dawn, if he does not come."

"Good!" exclaimed the Devi. "You have done well. And I will tell you why I have given these orders. My brother——" she faltered, choking, and the governor bowed his head, with the customary gesture of respect for a departed sovereign.

"The king of Vendhya was destroyed by magic," she said at last. "I have devoted my life to the destruction of his murderers. As he died he gave me a clue, and I have followed it. I have read the Book of Skelos, and talked with nameless hermits in the caves below Jhelai. I learned how, and by whom, he was destroyed. His enemies were the Black Seers of Mount Yimsha."

"Asura!" whispered Chunder Shan, paling.

20

Her eyes knifed him through. "Do you fear them?"

"Who does not, your Majesty?" he replied. "They are black devils, haunting the uninhabited hills beyond the Zhaibar. But the sages say that they seldom interfere in the lives of mortal men."

"Why they slew my brother I do not know," she answered. "But I have sworn on the altar of Asura to destroy them! And I need the aid of a man beyond the border. A Kshatriya army, unaided, would never reach Yimsha."

"Aye," muttered Chunder Shan. "You speak the truth there. It would be fight every step of the way, with hairy hillmen hurling down boulders from every height, and rushing us with their long knives in every valley. The Turanians fought their way through the Himelians once, but how many returned to Khurusun? Few of those who escaped the swords of the Kshatriyas, after the king, your brother, defeated their host on the Jhumda River, ever saw Secunderam again."

"And so I must control men across the border," she said, "men who know the way to Mount Yimsha——"

"But the tribes fear the Black Seers and shun the unholy mountain," broke in the governor.

"Does the chief, Conan, fear them?" she asked.

"Well, as to that," muttered the governor, "I doubt if there is anything that devil fears."

"So I have been told. Therefore he is the man I must deal with. He wishes the release of his seven men. Very well; their ransom shall be the heads of the Black Seers!" Her voice thrummed with hate as she uttered the last words, and her hands clenched at her sides. She looked an image of incarnate passion as she stood there with her head thrown high and her bosom heaving.

Again the governor knelt, for part of his wisdom was the knowledge that a woman in such an emotional tempest is as perilous as a blind cobra to any about her.

"It shall be as you wish, your Majesty." Then as she presented a calmer aspect, he rose and ventured to drop a word of warning. "I can not predict what the chief Conan's action will be. The tribesmen are always turbu-

21

lent, and I have reason to believe that emissaries from the Turanians are stirring them up to raid our borders. As your majesty knows, the Turanians have established themselves in Secunderam and other northern cities, though the hill tribes remain unconquered. King Yezdigerd has long looked southward with greedy lust and perhaps is seeking to gain by treachery what he could not win by force of arms. I have thought that Conan might well be one of his spies."

"We shall see," she answered. "If he loves his followers, he will be at the gates at dawn, to parley. I shall spend the night in the fortress. I came in disguise to Peshkhauri, and lodged my retinue at an inn instead of the palace. Besides my people, only yourself knows of my presence here."

"I shall escort you to your quarters, your Majesty," said the governor, and as they emerged from the doorway, he beckoned the warrior on guard there, and the man fell in behind them, spear held at salute.

The maid waited, veiled like her mistress, outside the door, and the group traversed a wide, winding corridor, lighted by smoky torches, and reached the quarters reserved for visiting notables—generals and viceroys, mostly; none of the royal family had ever honored the fortress before. Chunder Shan had a perturbed feeling that the suite was not suitable to such an exalted personage as the Devi, and though she sought to make him feel at ease in her presence, he was glad when she dismissed him and he bowed himself out. All the menials of the fort had been summoned to serve his royal guest—though he did not divulge her identity—and he stationed a squad of spearmen before her doors, among them the warrior who had guarded his own chamber. In his preoccupation he forgot to replace the man.

The governor had not been gone long from her when Yasmina suddenly remembered something else which she had wished to discuss with him, but had forgotten until that moment. It concerned the past actions of

22

one Kerim Shah, a nobleman from Iranistan, who had dwelt for a while in Peshkhauri before coming on to the court at Ayodhya. A vague suspicion concerning the man had been stirred by a glimpse of him in Peshkhauri that night. She wondered if he had followed her from Ayodhya. Being a truly remarkable Devi, she did not summon the governor to her again, but hurried out into the corridor, and hastened toward his chamber.

Chunder Shan, entering his chamber, closed the door and went to his table. There he took the letter he had been writing and tore it to bits. Scarcely had he finished when he heard something drop softly onto the parapet adjacent to the window. He looked up to see a figure loom briefly against the stars, and then a man dropped lightly into the room. The light glinted on a long sheen of steel in his hand.

"Shhhh!" he warned. "Don't make a noise, or I'll send the Devil a henchman!"

The governor checked his motion toward the sword on the table. He was within reach of the yard-long Zhaibar knife that glittered in the intruder's fist, and he knew the desperate quickness of a hillman.

The invader was a tall man, at once strong and supple. He was dressed like a hillman, but his dark features and blazing blue eyes did not match his garb. Chunder Shan had never seen a man like him; he was not an Easterner, but some barbarian from the West. But his aspect was as untamed and formidable as any of the hairy tribesmen who haunt the hills of Ghulistan.

"You come like a thief in the night," commented the governor, recovering some of his composure, although he remembered that there was no guard within call. Still, the hillman could not know that.

"I climbed a bastion," snarled the intruder. "A guard thrust his head over the battlement in time for me to rap it with my knife-hilt."

"You are Conan?"

"Who else? You sent word into the hills that you

23

wished for me to come and parley with you. Well, by Crom, I've come! Keep away from that table or I'll gut you."

"I merely wish to seat myself," answered the governor, carefully sinking into the ivory chair, which he wheeled away from the table. Conan moved restlessly before him, glancing suspiciously at the door, thumbing the razor edge of his three-foot knife. He did not walk like an Afghuli, and was bluntly direct where the East is subtle.

"You have seven of my men," he said abruptly. "You refused the ransom I offered. What the devil do you want?"

"Let us discuss terms," answered Chunder Shan cautiously.

"Terms?" There was a timbre of dangerous anger in his voice. "What do you mean? Haven't I offered you gold?"

Chunder Shan laughed.

"Gold? There is more gold in Peshkhauri than you ever saw."

"You're a liar," retorted Conan. "I've seen the *suk* of the goldsmiths in Khurusun."

"Well, more than any Afghuli ever saw," amended Chunder Shan. "And it is but a drop of all the treasure of Vendhya. Why should we desire gold? It would be more to our advantage to hang these seven thieves."

Conan ripped out a sulfurous oath and the long blade quivered in his grip as the muscles rose in ridges on his brown arm.

"I'll split your head like a ripe melon!"

A wild blue flame flickered in the hillman's eyes, but Chunder Shan shrugged his shoulders, though keeping an eye on the keen steel.

"You can kill me easily, and probably escape over the wall afterward. But that would not save the seven tribesmen. My men would surely hang them. And these men are headmen among the Afghulis."

"I know it," snarled Conan. "The tribe is baying like wolves at my heels because I have not procured their

24

release. Tell me in plain words what you want, because, by Crom! if there's no other way, I'll raise a horde and lead it to the very gates of Peshkhauri!"

Looking at the man as he stood squarely, knife in fist and eyes glaring, Chunder Shan did not doubt that he was capable of it. The governor did not believe any hill-horde could take Peshkhauri, but he did not wish a devastated countryside.

"There is a mission you must perform," he said, choosing his words with as much care as if they had been razors. "There——"

Conan had sprung back, wheeling to face the door at the same instant, lips asnarl. His barbarian ears had caught the quick tread of soft slippers outside the door. The next instant the door was thrown open and a slim, silk-robed form entered hastily, pulling the door shut—then stopping short at sight of the hillman.

Chunder Shan sprang up, his heart jumping into his mouth.

"Devil!" he cried involuntarily, losing his head momentarily in his fright.

"*Devil!*" It was like an explosive echo from the hillman's lips. Chander Shan saw recognition and intent flame up in the fierce blue eyes.

The governor shouted desperately and caught at his sword, but the hillman moved with the devastating speed of a hurricane. He sprang, knocked the governor sprawling with a savage blow of his knife-hilt, swept up the astounded Devi in one brawny arm and leaped for the window. Chunder Shan, struggling frantically to his feet, saw the man poise an instant on the sill in a flutter of silken skirts and white limbs that was his royal captive, and heard his fierce, exultant snarl: "Now dare to hang my men!" and then Conan leaped to the parapet and was gone. A wild scream floated back to the governor's ears.

"Guard! *Guard!*" screamed the governor, struggling up and running drunkenly to the door. He tore it open and reeled into the hall. His shouts re-echoed along the corridors, and warriors came running, gaping to see the governor holding his broken head, from which the blood streamed.

"Turn out the lancers!" he roared. "There has been an abduction!" Even in his frenzy he had enough sense left to withhold the full truth. He stopped short as he heard a sudden drum of hoofs outside, a frantic scream and a wild yell of barbaric exultation.

Followed by the bewildered guardsmen, the governor raced for the stair. In the courtyard of the fort a force of lancers always stood by saddled steeds, ready to ride at an instant's notice. Chunder Shan led his squadron flying after the fugitive, though his head swam so he had to hold with both hands to the saddle. He did not divulge the identity of the victim, but said merely that the noblewoman who had borne the royal signet ring had been carried away by the chief of the Afghulis. The abductor was out of sight and hearing, but they knew the path he would strike—the road that runs straight to the mouth of the Zhaibar. There was no moon; peasant huts rose dimly in the starlight. Behind them fell away the grim bastion of the fort, and the towers of Peshkhauri. Ahead of them loomed the black walls of the Himelians.

3. *Khemsa Uses Magic*

In the confusion that reigned in the fortress while the guard was being turned out, no one noticed that the girl who had accompanied the Devi slipped out the great arched gate and vanished in the darkness. She ran straight for the city, her garments tucked high. She did not follow the open road, but cut straight through fields and over slopes, avoiding fences and leaping irrigation ditches as surely as if it were broad daylight, and as easily as if she were a trained masculine runner. The hoof-drum of the guardsmen had faded away up the hill road before she reached the city wall. She did not go to the great gate, beneath whose arch men leaned on spears and craned their

26

necks into the darkness, discussing the unwonted activity about the fortress. She skirted the wall until she reached a certain point where the spire of a tower was visible above the battlements. Then she placed her hands to her mouth and voiced a low, weird call that carried strangely.

Almost instantly a head appeared at an embrasure and a rope came wriggling down the wall. She seized it, placed a foot in the loop at the end, and waved her arm. Then quickly and smoothly she was drawn up the sheer stone curtain. An instant later she scrambled over the merlons and stood up on a flat roof which covered a house that was built against the wall. There was an open trap there, and a man in a camel-hair robe who silently coiled the rope, not showing in any way the strain of hauling a full-grown woman up a forty-foot wall.

"Where is Kerim Shah?" she gasped, panting after her long run.

"Asleep in the house below. You have news?"

"Conan has stolen the Devi out of the fortress and carried her away into the hills!" She blurted out her news in a rush, the words stumbling over one another.

Khemsa showed no emotion, but merely nodded his turbaned head. "Kerim Shah will be glad to hear that," he said.

"Wait!" The girl threw her supple arms about his neck. She was panting hard, but not only from exertion. Her eyes blazed like black jewels in the starlight. Her upturned face was close to Khemsa's, but though he submitted to her embrace, he did not return it.

"Do not tell the Hyrkanian!" she panted. "Let us use this knowledge ourselves! The governor has gone into the hills with his riders, but he might as well chase a ghost. He has not told anyone that it was the Devi who was kidnapped. None in Peshkhauri or the fort knows it except us."

"But what good does it do us?" the man expostulated. "My masters sent me with Kerim Shah to aid him in every way——"

"Aid yourself!" she cried fiercely. "Shake off your yoke!"

"You mean—disobey my masters?" he gasped, and she felt his whole body turn cold under her arms.

"Aye!" she shook him in the fury of her emotion. "You too are a magician! Why will you be a slave, using your powers only to elevate others? Use your arts for yourself!"

"That is forbidden!" He was shaking as if with an ague. "I am not one of the Black Circle. Only by the command of the masters do I dare to use the knowledge they have taught me."

"But you *can* use it!" she argued passionately. "Do as I beg you! Of course Conan has taken the Devi to hold as hostage against the seven tribesmen in the governor's prison. Destroy them, so Chunder Shan can not use them to buy back the Devi. Then let us go into the mountains and take her from the Afghulis. They can not stand against your sorcery with their knives. The treasure of the Vendhyan kings will be ours as ransom—and then when we have it in our hands, we can trick them, and sell her to the king of Turan. We shall have wealth beyond our maddest dreams. With it we can buy warriors. We will take Khorbhul, oust the Turanians from the hills, and send our hosts southward; become king and queen of an empire!"

Khemsa too was panting, shaking like a leaf in her grasp; his face showed gray in the starlight, beaded with great drops of perspiration.

"I love you!" she cried fiercely, writhing her body against his, almost strangling him in her wild embrace, shaking him in her abandon. "I will make a king of you! For love of you I betrayed my mistress; for love of me betray your masters! Why fear the Black Seers? By your love for me you have broken one of their laws already! Break the rest! You are as strong as they!"

A man of ice could not have withstood the searing heat of her passion and fury. With an inarticulate cry he crushed her to him, bending her backward and showering gasping kisses on her eyes, face, and lips.

28

"I'll do it!" His voice was thick with laboring emotions. He staggered like a drunken man. "The arts they have taught me shall work for me, not for my masters. We shall be rulers of the world—of the world——"

"Come then!" Twisting lithely out of his embrace, she seized his hand and led him toward the trap-door. "First we must make sure that the governor does not exchange those seven Afghulis for the Devi."

He moved like a man in a daze, until they had descended a ladder and she paused in the chamber below. Kerim Shah lay on a couch motionless, an arm across his face as though to shield his sleeping eyes from the soft light of a brass lamp. She plucked Khemsa's arm and made a quick gesture across her own throat. Khemsa lifted his hand; then his expression changed and he drew away.

"I have eaten his salt," he muttered. "Besides, he can not interfere with us."

He led the girl through a door that opened on a winding stair. After their soft tread had faded into silence, the man on the couch sat up. Kerim Shah wiped the sweat from his face. A knife-thrust he did not dread, but he feared Khemsa as a man fears a poisonous reptile.

"People who plot on roofs should remember to lower their voices," he muttered. "But as Khemsa has turned against his masters, and as he was my only contact with them, I can count on their aid no longer. From now on I play the game in my own way."

Rising to his feet he went quickly to a table, drew pen and parchment from his girdle, and scribbled a few succinct lines:

To Khosru Khan, governor of Secunderam: the Cimmerian Conan has carried the Devi Yasmina to the villages of the Afghulis. It is an opportunity to get the Devi into our hands, as the king has so long desired. Send three thousand horsemen at once. I will meet them in the Valley of Gurashah with native guides.

And he signed it with a name that was not in the least like Kerim Shah.

Then from a golden cage he drew forth a carrier pigeon, to whose leg he made fast the parchment, rolled into a tiny cylinder and secured with gold wire. Then he went quickly to a casement and tossed the bird into the night. It wavered on fluttering wings, balanced, and was gone like a flitting shadow. Catching up helmet, sword, and cloak, Kerim Shah hurried out of the chamber and down the winding stair.

The prison quarters of Peshkhauri were separated from the rest of the city by a massive wall, in which was set a single iron-bound door under an arch. Over the arch burned a lurid red cresset, and beside the door squatted a warrior with spear and shield.

This warrior, leaning on his spear, and yawning from time to time, started suddenly to his feet. He had not thought he had dozed, but a man was standing before him, a man he had not heard approach. The man wore a camel-hair robe and a green turban. In the flickering light of the cresset his features were shadowy, but a pair of lambent eyes shone surprisingly in the lurid glow.

"Who comes?" demanded the warrior, presenting his spear. "Who are you?"

The stranger did not seem perturbed, though the spear-point touched his bosom. His eyes held the warrior's with strange intensity.

"What are you obliged to do?" he asked, strangely.

"To guard the gate!" The warrior spoke thickly and mechanically; he stood rigid as a statue, his eyes slowly glazing.

"You lie! You are obliged to obey me! You have looked into my eyes, and your soul is no longer your own. Open that door!"

Stiffly, with the wooden features of an image, the guard wheeled about, drew a great key from his girdle, turned it in the massive lock, and swung open the door. Then he stood at attention, his unseeing stare straight ahead of him.

A woman glided from the shadows and laid an eager hand on the mesmerist's arm.

"Bid him fetch us horses, Khemsa," she whispered.

"No need of that," answered the Rakhsha. Lifting his voice slightly he spoke to the guardsman. "I have no more use for you. Kill yourself!"

Like a man in a trance, the warrior thrust the butt of his spear against the base of the wall and placed the keen head against his body, just below the ribs. Then slowly, stolidly, he leaned against it with all his weight, so that it transfixed his body and came out between his shoulders. Sliding down the shaft he lay still, the spear jutting above him its full length, like a horrible stalk growing out of his back.

The girl stared down at him in morbid fascination, until Khemsa took her arm and led her through the gate. Torches lighted a narrow space between the outer wall and a lower inner one, in which were arched doors at regular intervals. A warrior paced this enclosure, and when the gate opened he came sauntering up, so secure in his knowledge of the prison's strength that he was not suspicious until Khemsa and the girl emerged from the archway. Then it was too late. The Rahksha did not waste time in hypnotism, though his action savored of magic to the girl. The guard lowered his spear threateningly, opening his mouth to shout an alarm that would bring spearmen swarming out of the guardrooms at either end of the alleyway. Khemsa flicked the spear aside with his left hand, as a man might flick a straw, and his right flashed out and back, seeming gently to caress the warrior's neck in passing. And the guard pitched on his face without a sound, his head lolling on a broken neck.

Khemsa did not glance at him, but went straight to one of the arched doors and placed his open hand against the heavy bronze lock. With a rending shudder the portal buckled inward. As the girl followed him through, she saw that the thick teakwood hung in splinters, the bronze bolts were bent and twisted from their sockets, and the great hinges broken and disjointed. A thousand-pound battering-ram with forty men to swing it could have shattered the barrier no more completely. Khemsa was drunk with freedom and the exercise of his power, glorying in his might and flinging his strength about as a young giant exercises his thews with unnecessary vigor in the exultant pride of his prowess.

The broken door let them into a small courtyard, lit by a cresset. Opposite the door was a wide grille of iron bars. A hairy hand was visible, gripping one of these bars, and in the darkness behind them glimmered the whites of eyes.

Khemsa stood silent for a space, gazing into the shadows from which those glimmering eyes gave back his stare with burning intensity. Then his hand went into his robe and came out again, and from his opening fingers a shimmering feather of sparkling dust shifted to the flags. Instantly a flare of green fire lighted the enclosure. In the brief glare the forms of seven men, standing motionless behind the bars, were limned in vivid detail; tall, hairy men in ragged hillmen's garments. They did not speak, but in their eyes blazed the fear of death, and their hairy fingers gripped the bars.

The fire died out but the glow remained, a quivering ball of lambent green that pulsed and shimmered on the flags before Khemsa's feet. The wide gaze of the tribesmen was fixed upon it. It wavered, elongated; it turned into a luminous green smoke spiraling upward. It twisted and writhed like a great shadowy serpent, then broadened and billowed out in shining folds and whirls. It grew to a cloud moving silently over the flags—straight toward the grille. The men watching its coming with dilated eyes; the bars quivered with the grip of their desperate fingers. Bearded lips parted but no sound came forth. The green cloud rolled on the bars and blotted them from sight. Like a fog it oozed through the grille and hid the men within. From the enveloping folds came a strangled gasp, as of a man plunged suddenly under the surface of water. That was all.

32

Khemsa touched the girl's arm, as she stood with parted lips and dilated eyes. Mechanically she turned away with him, looking back over her shoulder. Already the mist was thinning; close to the bars she saw a pair of sandaled feet, the toes turned upward—she glimpsed the indistinct outlines of seven still, prostrate shapes.

"And now for a steed swifter than the fastest horse ever bred in a mortal stable," Khemsa was saying. "We will be in Afghulistan before dawn."

4. An Encounter in the Pass

Yasmina Devi could never clearly remember the details of her abduction. The unexpectedness and violence stunned her; she had only a confused impression of a whirl of happenings—the terrifying grip of a mighty arm, the blazing eyes of her abductor, and his hot breath burning on her flesh. The leap through the window to the parapet, the mad race across battlements and roofs when the fear of falling froze her, the reckless descent of a rope bound to a merlon—he went down almost at a run, his captive folded limply over his brawny shoulder—all this was a befuddled tangle in the Devi's mind. She retained a more vivid memory of him running fleetly into the shadows of the trees, carrying her like a child, and vaulting into the saddle of a fierce Bhalkhana stallion which reared and snorted. Then there was a sensation of flying, and the racing hoofs were striking sparks of fire from the flinty road as the stallion swept up the slopes.

As the girl's mind cleared, her first sensations were furious rage and shame. She was appalled. The rulers of the golden kingdoms south of the Himelians were considered little short of divine; and she was the Devi of Vendyha! Fright was submerged in regal wrath. She cried out furiously and began struggling. She, Yasmina, to be carried on the saddle-bow of a hill chief, like a common wench of the market place! He merely hardened his massive thews slightly against her writhings, and for the first time in her life she experienced the coercion of superior physical strength. His arms felt like iron about her slender limbs. He glanced down at her and grinned hugely. His teeth glimmered whitely in the starlight. The reins lay loose on the stallion's flowing mane, and every thew and fiber of the great beast strained as he hurtled along the bolder-strewn trail. But Conan sat easily, almost carelessly, in the saddle, riding like a centaur.

"You hill-bred dog!" she panted, quivering with the impact of shame, anger, and the realization of helplessness. "You dare—you *dare!* Your life shall pay for this! Where are you taking me?"

"To the villages of Afghulistan," he answered, casting a glance over his shoulder.

Behind them, beyond the slopes they had traversed, torches were tossing on the walls of the fortress, and he glimpsed a flare of light that meant the great gate had been opened. And he laughed a deep-throated boom gusty as the hill wind.

"The Governor has sent his riders after us," he laughed. "By Crom, we will lead him a merry chase! What do you think, Devi—will they pay seven lives for a Kshatriya princess?"

"They will send an army to hang you and your spawn of devils," she promised him with conviction.

He laughed gustily and shifted her to a more comfortable position in his arms. But she took this as a fresh outrage, and renewed her vain struggles, until she saw that her efforts were only amusing him. Besides, her light silken garments, floating on the wind, were being outrageously disarranged by her struggles. She concluded that a scornful submission was the better part of dignity, and lapsed into a smoldering quiescence.

She felt even her anger being submerged by awe as they entered the mouth of the Pass, lowering like a black well mouth in the blacker walls that rose like colossal ramparts to bar their way. It was as if a gigantic knife had cut the Zhaïbar out of walls of solid rock. On either hand sheer slopes pitched up for thousands of feet, and the mouth of the Pass was dark as hate. Even Conan could not see with any accuracy, but he knew the road, even by night. And knowing that armed men were racing through the starlight after him, he did not check the stallion's speed. The great brute was not yet showing fatigue. He thundered along the road that followed the valley bed, labored up a slope, swept along a low ridge where treacherous shale on either hand lurked for the unwary, and came upon a trail that followed the lap of the left-hand wall.

Not even Conan could spy, in that darkness, an ambush set by Zhaibar tribesmen. As they swept past the black mouth of a gorge that opened into the Pass, a javelin swished through the air and thudded home behind the stallion's straining shoulder. The great beast let out his life in a shuddering sob and stumbled, going headlong in mid-stride. But Conan had recognized the flight and stroke of the javelin, and he acted with spring-steel quickness.

As the horse fell he leaped clear, holding the girl aloft to guard her from striking boulders. He lit on his feet like a cat, thrust her into a cleft of rock, and wheeled toward the outer darkness, drawing his knife.

Yasmina, confused by the rapidity of events, not quite sure just what had happened, saw a vague shape rush out of the darkness, bare feet slapping softly on the rock, ragged garments whipping on the wind of his haste. She glimpsed the flicker of steel, heard the lightning crack of stroke, parry, and counter-stroke, and the crunch of bone as Conan's long knife split the other's skull.

Conan sprang back, crouching in the shelter of the rocks. Out in the night men were moving and a stentorian voice roared: "What, you dogs! Do you flinch? In, curse you, and take them!"

Conan started, peered into the darkness and lifted his voice.

"Yar Afzal! Is it you?"

There sounded a startled imprecation, and the voice called warily.

"Conan? Is that you, Conan?"

"Aye!" The Cimmerian laughed. "Come forth, you old war-dog. I've slain one of your men."

There was movement among the rocks, a light flared dimly, and then a flame appeared and came bobbing toward him, and as it approached, a fierce bearded countenance grew out of the darkness. The man who carried it held it high, thrust forward, and craned his neck to peer among the boulders it lighted; the other hand gripped a great curved tulwar. Conan stepped forward, sheathing his knife, and the other roared a greeting.

"Aye, it is Conan! Come out of your rocks, dogs! It is Conan!"

Others pressed into the wavering circle of light—wild, ragged, bearded men, with eyes like wolves, and long blades in their fists. They did not see Yasmina, for she was hidden by Conan's massive body. But peeping from her covert, she knew icy fear for the first time that night. These men were more like wolves than human beings.

"What are you hunting in the Zhaïbar by night, Yar Afzal?" Conan demanded of the burly chief, who grinned like a bearded ghoul.

"Who knows what might come up the Pass after dark? We Wazulis are nighthawks. But what of you, Conan?"

"I have a prisoner," answered the Cimmerian. And moving aside he disclosed the cowering girl. Reaching a long arm into the crevice he drew her trembling forth.

Her imperious bearing was gone. She stared timidly at the ring of bearded faces that hemmed her in, and was grateful for the strong arm that clasped her possessively. The torch was thrust close to her, and there was a sucking intake of breath about the ring.

"She is my captive," Conan warned, glancing pointedly at the feet of the man he had slain, just visible within the ring of light. "I was taking her to Afghulistan, but now you have slain my horse, and the Kshatriyas are close behind me."

"Come with us to my village," suggested Yar Afzal.

36

"We have horses hidden in the gorge. They can never follow us in the darkness. They are close behind you, you say?"

"So close that I hear now the clink of their hoofs on the flint," answered Conan grimly.

Instantly there was movement; the torch was dashed out and the ragged shapes melted like phantoms into the darkness. Conan swept up the Devi in his arms, and she did not resist. The rocky ground hurt her slim feet in their soft slippers and she felt very small and helpless in that brutish, primordial blackness among those colossal, nighted crags.

Feeling her shiver in the wind that moaned down the defiles, Conan jerked a ragged cloak from its owner's shoulders and wrapped it about her. He also hissed a warning in her ear, ordering her to make no sound. She did not hear the distant clink of shod hoofs on rock that warned the keen-eared hillmen; but she was far too frightened to disobey, in any event.

She could see nothing but a few faint stars far above, but she knew by the deepening darkness when they entered the gorge mouth. There was a stir about them, the uneasy movement of horses. A few muttered words, and Conan mounted the horse of the man he had killed, lifting the girl up in front of him. Like phantoms except for the click of their hoofs, the band swept away up the shadowy gorge. Behind them on the trail they left the dead horse and the dead man, which were found less than half an hour later by the riders from the fortress, who recognized the man as a Wazuli and drew their own conclusions accordingly.

Yasmina, snuggled warmly in her captor's arms, grew drowsy in spite of herself. The motion of the horse, though it was uneven, uphill and down, yet possessed a certain rhythm which combined with weariness and emotional exhaustion to force sleep upon her. She had lost all sense of time or direction. They moved in soft thick darkness, in which she sometimes glimpsed vaguely gigantic walls sweeping up like black ramparts, or great crags shouldering the stars; at times she sensed echoing depths beneath them, or felt the wind of dizzy heights blowing cold about her. Gradually these things faded into a dreamy unwakefulness in which the clink of hoofs and the creak of saddles were like the irrelevant sounds in a dream.

She was vaguely aware when the motion ceased and she was lifted down and carried a few steps. There she was laid down on something soft and rustling, and something—a folded coat, perhaps—was thrust under her head, and the cloak in which she was wrapped was carefully tucked about her. She heard Yar Afzal laugh.

"A rare prize, Conan; fit mate for a chief of the Afghulis."

"Not for me," came Conan's answering rumble. "This wench will buy the lives of my seven headmen, blast their souls."

That was the last she heard as she sank into dreamless slumber.

She slept while armed men rode through the dark hills; and the fate of kingdoms hung in the balance. Through the shadowy gorges and defiles that night there rang the hoofs of galloping horses, and the starlight glimmered on helmets and curved blades, until the ghoulish shapes that haunt the crags stared into the darkness from ravine and boulder and wondered what things were afoot.

A band of these sat gaunt horses in the black pit-mouth of a gorge as the hurrying hoofs swept past. Their leader, a well-built man in a helmet and gilt-braided cloak, held up his hand warningly, until the riders had sped on. Then he laughed softly.

"They must have lost the trail! Or else they have found that Conan has already reached the Afghuli villages. It will take many riders to smoke out that hive. There will be squadrons riding up the Zhaibar by dawn."

"If there is fighting in the hills there will be looting," muttered a voice behind him, in the dialect of the Irakzai.

"There will be looting," answered the man with the helmet. "But first it is our business to reach the valley of

Gurashah and await the riders that will be galloping southward from Secunderam before daylight."

He lifted his reins and rode out of the defile, his men falling in behind him—thirty ragged phantoms in the starlight.

5. *The Black Stallion*

The sun was well up when Yasmina awoke. She did not start and stare blankly, wondering where she was. She awoke with full knowledge of all that had occurred. Her supple limbs were stiff from her long ride, and her firm flesh still seemed to feel the contact of the muscular arm that had borne her so far.

She was lying on a sheepskin covering a pallet of leaves on a hard-beaten dirt floor. A folded sheepskin coat was under her head, and she was wrapped in a ragged cloak. She was in a large room, the walls of which were crudely but strongly built of uncut rocks, plastered with sun-baked mud. Heavy beams supported a roof of the same kind, in which showed a trap-door up to which led a ladder. There were no windows in the thick walls, only loopholes. There was one door, a sturdy bronze affair that must have been looted from some Vendhyan border tower. Opposite it was a wide opening in the wall, with no door, but several strong wooden bars in place. Beyond them Yasmina saw a magnificent black stallion munching a pile of dried grass. The building was fort, dwelling place, and stable in one.

At the other end of the room a girl in the vest and baggy trousers of a hillwoman squatted beside a small fire, cooking strips of meat on an iron grid laid over blocks of stone. There was a sooty cleft in the wall a few feet from the floor, and some of the smoke found its way out there. The rest floated in blue wisps about the room.

The hill girl glanced at Yasmina over her shoulder, displaying a bold, handsome face, and then continued her cooking. Voices boomed outside; then the door was kicked open, and Conan strode in. He looked more enormous than ever with the morning sunlight behind him, and

39

Yasmina noted some details that had escaped her the night before. His garments were clean and not ragged. The broad Bakhariot girdle that supported his knife in its ornamented scabbard would have matched the robes of a prince, and there was a glint of fine Turanian mail under his shirt.

"Your captive is awake, Conan," said the Wazuli girl, and he grunted, strode up to the fire, and swept the strips of mutton off into a stone dish.

The squatting girl laughed up at him, with some spicy jest, and he grinned wolfishly, and hooking a toe under her haunches, tumbled her sprawling onto the floor. She seemed to derive considerable amusement from this bit of rough horseplay, but Conan paid no more heed to her. Producing a great hunk of bread from somewhere, with a copper jug of wine, he carried the lot to Yasmina, who had risen from her pallet and was regarding him doubt-fully.

"Rough fare for a Devi, girl, but our best," he grunted. "It will fill your belly, at least."

He set the platter on the floor, and she was suddenly aware of a ravenous hunger. Making no comment, she seated herself cross-legged on the floor, and taking the dish in her lap, she began to eat, using her fingers, which were all she had in the way of table utensils. After all, adaptability is one of the tests of true aristocracy. Conan stood looking down at her, his thumbs hooked in his girdle. He never sat cross-legged, after the Eastern fashion.

"Where am I?" she asked abruptly.

"In the hut of Yar Afzal, the chief of the Khurum Wazulis," he answered. "Afghulistan lies a good many miles farther on to the west. We'll hide here awhile. The Kshatriyas are beating up the hills for you—several of their squads have been cut up by the tribes already."

"What are you going to do?" she asked.

"Keep you until Chundar Shan is willing to trade back my seven cow-thieves," he grunted. "Women of the Wazulis are crushing ink out of *shoki* leaves, and after a while you can write a letter to the governor."

A touch of her old imperious wrath shook her, as she thought how maddeningly her plans had gone awry, leaving her captive of the very man she had plotted to get into her power. She flung down the dish, with the remnants of her meal, and sprang to her feet, tense with anger.

"I will not write a letter! If you do not take me back, they will hang your seven men, and a thousand more besides!"

The Wazuli girl laughed mockingly, Conan scowled, and then the door opened and Yar Afzal came swaggering in. The Wazuli chief was as tall as Conan, and of greater girth, but he looked fat and slow beside his hard compactness of the Cimmerian. He plucked his red-stained beard and stared meaningly at the Wazuli girl, and that wench rose and scurried out without delay. Then Yar Afzal turned to his guest.

"The damnable people murmur, Conan," quoth he. "They wish me to murder you and take the girl to hold for ransom. They say that anyone can tell by her garments that she is a noble lady. They say why should the Afghuli dogs profit by her, when it is the people who take the risk of guarding her?"

"Lend me your horse," said Conan. "I'll take her and go."

"Pish!" boomed Yar Afzal. "Do you think I can't handle my own people? I'll have them dancing in their shirts if they cross me! They don't love you—or any other outlander—but you saved my life once, and I will not forget. Come out, though, Conan; a scout has returned."

Conan hitched at his girdle and followed the chief outside. They closed the door after them, and Yasmina peeped through a loop-hole. She looked out on a level space before the hut. At the farther end of that space there was a cluster of mud and stone huts, and she saw naked children playing among the boulders, and the slim erect women of the hills going about their tasks.

Directly before the chief's hut a circle of hairy, ragged men squatted, facing the door. Conan and Yar Afzal stood

41

a few paces before the door, and between them and the ring of warriors another man sat cross-legged. This one was addressing his chief in the harsh accents of the Wazuli which Yasmina could scarcely understand, though as part of her royal education she had been taught the languages of Iranistan and the kindred tongues of Ghulistan.

"I talked with a Dagozai who saw the riders last night," said the scout. "He was lurking near when they came to the spot where we ambushed the lord Conan. He overheard their speech. Chunder Shan was with them. They found the dead horse, and one of the men recognized it as Conan's. Then they found the man Conan slew, and knew him for a Wazuli. It seemed to them that Conan had been slain and the girl taken by the Wazuli; so they turned aside from their purpose of following to Afghulistan. But they did not know from which village the dead man was come, and we had left no trail a Kshatriya could follow.

"So they rode to the nearest Wazuli village, which was the village of Jugra, and burnt it and slew many of the people. But the men of Khojur came upon them in darkness and slew some of them, and wounded the governor. So the survivors retired down the Zhaibar in the darkness before dawn, but they returned with reinforcements before sunrise, and there has been skirmishing and fighting in the hills all morning. It is said that a great army is being raised to sweep the hills about the Zhaibar. The tribes are whetting their knives and laying ambushes in every pass from here to Gurashah valley. Moreover, Kerim Shah has returned to the hills."

A grunt went around the circle, and Yasmina leaned closer to the loop-hole at the name she had begun to mistrust.

"Where went he?" demanded Yar Afzal.

"The Dagozai did not know; with him were thirty Irakzai of the lower villages. They rode into the hills and disappeared."

"These Irakzai are jackals that follow a lion for crumbs," growled Yar Afzal. "They have been lapping up the coins Kerim Shah scatters among the border tribes to buy men like horses. I like him not, for all he is our kinsman from Iranistan."

"He's not even that," said Conan. "I know him of old. He's an Hyrkanian, a spy of Yezdigerd's. If I catch him I'll hang his hide to a tamarisk."

"But the Kshatriyas!" clamored the men in the semicircle. "Are we to squat on our haunches until they smoke us out? They will learn at last in which Wazuli village the wench is held. We are not loved by the Zhaibari; they will help the Kshatriyas hunt us out."

"Let them come," grunted Yar Afzal. "We can hold the defiles against a host."

One of the men leaped up and shook his fist at Conan.

"Are we to take all the risks while he reaps the rewards?" he howled. "Are we to fight his battles for him?"

With a stride Conan reached him and bent slightly to stare full into his hairy face. The Cimmerian had not drawn his long knife, but his left hand grasped the scabbard, jutting the hilt suggestively forward.

"I ask no man to fight my battles," he said softly. "Draw your blade if you dare, you yapping dog!"

The Wazuli started back, snarling like a cat.

"Dare to touch me and here are fifty men to rend you apart!" he screeched.

"What!" roared Yar Afzal, his face purpling with wrath. His whiskers bristled, his belly swelled with his rage. "Are you chief of Khurum? Do the Wazulis take orders from Yar Afzal, or from a low-bred cur?"

The man cringed before his invincible chief, and Yar Afzal, striding up to him, seized him by the throat and choked him until his face was turning black. Then he hurled the man savagely against the ground and stood over him with his tulwar in his hand.

"Is there any who questions my authority?" he roared, and his warriors looked down sullenly as his bellicose glare swept their semicircle. Yar Afzal grunted scornfully and sheathed his weapon with a gesture that was the apex of insult. Then he kicked the fallen agitator with a concentrated vindictiveness that brought howls from his victim.

43

"Get down the valley to the watchers on the heights and bring word if they have seen anything," commanded Yar Afzal, and the man went, shaking with fear and grinding his teeth with fury.

Yar Afzal then seated himself ponderously on a stone, growling in his beard. Conan stood near him, legs braced apart, thumbs hooked in his girdle, narrowly watching the assembled warriors. They stared at him sullenly, not daring to brave Yar Afzal's fury, but hating the foreigner as only a hillman can hate.

"Now listen to me, you sons of nameless dogs, while I tell you what the lord Conan and I have planned to fool the Kshatriyas"—the boom of Yar Afzal's bull-like voice followed the discomfited warrior as he slunk away from the assembly.

The man passed by the cluster of huts, where women who had seen his defeat laughed at him and called stinging comments, and hastened on along the trail that wound among spurs and rocks toward the valley head.

Just as he rounded the first turn that took him out of sight of the village, he stopped short, gaping stupidly. He had not believed it possible for a stranger to enter the valley of Khurum without being detected by the hawk-eyed watchers along the heights; yet a man sat cross-legged on a low ledge beside the path—a man in a camel-hair robe and a green turban.

The Wazuli's mouth gaped for a yell, and his hand leaped to his knife-hilt. But at that instant his eyes met those of the stranger and the cry died in his throat, his fingers went limp. He stood like a statue, his own eyes glazed and vacant.

For minutes the scene held motionless; then the man on the ledge drew a cryptic symbol in the dust on the rock with his forefinger. The Wazuli did not see him place anything within the compass of that emblem, but presently something gleamed there—a round, shiny black ball that looked like polished jet. The man in the green turban took this up and tossed it the Wazuli, who mechanically caught it.

44

"Carry this to Yar Afzal," he said, and the Wazuli turned like an automaton and went back along the path, holding the black jet ball in his outstretched hand. He did not even turn his head to the renewed jeers of the women as he passed the huts. He did not seem to hear.

The man on the ledge gazed after him with a cryptic smile. A girl's head rose above the rim of the ledge and she looked at him with admiration and a touch of fear that had not been present the night before.

"Why did you do that?" she asked.

He ran his fingers through her dark locks caressingly.

"Are you still dizzy from your flight on the horse-of-air, that you doubt my wisdom?" he laughed. "As long as Yar Afzal lives, Conan will bide safe among the Wazuli fighting-men. Their knives are sharp, and there are many of them. What I plot will be safer, even for me, than to seek to slay him and take her from among them. It takes no wizard to predict what the Wazulis will do, and what Conan will do, when my victim hands the globe of Yezud to the chief of Khurum."

Back before the hut, Yar Afzal halted in the midst of some tirade, surprised and displeased to see the man he had sent up the valley, pushing his way through the throng.

"I bade you go to the watchers!" the chief bellowed. "You have not had time to come from them."

The other did not reply; he stood woodenly, staring vacantly into the chief's face, his palm outstretched holding the jet ball. Conan, looking over Yar Afzal's shoulder, murmured something and reached to touch the chief's arm, but as he did so, Yar Afzal, in a paroxysm of anger, struck the man with his clenched fist and felled him like an ox. As he fell, the jet sphere rolled to Yar Afzal's foot, and the chief, seeming to see it for the first time, bent and picked it up. The men, staring perplexedly at their senseless comrade, saw their chief bend, but they did not see what he picked up from the ground.

Yar Afzal straightened, glanced at the jet, and made a motion to thrust it into his girdle.

"Carry that fool to his hut," he growled. "He has the look of a lotus-eater. He returned me a blank stare. I—aie!"

In his right hand, moving toward his girdle, he had suddenly felt movement where movement should not be. His voice died away as he stood and glared at nothing; and inside his clenched right hand he felt the quivering of *change*, of *motion*, of *life*. He no longer held a smooth shining sphere in his fingers. And he dared not look; his tongue clove to the roof of his mouth, and he could not open his hand. His astonished warriors saw Yar Afzal's eyes distend, the color ebb from his face. Then suddenly a bellow of agony burst from his bearded lips; he swayed and fell as if struck by lightning, his right arm tossed out in front of him. Face down, he lay, and from between his opening fingers crawled a spider—a hideous, black, hairy-legged monster whose body shone like black jet. The men yelled and gave back suddenly, and the creature scuttled into a crevice of the rocks and disappeared.

The warriors started up, glaring wildly, and a voice rose above their clamor, a far-carrying voice of command which came from none knew where. Afterward each man there —who still lived—denied that he had shouted, but all there heard it.

"Yar Afzal is dead! Kill the outlander!"

That shout focused their whirling minds as one. Doubt, bewilderment and fear vanished in the uproaring surge of the blood-lust. A furious yell rent the skies as the tribesmen responded instantly to the suggestion. They came headlong across the open space, cloaks flapping, eyes blazing, knives lifted.

Conan's action was as quick as theirs. As the voice shouted he sprang for the hut door. But they were closer to him than he was to the door, and with one foot on the sill he had to wheel and parry the swipe of a yard-long blade. He split the man's skull—ducked another swinging knife and gutted the wielder—felled a man with his left

46

fist and stabbed another in the belly—and heaved back mightily against the closed door with his shoulders. Hacking blades were nicking chips out of the jambs about his ears, but the door flew open under the impact of his shoulders, and he went stumbling backward into the room. A bearded, tribesman, thrusting with all his fury as Conan sprang back, over-reached and pitched headfirst through the doorway. Conan stooped, grasped the slack of his garments and hauled him clear, and slammed the door in the faces of the men who came surging into it. Bones snapped under the impact, and the next instant Conan slammed the bolts into place and whirled with desperate haste to meet the man, who sprang from the floor and tore into action like a madman.

Yasmina cowered in a corner, staring in horror as the two men fought back and forth across the room, almost trampling her at times; the flash and clangor of their blades filled the room, and outside the mob clamored like a wolf-pack, hacking deafeningly at the bronze door with their long knives, and dashing huge rocks against it. Somebody fetched a tree trunk, and the door began to stagger under the thunderous assault. Yasmina clasped her ears, staring wildly. Violence and fury within, cataclysmic madness without. The stallion in his stall neighed and reared, thundering with his heels against the walls. He wheeled and launched his hoofs through the bars just as the tribesman, backing away froom Conan's murderous swipes, stumbled against them. His spine cracked in three places like a rotten branch and he was hurled headlong against the Cimmerian, bearing him backward so that they both crashed to the beaten floor.

Yasmina cried out and ran forward; to her dazed sight it seemed that both were slain. She reached them just as Conan threw aside the corpse and rose. She caught his arm, trembling from head to foot.

"Oh, you live! I thought—I thought you were dead!"

He glanced down at her quickly, into the pale, upturned face and the wide staring dark eyes.

"Why are you trembling?" he demanded. "Why should you care if I live or die?"

A vestige of her poise returned to her, and she drew away, making a rather pitiful attempt at playing the Devi.

"You are preferable to those wolves howling without," she answered, gesturing toward the door, the stone sill of which was beginning to splinter away.

"That won't hold long," he muttered, then turned and went swiftly to the stall of the stallion.

Yasmina clenched her hands and caught her breath as she saw him tear aside the splintered bars and go into the stall with the maddened beast. The stallion reared above him, neighing terribly, hoofs lifted, eyes and teeth flashing and ears laid back, but Conan leaped and caught his mane with a display of sheer strength that seemed impossible, and dragged the beast down on his forelegs. The steed snorted and quivered, but stood still while the man bridled him and clapped on the gold-worked saddle, with the wide silver stirrups.

Wheeling the beast around in the stall, Conan called quickly to Yasmina, and the girl came, sidling nervously past the stallion's heels. Conan was working at the stone wall, talking swiftly as he worked.

"A secret door in the wall here, that not even the Wazuli know about. Yar Afzal showed it to me once when he was drunk. It opens out into the mouth of the ravine behind the hut. Ha!"

As he tugged at a projection that seemed casual, a whole section of the wall slid back on oiled iron runners. Looking through, the girl saw a narrow defile opening in a sheer stone cliff within a few feet of the hut's back wall. Then Conan sprang into the saddle and hauled her up before him. Behind them the great door groaned like a living thing and crashed in, and a yell rang to the roof as the entrance was instantly flooded with hairy faces and knives in hairy fists. And then the great stallion went through the wall like a javelin from a catapult, and thundered into the defile, running low, foam flying from the bit-rings.

That move came as an absolute surprise to the Wazulis. It was a surprise, too, to those stealing down the ravine. It happened so quickly—the hurricane-like charge of the great horse—that a man in a green turban was unable to get out of the way. He went down under the frantic hoofs, and a girl screamed. Conan got one glimpse of her as they thundered by—a slim, dark girl in silk trousers and a jeweled breast-band, flattening herself against the ravine wall. Then the black horse and his riders were gone up the gorge like the spume blown before a storm, and the men who came tumbling through the wall into the defile after them met that which changed their yells of bloodlust to shrill screams of fear and death.

6. *The Mountain of the Black Seers*

"Where now?" Yasmina was trying to sit erect on the rocking saddlebow, clutching her captor. She was conscious of a recognition of shame that she should not find unpleasant the feel of his muscular flesh under her fingers.

"To Afghulistan," he answered. "It's a perilous road, but the stallion will carry us easily, unless we fall in with some of your friends, or my tribal enemies. Now that Yar Afzal is dead, those damned Wazulis will be on our heels. I'm surprised we haven't sighted them behind us already."

"Who was that man you rode down?" she asked.

"I don't know. I never saw him before. He's no Ghuli, that's certain. What the devil he was doing there is more than I can say. There was a girl with him, too."

"Yes." Her gaze was shadowed. "I can not understand that. That girl was my maid, Gitara. Do you suppose she was coming to aid me? That the man was a friend? If so, the Wazulis have captured them both."

"Well," he answered, "there's nothing we can do. If we go back, they'll skin us both. I can't understand how a girl like that could get this far into the mountains with only one man—and he a robed scholar, for that's what he

49

looked like. There's something infernally queer in all this. That fellow Yar Afzal beat and sent away—he moved like a man walking in his sleep. I've seen the priests of Zamora perform their abominable rituals in their forbidden temples, and their victims had a stare like that man. The priests looked into their eyes and muttered incantations, and then the people became like walking dead men, with glassy eyes, doing as they ordered.

"And then I saw what the fellow had in his hand, which Yar Afzal picked up. It was like a big black jet bead, such as the temple girls of Yezud wear when they dance before the black stone spider which is their god. Yar Afzal held it in his hand, and he didn't pick up anything else. Yet when he fell dead, a spider, like the god at Yezud, only smaller, ran out of his fingers. And then, when the Wazulis stood uncertain there, a voice cried out for them to kill me, and I know that voice didn't come from any of the warriors, nor from the women who watched by the huts. It seemed to come from *above*."

Yasmina did not reply. She glanced at the stark outlines of the mountains all about them and shuddered. Her soul shrank from their gaunt brutality. This was a grim, naked land where anything might happen. Age-old traditions invested it with shuddery horror for anyone born in the hot, luxuriant southern plains.

The sun was high, beating down with fierce heat, yet the wind that blew in fitful gusts seemed to sweep off slopes of ice. Once she heard a strange rushing above them that was not the sweep of the wind, and from the way Conan looked up, she knew it was not a common sound to him, either. She thought that a strip of the cold blue sky was momentarily blurred, as if some all but invisible object had swept between it and herself, but she could not be sure. Neither made any comment, but Conan loosened his knife in his scabbard.

They were following a faintly marked path dipping down into ravines so deep the sun never struck bottom, laboring up steep slopes where loose shale threatened to slide from beneath their feet, and following knife-edge ridges with blue-hazed echoing depths on either hand.

The sun had passed its zenith when they crossed a narrow trail winding among the crags. Conan reined the horse aside and followed it southward, going almost at right angles to their former course.

"A Galzai village is at one end of this trail," he explained. "Their women follow it to a well, for water. You need new garments."

Glancing down at her filmy attire, Yasmina agreed with him. Her cloth-of-gold slippers were in tatters, her robes and silken under-garments torn to shreds that scarcely held together decently. Garments meant for the streets of Peshkhauri were scarcely appropriate for the crags of the Himelians.

Coming to a crook in the trail, Conan dismounted, helped Yasmina down and waited. Presently he nodded, though she heard nothing.

"A woman coming along the trail," he remarked. In sudden panic she clutched his arm.

"You will not—not kill her?"

"I don't kill women ordinarily," he grunted; "though some of these hillwomen are she-wolves. No," he grinned as at a huge jest. "By Crom, I'll *pay* for her clothes! How is that?" He displayed a handful of gold coins, and replaced all but the largest. She nodded, much relieved. It was perhaps natural for men to slay and die; her flesh crawled at the thought of watching the butchery of a woman.

Presently, a woman appeared around the crook of the trail—a tall, slim Galzai girl, straight as a young sapling, bearing a great empty gourd. She stopped short and the gourd fell from her hands when she saw them; she wavered as though to run, then realized that Conan was too close to her to allow her to escape, and so stood still, staring at them with a mixed expression of fear and curiosity.

Conan displayed the gold coin.

"If you will give this woman your garments," he said, "I will give you this money."

The response was instant. The girl smiled broadly with surprise and delight, and, with the disdain of a hillwoman for prudish conventions, promptly yanked off her sleeveless embroidered vest, slipped down her wide trousers and stepped out of them, twitched off her wide-sleeved shirt, and kicked off her sandals. Bundling them all in a bunch, she proffered them to Conan, who handed them to the astonished Devi.

"Get behind that rock and put these on," he directed, further proving himself no native hillman. "Fold your robes up into a bundle and bring them to me when you come out."

"The money!" clamored the hill girl, stretching out her hands eagerly. "The gold you promised me!"

Conan flipped the coin to her, she caught it, bit, then thrust it into her hair, bent and caught up the gourd and went on down the path, as devoid of self-consciousness as of garments. Conan waited with some impatience while the Devi, for the first time in her pampered life, dressed herself. When she stepped from behind the rock he swore in surprise, and she felt a curious rush of emotions at the unrestrained admiration burning in his fierce blue eyes. She felt shame, embarrassment, yet a stimulation of vanity she had never before experienced, and a tingling when meeting the impact of his eyes. He laid a heavy hand on her shoulder and turned her about, staring avidly at her from all angles.

"By Crom!" said he. "In those smoky, mystic robes you were aloof and cold and far off as a star! Now you are a woman of warm flesh and blood! You went behind that rock as the Devi of Vendhya; you come out as a hill girl —though a thousand times more beautiful than any wench of the Zhaibar! You were a goddess—now you are real!"

He spanked her resoundingly, and she, recognizing this as merely another expression of admiration, did not feel outraged. It was indeed as if the changing of her garments had wrought a change in her personality. The feelings and sensations she had suppressed rose to domination in her now, as if the queenly robes she had cast off had been material shackles and inhibitions.

But Conan, in his renewed admiration, did not forget that peril lurked all about them. The farther they drew away from the region of the Zhaibar, the less likely he was to encounter any Kshatriya troops. On the other hand, he had been listening all throughout their flight for sounds that would tell him the vengeful Wazulis of Khurum were on their heels.

Swinging the Devi up, he followed her into the saddle and again reined the stallion westward. The bundle of garments she had given him, he hurled over a cliff, to fall into the depths of a thousand-foot gorge.

"Why did you do that?" she asked. "Why did you not give them to the girl?"

"The riders from Peshkhauri are combing these hills," he said. "They'll be ambushed and harried at every turn, and by way of reprisal they'll destroy every village they can take. They may turn westward any time. If they found a girl wearing your garments, they'd torture her into talking, and she might put them on my trail."

"What will she do?" asked Yasmina.

"Go back to her village and tell her people that a stranger attacked her," he answered. "She'll have them on our track, all right. But she had to go on and get the water first; if she dared go back without it, they'd whip the skin off her. That gives us a long start. They'll never catch us. By nightfall we'll cross the Afghuli border."

"There are no paths or signs of human habitation in these parts," she commented. "Even for the Himelians this region seems singularly deserted. We have not seen a trail since we left the one where we met the Galzai woman."

For answer he pointed to the northwest, where she glimpsed a peak in a notch of the crags.

"Yimsha," grunted Conan. "The tribes build their villages as far from that mountain as they can."

She was instantly rigid with attention.

53

"Yimsha!" she whispered. "The mountain of the Black Seers!"

"So they say," he answered. "This is as near as I ever approached it. I have swung north to avoid any Kshatriya troops that might be prowling through the hills. The regular trail from Khurum to Afghulistan lies farther south. This is an ancient one, and seldom used."

She was staring intently at the distant peak. Her nails bit into her pink palms.

"How long would it take to reach Yimsha from this point?"

"All the rest of the day, and all night," he answered, and grinned. "Do you want to go there? By Crom, it's no place for an ordinary human, from what the hill people say."

"Why do they not gather and destroy the devils that inhabit it?" she demanded.

"Wipe out wizards with swords? Anyway, they never interfere with people, unless the people interfere with them. I never saw one of them, though I've talked with men who swore they had. They say they've glimpsed people from the tower among the crags at sunset or sunrise—tall, silent men in black robes."

"Would you be afraid to attack them?"

"I?" The idea seemed a new one to him. "Why, if they imposed upon me, it would be my life or theirs. But I have nothing to do with them. I came to these mountains to raise a following of human beings, not to war with wizards."

Yasmina did not at once reply. She stared at the peak as at a human enemy, feeling all her anger and hatred stir in her bosom anew. And another feeling began to take dim shape. She had plotted to hurl against the masters of Yimsha the man in whose arms she was now carried. Perhaps there was another way, besides the method she had planned, to accomplish her purpose. She could not mistake the look that was beginning to dawn in this wild man's eyes as they rested on her. Kingdoms

54

have fallen when a woman's slim white hands pulled the strings of destiny. Suddenly she stiffened, pointing.

"Look!"

Just visible on the distant peak there hung a cloud of peculiar aspect. It was a frosty crimson in color, veined with sparkling gold. This cloud was in motion; it rotated, and as it whirled it contracted. It dwindled to a spinning taper that flashed in the sun. And suddenly it detached itself from the snow-tipped peak, floated out over the void like a gay-hued feather, and became invisible against the cerulean sky.

"What could that have been?" asked the girl uneasily, as a shoulder of rock shut the distant mountain from view; the phenomenon had been disturbing, even its beauty.

"The hillmen call it Yimsha's Carpet, whatever that means," answered Conan. "I've seen five hundred of them running as if the devil were at their heels, to hide themselves in caves and crags, because they saw that crimson cloud float up from the peak. What in——"

They had advanced through a narrow, knife-cut gash between turreted walls and emerged upon a broad ledge, flanked by a series of rugged slopes on one hand, and a gigantic precipice on the other. The dim trail followed this ledge, bent around a shoulder and reappeared at intervals far below, working a tedious way downward. And emerging from the gut that opened upon the ledge, the black stallion halted short, snorting. Conan urged him on impatiently, and the horse snorted and threw his head up and down, quivering and straining as if against an invisible barrier.

Conan swore and swung off, lifting Yasmina down with him. He went forward, with a hand thrown out before him as if expecting to encounter unseen resistance, but there was nothing to hinder him, though when he tried to lead the horse, it neighed shrilly and jerked back. Then Yasmina cried out, and Conan wheeled, hand starting to knife-hilt.

Neither of them had seen him come, but he stood there, with his arms folded, a man in a camel-hair robe and a green turban. Conan grunted with surprise to recognize the man the stallion had spurned in the ravine outside the Waznli village.

"Who the devil are you?" he demanded.

The man did not answer. Conan noticed that his eyes were wide, fixed, and of a peculiar luminous quality. And those eyes held his like a magnet.

Khemsa's sorcery was based on hypnotism, as is the case with most Eastern magic. The way has been prepared for the hypnotist for untold centuries of generations who have lived and died in the firm convicton of the reality and power of hypnotism, building up, by mass thought and practice, a colossal though intangible atmosphere against which the individual, steeped in the traditions of the land, finds himself helpless.

But Conan was not a son of the East. Its traditions were meaningless to him; he was the product of an utterly alien atmosphere. Hypnotism was not even a myth in Cimmeria. The heritage that prepared a native of the East for submission to the mesmerist was not his.

He was aware of what Khemsa was trying to do to him; but he felt the impact of the man's uncanny power only as a vague impulsion, a tugging and pulling that he could shake off as a man shakes spider webs from his garments.

Aware of hostility and black magic, he ripped out his long knife and lunged, as quick on his feet as a mountain lion.

But hypnotism was not all of Khemsa's magic. Yasmina, watching, did not see by what roguery of movement or illusion the man in the green turban avoided the terrible disemboweling thrust. But the keen blade whickered between side and lifted arm, and to Yasmina it seemed that Khemsa merely brushed his open palm lightly against Conan's bullneck. But the Cimmerian went down like a slain ox.

Yet Conan was not dead; breaking his fall with his left

hand, he slashed at Khemsa's legs even as he went down, and the Rakhsha avoided the scythe-like swipe only by a most unwizardly bound backward. Then Yasmina cried out sharply as she saw a woman she recognized as Gitara glide out from among the rocks and come up to the man. The greeting died in the Devi's throat as she saw the malevolence in the girl's beautiful face.

Conan was rising slowly, shaken and dazed by the cruel craft of that blow which, delivered with an art forgotten of men before Atlantis sank, would have broken like a rotten twig the neck of a lesser man. Khemsa gazed at him cautiously and a trifle uncertainly. The Rakhsha had learned the full flood of his own power when he faced at bay the knives of the maddened Wazulis in the ravine behind Khurum village; but the Cimmerian's resistance had perhaps shaken his newfound confidence a trifle. Sorcery thrives on success, not on failure.

He stepped forward, lifting his hand—then halted as if frozen, head tilted back, eyes wide open, hand raised. In spite of himself Conan followed his gaze, and so did the women—the girl cowering by the trembling stallion, and the girl beside Khemsa.

Down the mountain slopes, like a whirl of shining dust blown before the wind, a crimson, conoid cloud came dancing. Khemsa's dark face turned ashen; his hand began to tremble, then sank to his side. The girl beside him, sensing the change in him, stared at him inquiringly.

The crimson shape left the mountain slope and came down in a long arching swoop. It struck the ledge between Conan and Khemsa, and the Rakhsha gave back with a stifled cry. He backed away, pushing the girl Gitara back with groping, fending hands.

The crimson cloud balanced like a spinning top for an instant, whirling in a dazzling sheen on its point. Then without warning it was gone, vanished as a bubble vanishes when burst. There on the ledge stood four men. It was miraculous, incredible, impossible, yet it was true. They were not ghosts or phantoms. They were four tall men, with shaven, vulture-like heads, and black robes that hid their feet. Their hands were concealed by their wide sleeves. They stood in silence, their naked heads nodding slightly in unison. They were facing Khemsa, but behind them Conan felt his own blood turning to ice in his veins. Rising, he backed stealthily away, until he felt the stallion's shoulder trembling against his back, and the Devi crept into the shelter of his arm. There was no word spoken. Silence hung like a stifling pall.

All four of the men in black robes stared at Khemsa. Their vulture-like faces were immobile, their eyes introspective and contemplative. But Khemsa shook like a man in an ague. His feet were braced on the rock, his calves straining as if in physical combat. Sweat ran in streams down his dark face. His right hand locked on something under his brown robe so desperately that the blood ebbed from that hand and left it white. His left hand fell on the shoulder of Gitara and clutched in agony like the grasp of a drowning man. She did not flinch or whimper, though his fingers dug like talons into her firm flesh.

Conan had witnessed hundreds of battles in his wild life, but never one like this, wherein four diabolical wills sought to beat down one lesser but equally devilish will that opposed them. But he only faintly sensed the monstrous quality of that hideous struggle. With his back to the wall, driven to bay by his former masters, Khemsa was fighting for his life with all the dark power, all the frightful knowledge they had taught him through long, grim years of neophytism and vassalage.

He was stronger than even he had guessed, and the free exercise of his powers in his own behalf had tapped unsuspected reservoirs of forces. And he was nerved to super-energy by frantic fear and desperation. He reeled before the merciless impact of those hypnotic eyes, but he held his ground. His features were distorted into a bestial grin of agony, and his limbs were twisted as in a rack. It was a war of souls, of frightful brains steeped in lore forbidden to men for a million years, of mentalities which had plumbed the abysses and explored the dark stars where spawn the shadows.

58

Yasmina understood this better than did Conan. And she dimly understood why Khemsa could withstand the concentrated impact of those four hellish wills which might have blasted into atoms the very rock on which he stood. The reason was the girl that he clutched with the strength of his despair. She was like an anchor to his staggering soul, battered by the waves of those psychic emanations. His weakness was now his strength. His love for the girl, violent and evil though it might be, was yet a tie that bound him to the rest of humanity, providing an earthly leverage for his will, a chain that his inhuman enemies could not break; at least not break through Khemsa.

They realized that before he did. And one of them turned his gaze from the Rakhsha full upon Gitara: There was no battle there. The girl shrank and wilted like a leaf in the drouth. Irresistibly impelled, she tore herself from her lover's arms before he realized what was happening. Then a hideous thing came to pass. She began to back toward the precipice, facing her tormentors, her eyes wide and blank as dark gleaming glass from behind which a lamp has been blown out. Khemsa groaned and staggered toward her, falling into the trap set for him. A divided mind could not maintain the unequal battle. He was beaten, a straw in their hands. The girl went backward, walking like an automaton, and Khemsa reeled drunkenly after her, hands vainly outstretched, groaning, slobbering in his pain, his feet moving heavily like dead things.

On the very brink she paused, standing stiffly, her heels on the edge, and he fell on his knees and crawled whimpering toward her, groping for her, to drag her back from destruction. And just before his clumsy fingers touched her, one of the wizards laughed, like the sudden, bronze note of a bell in Hell. The girl reeled suddenly and, consummate climax of exquisite cruelty, reason and understanding flooded back into her eyes, which flared with awful fear. She screamed, clutched wildly at her lover's staining hands, and then, unable to save herself, fell headlong with a moaning cry.

Khemsa hauled himself to the edge and stared over, haggardly, his lips working as he mumbled to himself. Then he turned and stared for a long minute at his torturers, with wide eyes that held no human light. And then with a cry that almost burst the rocks, he reeled up and came rushing toward them, a knife lifted in his hand.

One of the Rakhshas stepped forward and stamped his foot, and as he stamped, there came a rumbling that grew swiftly to a grinding roar. Where his foot struck, a crevice opened in the solid rock that widened instantly. Then, with a deafening crash, a whole section of the ledge gave way. There was a last glimpse of Khemsa, with arms wildly upflung, and then he vanished amidst the roar of the avalanche that thundered down into the abyss.

The four looked contemplatively at the ragged edge of rock that formed the new rim of the precipice, and then turned suddenly. Conan, thrown off his feet by the shudder of the mountain, was rising, lifting Yasmina. He seemed to move as slowly as his brain was working. He was befogged and stupid. He realized that there was desperate need for him to lift the Devi on the black stallion, and ride like the wind, but an unaccountable sluggishness weighted his every thought and action.

And now the wizards had turned toward him; they raised their arms, and to his horrified sight, he saw their outlines fading, dimming, becoming hazy and nebulous, as a crimson smoke billowed around their feet and rose about them. They were blotted out by a sudden whirling cloud—and then he realized that he too was enveloped in a blinding crimson mist—he heard Yasmina scream, and the stallion cried out like a woman in pain. The Devi was torn from his arm, and as he lashed out with his knife blindly, a terrific blow like a gust of storm wind knocked him sprawling against a rock. Dazedly he saw a crimson conoid cloud spinning up and over the mountain slopes. Yasmina was gone, and so were the four men in black. Only the terrified stallion shared the ledge with him.

7. On to Yimsha

As mists vanish before a strong wind, the cobwebs vanished from Conan's brain. With a searing curse he leaped into the saddle and the stallion reared neighing beneath him. He glared up the slopes, hesitated, and then turned down the trail in the direction he had been going when halted by Khemsa's trickery. But now he did not ride at a measured gait. He shook loose the reins and the stallion went like a thunderbolt, as if frantic to lose hysteria in violent physical exertion. Across the ledge and around the crag and down the narrow trail threading the great steep they plunged at breakneck speed. The path followed a fold of rock, winding interminably down from tier to tier of striated escarpment, and once, far below, Conan got a glimpse of the ruin that had fallen—a mighty pile of broken stone and boulders at the foot of a gigantic cliff.

The valley floor was still far below him when he reached a long and lofty ridge that led out from the slope like a natural causeway. Out upon this he rode, with an almost sheer drop on either hand. He could trace ahead of him the trail he had to follow; far ahead it dropped down from the ridge and made a great horseshoe back into the river bed at his left hand. He cursed the necessity of traversing those miles, but it was the only way. To try to descend to the lower lap of the trail here would be to attempt the impossible. Only a bird could get to the river-bed with a whole neck.

So he urged on the wearying stallion, until a clink of hoofs reached his ears, welling up from below. Pulling up short and reining to the lip of the cliff, he stared down into the dry river-bed that wound along the foot of the ridge. Along that gorge rode a motley throng—bearded men on half-wild horses, five hundred strong, bristling with weapons. And Conan shouted suddenly, leaning over the edge of the cliff, three hundred feet above them.

At his shout they reined back, and five hundred bearded

faces were tilted up toward him; a deep, clamorous roar filled the canyon. Conan did not waste words.

"I was riding for Ghor!" he roared. "I had not hoped to meet you dogs on the trail. Follow me as fast as your nags can push! I'm going to Yimsha, and——"

"Traitor!" The howl was like a dash of ice-water in his face.

"What?" He glared down at them, jolted speechless. He saw wild eyes blazing up at him, faces contorted with fury, fists brandishing blades.

"Traitor!" they roared back, wholeheartedly. "Where are the seven chiefs held captive in Peshkhauri?"

"Why, in the governor's prison, I suppose," he answered.

A bloodthirsty yell from a hundred throats answered him, with such a waving of weapons and a clamor that he could not understand what they were saying. He beat down the din with a bull-like roar, and bellowed: "What devil's play is this? Let one of you speak, so I can understand what you mean!"

A gaunt old chief elected himself to this position, shook his tulwar at Conan as a preamble, and shouted accusingly: "You would not let us go raiding Peshkhauri to rescue our brothers!"

"No, you fools!" roared the exasperated Cimmerian. "Even if you'd breached the wall, which is unlikely, they'd have hanged the prisoners before you could reach them."

"And you went alone to traffic with the governor!" yelled the Afghuli, working himself into a frothing frenzy.

"Well?"

"Where are the seven chiefs?" howled the old chief, making his tulwar into a glimmering wheel of steel about his head. "Where are they? Dead!"

"What!" Conan nearly fell off his horse in his surprise.

"Aye, dead!" five hundred bloodthirsty voices assured him.

The old chief brandished his arms and got the floor

again. "They were not hanged!" he screeched. "A Wazuli in another cell saw them die! The governor sent a wizard to slay them by craft!"

"That must be a lie," said Conan. "The governor would not dare. Last night I talked with him——"

The admission was unfortunate. A yell of hate and accusation split the skies.

"Aye! You went to him alone! To betray us! It is no lie. The Wazuli escaped through the doors the wizard burst in his entry, and told the tale to our scouts whom he met in the Zhaibar. They had been sent forth to search for you, when you did not return. When they heard the Wazuli's tale, they returned with all haste to Ghor, and we saddled our steeds and girt our swords!"

"And what do you fools mean to do?" demanded the Cimmerian.

"To avenge our brothers!" they howled. "Death to the Kshatriyas! Slay him, brothers, he is a traitor!"

Arrows began to rattle around him. Conan rose in his stirrups, striving to make himself heard above the tumult, and then, with a roar of mingled rage, defiance, and disgust, he wheeled and galloped back up the trail. Behind him and below him the Afghulis came pelting, mouthing their rage, too furious even to remember that the only way they could reach the height whereon he rode was to traverse the river-bed in the other direction, make the broad bend, and follow the twisting trail up over the ridge. When they did remember this, and turned back, their repudiated chief had almost reached the point where the ridge joined the escarpment.

At the cliff he did not take the trail by which he had descended, but turned off on another, a mere trace along a rock-fault, where the stallion scrambled for footing. He had not ridden far when the stallion snorted and shied back from something lying in the trail. Conan stared down on the travesty of a man, a broken, shredded, bloody heap that gibbered and gnashed splintered teeth.

Only the dark gods that rule over the grim destinies of

wizards know how Khemsa dragged his shattered body from beneath that awful cairn of fallen rocks and up the steep slope to the trail.

Impelled by some obscure reason, Conan dismounted and stood looking down at the ghastly shape, knowing that he was witness of a thing miraculous and opposed to nature. The Rakhsha lifted his gory head, and his strange eyes, glazed with agony and approaching death, rested on Conan with recognition.

"Where are they?" It was a racking croak not even remotely resembling a human voice.

"Gone back to their damnable castle on Yimsha," grunted Conan. "They took the Devi with them."

"I will go!" muttered the man. "I will follow them! They killed Gitara; I will kill them—the acolytes, the Four of the Black Circle, the Master himself! Kill—kill them all!" He strove to drag his mutilated frame along the rock, but not even his indomitable will could animate that gory mass longer, where the splintered bones hung together only by torn tissue and ruptured fiber.

"Follow them!" raved Khemsa, drooling a bloody slaver. "Follow!"

"I'm going to," growled Conan. "I went to fetch my Afghulis, but they've turned on me. I'm going on to Yimsha alone. I'll have the Devi back if I have to tear down that damned mountain with my bare hands. I didn't think the governor would dare kill my headmen, when I had the Devi, but it seems he did. I'll have his head for that. She's no use to me now as a hostage, but——"

"The curse of Yizil on them!" gasped Khemsa. "Go! I —Khemsa—am dying. Wait—take my girdle."

He tried to fumble with a mangled hand at his tatters, and Conan, understanding what he sought to convey, bent and drew from about his gory waist a girdle of curious aspect.

"Follow the golden vein through the abyss," muttered Khemsa. "Wear the girdle. I had it from a Stygian priest. It will aid you, though it failed me at last. Break the crystal globe with the four golden pomegranates. Beware of

64

the Master's transmutations—I am going to Gitara—she is waiting for me in Hell—*aie, ya Skelos yar!*" And so he died.

Conan stared down at the girdle. The hair of which it was woven was not horsehair. He was convinced that it was woven of the thick black tresses of a woman. Set in the thick mesh were tiny jewels such as he had never seen before. The buckle was strangely made, in the form of a golden serpent head, flat, wedge-shaped, and scaled with curious art. A strong shudder shook Conan as he handled it, and he turned as though to cast it over the precipice; then he hesitated, and finally buckled it about his waist, under the Bakhariot girdle. Then he mounted and pushed on.

The sun had sunk behind the crags. He climbed the trail in the vast shadow of the cliffs that was thrown out like a dark blue mantle over valleys and ridges far below. He was not far from the crest when, edging around the shoulder of a jutting crag, he heard the clink of shod hoofs ahead of him. He did not turn back. Indeed, so narrow was the path that the stallion could not have wheeled his great body upon it. He rounded the jut of the rock and came upon a portion of the path that broadened somewhat. A chorus of threatening yells broke on his ear, but his stallion pinned a terrified horse hard against the rock, and Conan caught the arm of the rider in an iron grip, checking the lifted sword in midair.

"Kerim Shah!" muttered Conan, red glints smoldering luridly in his eyes. The Turanian did not struggle; they sat their horses almost breast to breast, Conan's fingers locking the other's sword arm. Behind Kerim Shah filed a group of lean Irakzai on gaunt horses. They glared like wolves, fingering bows and knives, but rendered uncertain because of the narrowness of the path and the perilous proximity of the abyss that yawned beneath them.

"Where is the Devi?" demanded Kerim Shah.

"What's it to you, you Hyrkanian spy?" snarled Conan.

"I know you have her," answered Kerim Shah. "I was

on my way northward with some tribesmen when we were ambushed by enemies in Shalizah Pass. Many of my men were slain, and the rest of us harried through the hills like jackals. When we had beaten off our pursuers, we turned westward, toward Amir Jehun Pass, and this morning we came upon a Wazuli wandering through the hills. He was quite mad, but I learned much from his incoherent gibberings before he died. I learned that he was the sole survivor of a band which followed a chief of the Afghulis and a captive Kshatriya woman into a gorge behind Khurum village. He babbled much of a man in a green turban whom the Afghuli rode down, but who, when attacked by the Wazulis who pursued, smote them with a nameless doom what wiped them out as a gust of wind-driven fire wipes out a cluster of locusts.

"How that one man escaped, I do not know, nor did he; but I knew from his maunderings that Conan of Ghor had been in Khurum with his royal captive. And as we made our way through the hills, we overtook a naked Galzai girl bearing a gourd of water, who told us a tale of having been stripped and ravished by a giant foreigner in the garb of an Afghuli chief, who, she said, gave her garments to a Vendhyan woman who accompanied him. She said you rode westward."

Kerim Shah did not consider it necessary to explain that he had been on his way to keep his rendezvous with the expected troops from Secunderam when he found his way barred by hostile tribesmen. The road to Gurashah valley through Shalizah Pass was longer than the road that wound through Amir Jehun Pass, but the latter traversed part of the Afghuli country, which Kerim Shah had been anxious to avoid until he came with an army. Barred from the Shalizah road, however, he had turned to the forbidden route, until news that Conan had not yet reached Afghulistan with his captive had caused him to turn southward and push on recklessly in the hope of overtaking the Cimmerian in the hills.

"So you had better tell me where the Devi is," suggested Kerim Shah. "We outnumber you—"

"Let one of your dogs nock a shaft and I'll throw you over the cliff," Conan promised. "It wouldn't do you any good to kill me, anyhow. Five hundred Afghulis are on my trail, and if they find you've cheated them, they'll flay you alive. Anyway, I haven't got the Devi. She's in the hands of the Black Seers of Yimsha."

"*Tarim!*" swore Kerim Shah softly, shaken out of his poise for the first time. "Khemsa—"

"Khemsa's dead," grunted Conan. "His masters sent him to Hell on a landslide. And now get out of my way. I'd be glad to kill you if I had the time, but I'm on my way to Yimsha."

"I'll go with you," said the Turanian abruptly.

Conan laughed at him. "Do you think I'd trust you, you Hyrkanian dog?"

"I don't ask you to," returned Kerim Shah. "We both want the Devi. You know my reason; King Yezdigerd desires to add her kingdom to his empire, and herself in his seraglio. And I knew you, in the days when you were a hetman of the *kozak* steppes; so I know your ambition is wholesale plunder. You want to loot Vendhya, and to twist out a huge ransom for Yasmina. Well, let us for the time being, without any illusion about each other, unite our forces, and try to rescue the Devi from the Seers. If we succeed, and live, we can fight it out to see who keeps her."

Conan narrowly scrutinized the other for a moment, and then nodded, releasing the Turanian's arm. "Agreed; what about your men?"

Kerim Shah turned to the silent Irakzai and spoke briefly: "This chief and I are going to Yimsha to fight the wizards. Will you go with us, or stay here to be flayed by the Afghulis who are following this man?"

They looked at him with eyes grimly fatalistic. They were doomed and they knew it—had known it ever since the singing arrows of the ambushed Dagozai had driven them back from the pass of Shalizah. The men of the lower Zhaibar had too many reeking blood-feuds among the crag-dwellers. They were too small a band to fight

67

their way back through the hills to the villages of the border, without the guidance of the crafty Turanian. They counted themselves as dead already, so they made the reply that only dead men would make: "We will go with thee and die on Yimsha."

"Then in Crom's name let us be gone," grunted Conan, fidgeting with impatience as he stared into the blue gulfs of the deepening twilight. "My wolves were hours behind me, but we've lost a devilish lot of time."

Kerim Shah backed his steed from between the black stallion and the cliff, sheathed his sword and cautiously turned the horse. Presently the band was filing up the path as swiftly as they dared. They came out upon the crest nearly a mile east of the spot where Khemsa had halted the Cimmerian and the Devi. The path they had traversed was a perilous one, even for hillmen, and for that reason Conan had avoided it that day when carrying Yasmina, though Kerim Shah, following him, had taken it supposing the Cimmerian had done likewise. Even Conan sighed with relief when the horses scrambled up over the last rim. They moved like phantom riders through an enchanted realm of shadows. The soft creak of leather, the clink of steel marked their passing, then again the dark mountain slopes lay naked and silent in the starlight.

8. Yasmina Knows Stark Terror

Yasmina had time but for one scream when she felt herself enveloped in that crimson whirl and torn from her protector with appalling force. She screamed once, and then she had no breath to scream. She was blinded, deafened, rendered mute and eventually senseless by the terrific rushing of the air about her. There was a dazed consciousness of dizzy height and numbing speed, a confused impression of natural sensations gone mad, and then vertigo and oblivion.

A vestige of these sensations clung to her as she recovered consciousness; so she cried out and clutched

68

wildly as though to stay a headlong and involuntary flight. Her fingers closed on soft fabric, and a relieving sense of stability pervaded her. She took cognizance of her surroundings.

She was lying on a dais covered with black velvet. This dais stood in a great, dim room whose walls were hung with dusky tapestries across which crawled dragons reproduced with repellent realism. Floating shadows merely hinted at the lofty ceiling, and gloom that lent itself to illusion lurked in the corners. There seemed to be neither windows nor doors in the walls, or else they were concealed by the nighted tapestries. Where the dim light came from, Yasmina could not determine. The great room was a realm of mysteries, of shadows, and shadowy shapes in which she could not have sworn to observe movement, yet which invaded her mind with a dim and formless terror.

But her gaze fixed itself on a tangible object. On another, smaller dais of jet, a few feet away, a man sat cross-legged, gazing contemplatively at her. His long black velvet robe, embroidered with gold thread, fell loosely about him, masking his figure. His hands were folded in his sleeves. There was a velvet cap upon his head. His face was calm, placid, not unhandsome, his eyes lambent and slightly oblique. He did not move a muscle as he sat regarding her, nor did his expression alter when he saw she was conscious.

Yasmina felt fear crawl like a trickle of ice-water down her supple spine. She lifted herself on her elbows and stared apprehensively at the stranger.

"Who are you?" she demanded. Her voice sounded brittle and inadequate.

"I am the Master of Yimsha." The tone was rich and resonant, like the mellow notes of a temple bell.

"Why did you bring me here?" she demanded.

"Were you not seeking me?"

"If you are one of the Black Seers—yes!" she answered recklessly, believing that he could read her thoughts anyway.

He laughed softly, and chills crawled up and down her spine again.

"You would turn the wild children of the hills against the Seers of Yimsha!" he smiled. "I have read it in your mind, princess. Your weak, human mind, filled with petty dreams of hate and revenge."

"You slew my brother!" A rising tide of anger was vying with her fear; her hands were clenched, her lithe body rigid. "Why did you persecute him? He never harmed you. The priests say the Seers are above meddling in human affairs. Why did you destroy the king of Vendhya?"

"How can an ordinary human understand the motives of a Seer?" returned the Master calmly. "My acolytes in the temples of Turan, who are the priests behind the priests of Tarim, urged me to bestir myself in behalf of Yezdigerd. For reasons of my own, I complied. How can I explain my mystic reasons to your puny intellect? You could not understand."

"I understand this: my brother died!" Tears of grief and rage shook in her voice. She rose upon her knees and stared at him with wide blazing eyes, as supple and dangerous in that moment as a she-panther.

"As Yezdigerd desired," agreed the Master calmly. "For a while it was my whim to further his ambitions."

"Is Yezdigerd your vassal?" Yasmina tried to keep the timbre of her voice unaltered. She had felt her knee pressing something hard and symmetrical under a fold of velvet. Subtly she shifted her position, moving her hand under the fold.

"Is the dog that licks up the offal in the temple yard the vassal of the god?" returned the Master.

He did not seem to notice the actions she sought to dissemble. Concealed by the velvet, her fingers closed on what she knew was the golden hilt of a dagger. She bent her head to hide the light of triumph in her eyes.

"I am weary of Yezdigerd," said the Master. "I have turned to other amusements—ha!"

With a fierce cry Yasmina sprang like a jungle cat, stabbing murderously. Then she stumbled and slid to the floor, where she cowered, staring up at the man on the dais. He had not moved; his cryptic smile was unchanged. Tremblingly she lifted her hand and stared at it with dilated eyes. There was no dagger in her fingers; they grasped a stalk of golden lotus, the crushed blossoms drooping on the bruised stem.

She dropped it as if it had been a viper, and scrambled away from the proximity of her tormenter. She returned to her own dais, because that was at least more dignified for a queen than groveling on the floor at the feet of a sorcerer, and eyed him apprehensively, expecting reprisals.

But the Master made no move.

"All substance is one to him who holds the key of the cosmos," he said cryptically. "To an adept nothing is immutable. At will, steel blossoms bloom in unnamed gardens, or flower-swords flash in the moonlight."

"You are a devil," she sobbed.

"Not I!" he laughed. "I was born on this planet, long ago. Once I was a common man, nor have I lost all human attributes in the numberless eons of my adeptship. A human steeped in the dark arts is greater than a devil. I am of human origin, but I rule demons. You have seen the Lords of the Black Circle—it would blast your soul to hear from what far realm I summoned them and from what doom I guard them with ensorceled crystal and golden serpents.

"But only I can rule them. My foolish Khemsa thought to make himself great—poor fool, bursting material doors and hurtling himself and his mistress through the air from hill to hill! Yet if he had not been destroyed, his power might have grown to rival mine."

He laughed again. "And you, poor, silly thing! Plotting to send a hairy hill chief to storm Yimsha! It was such a jest that I myself could have designed, had it occurred to me, that you should fall into his hands. And I read in your childish mind an intention to seduce by your feminine wiles to attempt your purpose, anyway.

"But for all your stupidity, you are a woman fair to look upon. It is my whim to keep you for my slave."

The daughter of a thousand proud emperors gasped with shame and fury at the word.

"You dare not!"

His mocking laughter cut her like a whip across her naked shoulders.

"The king dares not trample a worm in the road? Little fool, do you not realize that your royal pride is no more to me than a straw blown on the wind? I, who have known the kisses of the queens of Hell! You have seen how I deal with a rebel!"

Cowed and awed, the girl crouched on the velvet-covered dais. The light grew dimmer and more phantom-like. The features of the Master became shadowy. His voice took on a newer tone of command.

"I will never yield to you!" Her voice trembled with fear but it carried a ring of resolution.

"You will yield," he answered with horrible conviction. "Fear and pain shall teach you. I will lash you with horror and agony to the last quivering ounce of your endurance, until you become as melted wax to be bent and molded in my hands as I desire. You shall know such discipline as no mortal woman ever knew, until my slightest command is to you as the unalterable will of the gods. And first, to humble your pride, you shall travel back through the lost ages, and view all the shapes that have been you. *Aie, yil la khosa!*"

At these words the shadowy room swam before Yasmina's affrighted gaze. The roots of her hair prickled her scalp, and her tongue clove to her palate. Somewhere a gong sounded a deep, ominous note. The dragons on the tapestries glowed like blue fire, and then faded out. The Master on his dais was but a shapeless shadow. The dim light gave way to soft, thick darkness, almost tangible, that pulsed with strange radiations. She could no longer see the Master. She could see nothing. She had a strange sensation that the walls and ceiling had withdrawn immensely from her.

Then somewhere in the darkness a glow began, like a

firefly that rhythmically dimmed and quickened. It grew to a golden ball, and as it expanded its light grew more intense, flaming whitely. It burst suddenly, showering the darkness with white sparks that did not illumine the shadows. But like an impression left in the gloom, a faint luminance remained, and revealed a slender dusky shaft shooting up from the shadowy floor. Under the girl's dilated gaze it spread, took shape; stems and broad leaves appeared, and great black poisonous blossoms that towered above her as she cringed against the velvet. A subtle perfume pervaded the atmosphere. It was the dread figure of the black lotus that had grown up as she watched, as it grows in the haunted, forbidden jungles of Khitai.

The broad leaves were murmurous with evil life. The blossoms bent toward her like sentient things, nodding serpent-like on pliant stems. Etched against soft, impenetrable darkness, it loomed over her, gigantic, blackly visible in some mad way. Her brain reeled with the drugging scent and she sought to crawl from the dais. Then she clung to it as it seemed to be pitching at an impossible slant. She cried out with terror and clung to the velvet, but she felt her fingers ruthlessly torn away. There was a sensation as of all sanity and stability crumbling and vanishing. She was a quivering atom of sentiency driven through a black, roaring, icy void by a thundering wind that threatened to extinguish her feeble flicker of animate life like a candle blown out in a storm.

Then there came a period of blind impulse and movement, when the atom that was she mingled and merged with myriad other atoms of spawning life in the yeasty morass of existence, molded by formative forces until she emerged again a conscious individual, whirling down an endless spiral of lives.

In a mist of terror she relived all her former existences, recognized and *was* again all the bodies that had carried her ego throughout the changing ages. She bruised her feet again over the long, weary road of life that stretched out behind her into the immemorial Past. Back beyond the dimmest dawns of Time she crouched shuddering in pri-

73

mordial jungles, hunted by slavering beasts of prey. Skin-clad, she waded thigh-deep in rice-swamps, battling with squawking waterfowl for the precious grains. She labored with the oxen to drag the pointed stick through the stubborn soil, and she crouched endlessly over looms in peasant huts.

She saw walled cities burst into flame, and fled screaming before the slayers. She reeled naked and bleeding over burning sands, dragged at the slaver's stirrup, and she knew the grip of hot, fierce hands on her writhing flesh, the shame and agony of brutal lust. She screamed under the bite of the lash, and moaned on the rack; mad with terror she fought against the hands that forced her head inexorably down on the bloody block.

She knew the agonies of childbirth, and the bitterness of love betrayed. She suffered all the woes and wrongs and brutalities that man has inflicted on woman throughout the eons; and she endured all the spite and malice of woman for woman. And like the flick of a fiery whip throughout was the consciousness she retained of her Devi-ship. She was all the women she had ever been, yet in her knowing she was Yasmina. This consciousness was not lost in the throes of reincarnation. At one and the same time she was a naked slave-wench groveling under the whip, and the proud Devi of Vendhya. And she suffered not only as the slave-girl suffered, but as Yasmina, to whose pride the whip was like a white-hot brand.

Life merged into life in flying chaos, each with its burden of woe and shame and agony, until she dimly heard her own voice screaming unbearably, like one long-drawn cry of suffering echoing down the ages.

Then she awakened on the velvet-covered dais in the mystic room.

In a ghostly gray light she saw again the dais and the cryptic robed figure seated upon it. The hooded head was bent, the high shoulders faintly etched against the uncertain dimness. She could make out no details clearly, but the hood, where the velvet cap had been, stirred a form-

74

less uneasiness in her. As she stared, there stole over her a nameless fear that froze her tongue to her palate—a feeling that it was not the Master who sat so silently on that black dais.

Then the figure moved and rose upright, towering above her. It stooped over her and the long arms in their wide black sleeves bent about her. She fought against them in speechless fright, surprised by their lean hardness. The hooded head bent down toward her averted face. And she screamed, and screamed again in poignant fear and loathing. Bony arms gripped her lithe body, and from that hood looked forth a countenance of death and decay—features like rotting parchment on a moldering skull.

She screamed again, and then, as those champing, grinning jaws bent toward her lips, she lost consciousness. . . .

9. *The Castle of the Wizards*

The sun had risen over the white Himelian peaks. At the foot of a long slope, a group of horsemen halted and stared upward. High above them a stone tower poised on the pitch of the mountainside. Beyond and above that gleamed the walls of a greater keep, near the line where the snow began that capped Yimsha's pinnacle. There was a touch of unreality about the whole—purple slopes pitching up to that fantastic castle, toy-like with distance, and above it the white glistening peak shouldering the cold blue.

"We'll leave the horses here," grunted Conan. "That treacherous slope is safer for a man on foot. Besides, they're done."

He swung down from the black stallion which stood with wide-braced legs and drooping head. They had pushed hard throughout the night, gnawing at scraps from saddle-bags, and pausing only to give the horses the rests they had to have.

"That first tower is held by the acolytes of the Black

Seers," said Conan. "Or so men say; watch-dogs for their masters—lesser sorcerers. They won't sit sucking their thumbs as we climb this slope."

Kerim Shah glanced up the mountain, then back the way they had come; they were already far up on Yimsha's side, and a vast expanse of lesser peaks and crags spread out beneath them. Among those labyrinths the Turanian sought in vain for a movement of color that would betray men. Evidently the pursuing Afghulis had lost their chief's trail in the night.

"Let us go, then."

They tied the weary horses in a clump of tamarisk and without further comment turned up the slope. There was no cover. It was a naked incline, strewn with boulders not big enough to conceal a man. But they did conceal something else.

The party had not gone fifty steps when a snarling shape burst from behind a rock. It was one of the gaunt savage dogs that infested the hill villages, and its eyes glared redly, its jaws dripped foam. Conan was leading, but it did not attack him. It dashed past him and leaped at Kerim Shah. The Turanian leaped aside, and the great dog flung itself upon the Irakzai behind him. The man yelled and threw up his arm, which was torn by the brute's fangs as it bore him backward, and the next instant half a dozen tulwars were hacking at the beast. Yet not until it was literally dismembered did the hideous creature cease its efforts to seize and rend its attackers.

Kerim Shah bound up the wounded warrior's gashed arm, looked at him narrowly, and then turned away without a word. He rejoined Conan, and they renewed the climb in silence.

Presently Kerim Shah said: "Strange to find a village dog in this place."

"There's no offal here," grunted Conan.

Both turned their heads to glance back at the wounded warrior toiling after them among his companions. Sweat glistened on his dark face and his lips were drawn back

76

from his teeth in a grimace of pain. Then both looked again at the stone tower squatting above them.

A slumberous quiet lay over the uplands. The tower showed no sign of life, nor did the strange pyramidal structure beyond it. But the men who toiled upward went with the tenseness of men walking on the edge of a crater. Kerim Shah had unslung the powerful Turanian bow that killed at five hundred paces, and the Irakzai looked to their own lighter and less lethal bows.

But they were not within bow-shot of the tower when something shot down out of the sky without warning. It passed so close to Conan that he felt the wind of the rushing wings, but it was an Irakzai who staggered and fell, blood jetting from a severed jugular. A hawk with wings like burnished steel shot up again, blood dripping from the scimitar-beak, to reel against the sky as Kerim Shah's bowstring twanged. It dropped like a plummet, but no man saw where it struck the earth.

Conan bent over the victim of the attack, but the man was already dead. No one spoke; useless to comment on the fact that never before had a hawk been known to swoop on a man. Red rage began to vie with fatalistic lethargy in the wild souls of the Irakzai. Hairy fingers nocked arrows and men glared vengefully at the tower whose very silence mocked them.

But the next attack came swiftly. They all saw it—a white puffball of smoke that tumbled over the tower-rim and came drifting and rolling down the slope toward them. Others followed it. They seemed harmless, mere woolly globes of cloudy foam, but Conan stepped aside to avoid contact with the first. Behind him one of the Irakzai reached out and thrust his sword into the unstable mass. Instantly a sharp report shook the mountainside. There was a burst of blinding flame, and then the puffball had vanished, and of the too-curious warrior remained only a heap of charred and blackened bones. The crisped hand still gripped the ivory sword-hilt, but the blade was gone—melted and destroyed by that awful

77

heat. Yet men standing almost within reach of the victim had not suffered except to be dazzled and half blinded by the sudden flare.

"Steel touches it off," grunted Conan. "Look out—here they come!"

The slope above them was almost covered by the billowing spheres. Kerim Shah bent his bow and sent a shaft into the mass, and those touched by the arrow burst like bubbles in spurting flame. His men followed his example and for the next few minutes it was as if a thunderstorm raged on the mountain slope, with bolts of lightning striking and bursting in showers of flame. When the barrage ceased, only a few arrows were left in the quivers of the archers.

They pushed on grimly, over soil charred and blackened, where the naked rock had in places been turned to lava by the explosion of those diabolical bombs.

Now they were almost within arrowflight of the silent tower, and they spread their line, nerves taut, ready for any horror that might descend upon them.

On the tower appeared a single figure, lifting a ten-foot bronze horn. Its strident bellow roared out across the echoing slopes, like the blare of trumpets on Judgment Day. And it began to be fearfully answered. The ground trembled under the feet of the invaders, and rumblings and grindings welled up from the subterranean depths.

The Irakzai screamed, reeling like drunken men on the shuddering slope, and Conan, eyes glaring, charged recklessly up the incline, knife in hand, straight at the door that showed in the tower-wall. Above him the great horn roared and bellowed in brutish mockery. And then Kerim Shah drew a shaft to his ear and loosed.

Only a Turanian could have made that shot. The bellowing of the horn ceased suddenly, and a high, thin scream shrilled in its place. The green-robed figure on the tower staggered, clutching at the long shaft which quivered in its bosom, and then pitched across the parapet. The great horn tumbled upon the battlement and hung precariously, and another robed figure rushed to seize it, shrieking in horror. Again the Turanian bow twanged, and again it was answered by a death-howl. The second acolyte, in falling, struck the horn with his elbow and knocked it clattering over the parapet to shatter on the rocks far below.

At such headlong speed had Conan covered the ground that before the clattering echoes of that fall had died away, he was hacking at the door. Warned by his savage instinct, he gave back suddenly as a tide of molten lead splashed down from above. But the next instant he was back again, attacking the panels with redoubled fury. He was galvanized by the fact that his enemies had resorted to earthly weapons. The sorcery of the acolytes was limited. Their necromantic resources might well be exhausted.

Kerim Shah was hurrying up the slope, his hillmen behind him in a straggling crescent. They loosed as they ran, their arrows splintering against the walls or arching over the parapet.

The heavy teak portal gave way beneath the Cimmerian's assault, and he peered inside warily, expecting anything. He was looking into a circular chamber from which a stair wound upward. On the opposite side of the chamber a door gaped open, revealing the outer slope—and the backs of half a dozen green-robed figures in full retreat.

Conan yelled, took a step into the tower, and then native caution jerked him back, just as a great block of stone fell crashing to the floor where his foot had been an instant before. Shouting to his followers, he raced around the tower.

The acolytes had evacuated their first line of defense. As Conan rounded the tower he saw their green robes twinkling up the mountain ahead of him. He gave chase, panting with earnest blood-lust, and behind him Kerim Shah and the Irakzai came pelting, the latter yelling like wolves at the flight of their enemies, their fatalism momentarily submerged by temporary triumph.

The tower stood on the lower edge of a narrow plateau whose upward slant was barely perceptible. A few hundred yards away, this plateau ended abruptly in a chasm, which had been invisible farther down the mountain. Into this chasm the acolytes apparently leaped without checking their speed. Their pursuers saw the green robes flutter and disappear over the edge.

A few moments later they themselves were standing on the brink of the mighty moat that cut them off from the castle of the Black Seers. It was a sheer-walled ravine that extended in either direction as far as they could see, apparently girdling the mountain, some four hundred yards in width and five hundred feet deep. And in it, from rim to rim, a strange, translucent mist sparkled and shimmered.

Looking down, Conan grunted. Far below him, moving across the glimmering floor, which shone like burnished silver, he saw the forms of the green-robed acolytes. Their outline was wavering and indistinct, like figures seen under deep water. They walked in single file, moving toward the opposite wall.

Kerim Shah nocked an arrow and sent it singing downward. But when it struck the mist that filled the chasm it seemed to lose momentum and direction, wandering widely from its course.

"If they went down, so can we!" grunted Conan, while Kerim Shah stared after his shaft in amazement. "I saw them last at this spot——"

Squinting down he saw something shining like a golden thread across the canyon floor far below. The acolytes seemed to be following this thread, and there suddenly came to him Khemsa's cryptic words—"Follow the golden vein!" On the brink, under his very hand as he crouched, he found it, a thin vein of sparkling gold running from an outcropping of ore to the edge and down across the silvery floor. And he found something else, which had before been invisible to him because of the peculiar refraction of the light. The gold vein followed a narrow ramp

80

which slanted down into the ravine, fitted with niches for hand and foot hold.

"Here's where they went down," he grunted to Kerim Shah. "They're no adepts, to waft themselves through the air! We'll follow them——"

It was at that instant that the man who had been bitten by the mad dog cried out horribly and leaped at Kerim Shah, foaming and gnashing his teeth. The Turanian, quick as a cat on his feet, sprang aside and the madman pitched head-first over the brink. The others rushed to the edge and glared after him in amazement. The maniac did not fall plummetlike. He floated slowly down through the rosy haze like a man sinking in deep water. His limbs moved like a man trying to swim, and his features were purple and convulsed beyond the contortions of his madness. Far down at last on the shining floor his body settled and lay still.

"There's death in that chasm," muttered Kerim Shah, drawing back from the rosy mist that shimmered almost at his feet. "What now, Conan?"

"On!" answered the Cimmerian grimly. "Those acolytes are human; if the mist doesn't kill them, it won't kill me."

He hitched his belt, and his hands touched the girdle Khemsa had given him; he scowled, then smiled bleakly. He had forgotten that girdle; yet thrice had death passed him by to strike another victim.

The acolytes had reached the farther wall and were moving up it like great green flies. Letting himself upon the ramp, he descended warily. The rosy cloud lapped about his ankles, ascending as he lowered himself. It reached his knees, his thighs, his waist, his armpits. He felt it as one feels a thick heavy fog on a damp night. With it lapping about his chin he hesitated, and then ducked under. Instantly his breath ceased; all air was shut off from him and he felt his ribs caving in on his vitals. With a frantic effort he heaved himself up, fighting for life. His head rose above the surface and he drank air in great gulps.

81

Kerim Shah leaned down toward him, spoke to him, but Conan neither heard nor heeded. Stubbornly, his mind fixed on what the dying Khemsa had told him, the Cimmerian groped for the gold vein, and found that he had moved off it in his descent. Several series of hand-holds were niched in the ramp. Placing himself directly over the thread, he began climbing down once more. The rosy mist rose about him, engulfed him. Now is head was under, but he was still drinking pure air. Above him he saw his companions staring down at him, their features blurred by the haze that shimmered over his head. He gestured for them to follow and went down swiftly, without waiting to see whether they complied or not.

Kerim Shah sheathed his sword without comment and followed, and the Irakzai, more fearful of being left alone than of the terrors that might lurk below, scrambled after him. Each man clung to the golden thread as they saw the Cimmerian do.

Down the slanting ramp they went to the ravine floor and moved out across the shining level, treading the gold vein like rope-walkers. It was as if they walked along an invisible tunnel through which air circulated freely. They felt death pressing in on them above and on either hand, but it did not touch them.

The vein crawled up a similar ramp on the other wall up which the acolytes had disappeared, and up it they went with taut nerves, not knowing what might be waiting for them among the jutting spurs of rock that fanged the lip of the precipice.

It was the green-robed acolytes who awaited them, with knives in their hands. Perhaps they had reached the limits to which they could retreat. Perhaps the Stygian girdle about Conan's waist could have told why their necromantic spells had proven so weak and so quickly exhausted. Perhaps it was a knowledge of death decreed for failure that sent them leaping from among the rocks, eyes glaring and knives glittering, resorting in their desperation to material weapons.

There among the rocky fangs on the precipice lip was

no war of wizard craft. It was a whirl of blades, where real steel bit and real blood spurted, where sinewy arms dealt forthright blows that severed quivering flesh, and men went down to be trodden under foot as the fight raged over them.

One of the Irakzai bled to death among the rocks, but the acolytes were down—slashed and hacked asunder or hurled over the edge to float sluggishly down to the silver floor that shone so far below.

Then the conquerors shook blood and sweat from their eyes, and looked at one another. Conan and Kerim Shah still stood upright and four of the Irakzai.

They stood among the rocky teeth that serrated the precipice brink, and from that spot a path wound up a gentle slope to a broad stair, consisting of half a dozen steps, a hundred feet across, cut out of a green jade-like substance. They led up to a broad stage or roofless gallery of the same polished stone, and above it rose, tier upon tier, the castle of the Black Seers. It seemed to have been carved out of the sheer stone of the mountain. The architecture was faultless, but unadorned. The many casements were barred and masked with curtains within. There was no sign of life, friendly or hostile.

They went up the path in silence, and warily as men treading the lair of a serpent. The Irakzai were dumb, like men marching to a certain doom. Even Kerim Shah was silent. Only Conan seemed unaware what a monstrous dislocating and uprooting of accepted thought and action their invasion constituted, what an unprecedented violation of tradition. He was not of the East; and he came of a breed who fought devils and wizards as promptly and matter-of-factly as they battled human foes.

He strode up the shining stairs and across the wide green gallery straight toward the great golden-bound teak door that opened upon it. He cast but a single glance upward at the higher tiers of the great pyramidal structure towering above him. He reached a hand for the bronze prong that jutted like a handle from the door—then

83

checked himself, grinning hardly. The handle was made in the shape of a serpent, head lifted on arched neck; and Conan had a suspicion that that metal head would come to grisly life under his hand.

He struck it from the door with one blow, and its bronze clink on the glassy floor did not lessen his caution. He flipped it aside with his knife-point, and again turned to the door. Utter silence reigned over the towers. Far below them the mountain slopes fell away into a purple haze of distance. The sun glittered on snow-clad peaks on either hand. High above, a vulture hung like a black dot in the cold blue of the sky. But for it, the men before the gold-bound door were the only evidence of life, tiny figures on a green jade gallery poised on the dizzy height, with that fantastic pile of stone towering above them.

A sharp wind off the snow slashed them, whipping their tatters about. Conan's long knife splintering through the teak panels roused the startled echoes. Again and again he struck, hewing through polished wood and metal bands alike. Through the sundered ruins he glared into the interior, alert and suspicious as a wolf. He saw a broad chamber, the polished stone walls untapestried, the mosaic floor uncarpeted. Square, polished ebon stools and a stone dais formed the only furnishings. The room was empty of human life. Another door showed in the opposite wall.

"Leave a man on guard outside," grunted Conan. "I'm going in."

Kerim Shah designated a warrior for that duty, and the man fell back toward the middle of the gallery, bow in hand. Conan strode into the castle, followed by the Turanian and the three remaining Irakzai. The one outside spat, grumbled in his beard, and started suddenly as a low mocking laugh reached his ears.

He lifted his head and saw, on the tier above him, a tall, black-robed figure, naked head nodding slightly as he stared down. His whole attitude suggested mockery and malignity. Quick as a flash the Irakzai bent his bow and loosed, and the arrow streaked upward to strike full

84

in the black-robed breast. The mocking smile did not alter. The Seer plucked out the missile and threw it back at the bowman, not as a weapon is hurled, but with a contemptuous gesture. The Irakzai dodged, instinctively throwing up his arm. His fingers closed on the revolving shaft.

· Then he shrieked. In his hand the wooden shaft suddenly *writhed*. Its rigid outline became pliant, melting in his grasp. He tried to throw it from him, but it was too late. He held a living serpent in his naked hand, and already it had coiled about his wrist and its wicked wedge-shaped head darted at his muscular arm. He screamed again and his eyes became distended, his features purple. He went to his knees shaken by an awful convulsion, and then lay still.

The men inside had wheeled at his first cry. Conan took a swift stride toward the open doorway, and then halted short, baffled. To the men behind him it seemed that he strained against empty air. But though he could see nothing, there was a slick, smooth, hard surface under his hands, and he knew that a sheet of crystal had been let down in the doorway. Through it he saw the Irakzai lying motionless on the glassy gallery, an ordinary arrow sticking in his arm.

Conan lifted his knife and smote, and the watchers were dumfounded to see his blow checked apparently in midair, with the loud clang of steel that meets an unyielding substance. He wasted no more effort. He knew that not even the legendary tulwar of Amir Khurum could shatter that invisible curtain.

In a few words he explained the matter to Kerim Shah, and the Turanian shrugged his shoulders. "Well, if our exit is barred, we must find another. In the meanwhile our way lies forward, does it not?"

With a grunt the Cimmerian turned and strode across the chamber to the opposite door, with a feeling of treading on the threshold of doom. As he lifted his knife to shatter the door, it swung silently open as if of its own accord. He strode into a great hall, flanked with tall glassy columns. A hundred feet from the door began the broad jade-green steps of a stair that tapered toward the top like the side of a pyramid. What lay beyond that stair he could not tell. But between him and its shimmering foot stood a curious altar of gleaming black jet. Four great golden serpents twined their tails about this altar and reared their wedge-shaped heads in the air, facing the four quarters of the compass like the enchanted guardians of a fabled treasure. But on the altar, between the arching necks, stood only a crystal globe filled with a cloudy smoke-like substance, in which floated four golden pomegranates.

The sight stirred some dim recollection in his mind; then Conan heeded the altar no longer, for on the lower steps of the stair stood four black-robed figures. He had not seen them come. They were simply there, tall, gaunt, their vulture-heads nodding in unison, their feet and hands hidden by their flowing garments.

One lifted his arm and the sleeve fell away revealing his hand—and it was not a hand at all. Conan halted in mid-stride, compelled against his will. He had encountered a force differing subtly from Khemsa's mesmerism, and he could not advance, though he felt it in his power to retreat if he wished. His companions had likewise halted, and they seemed even more helpless than he, unable to move in either direction.

The Seer whose arm was lifted beckoned to one of the Irakzai, and the man moved toward him like one in a trance, eyes staring and fixed, blade hanging in limp fingers. As he pushed past Conan, the Cimmerian threw an arm across his breast to arrest him. Conan was so much stronger than the Irakzai that in ordinary circumstances he could have broken his spine between his hands. But now the muscular arm was brushed aside like a straw and the Irakzai moved toward the stair, treading jerkily and mechanically. He reached the steps and knelt stiffly, proffering his blade and bending his head. The Seer took the sword. It flashed as he swung it up and down. The Irakzai's head tumbled from his shoulders and thudded heavily on the black marble floor. An arch of blood jetted from

86

the severed arteries and the body slumped over and lay with arms spread wide.

Again a malformed hand lifted and beckoned, and another Irakzai stumbled stiffly to his doom. The ghastly drama was re-enacted and another headless form lay beside the first.

As the third tribesman clumped his way past Conan to his death, the Cimmerian, his veins bulging in his temples with his efforts to break past the unseen barrier that held him, was suddenly aware of allied forces, unseen, but waking into life about him. This realization came without warning, but so powerfully that he could not doubt his instinct. His left hand slid involuntarily under his Bakhariot belt and closed on the Stygian girdle. And as he gripped it he felt new strength flood his numbed limbs; the will to live was a pulsing white-hot fire, matched by the intensity of his burning rage.

The third Irakzai was a decapitated corpse, and the hideous finger was lifting again when Conan felt the bursting of the invisible barrier. A fierce, involuntary cry burst from his lips as he leaped with the explosive suddenness of pent-up ferocity. His left hand gripped the sorcerer's girdle as a drowning man grips a floating log, and the long knife was a sheen of light in his right. The men on the steps did not move. They watched calmly, cynically; if they felt surprise they did not show it. Conan did not allow himself to think what might chance when he came within knife-reach of them. His blood was pounding in his temples, a mist of crimson swam before his sight. He was afire with the urge to kill—to drive his knife deep into flesh and bone, and twist the blade in blood and entrails.

Another dozen strides would carry him to the steps where the sneering demons stood. He drew his breath deep, his fury rising redly as his charge gathered momentum. He was hurtling past the altar with its golden serpents when like a levin-flash there shot across his mind again as vividly as if spoken in his external ear, the cryptic words of Khemsa: *"Break the crystal ball!"*

87

His reaction was almost without his own volition. Execution followed impulse so spontaneously that the greatest sorcerer of the age would not have had time to read his mind and prevent his action. Wheeling like a cat from his headlong charge, he brought his knife crashing down upon the crystal. Instantly the air vibrated with a peal of terror, whether from the stairs, the altar, or the crystal itself he could not tell. Hisses filled his ears as the the golden serpents, suddenly vibrant with hideous life, writhed and smote at him. But he was fired to the speed of a maddened tiger. A whirl of steel sheared through the hideous trunks that waved toward him, and he smote the crystal sphere again and yet again. And the globe burst with a noise like a thunder-clap, raining fiery shards on the black marble, and the gold pomegranates, as if released from captivity, shot upward toward the lofty roof and were gone.

A mad screaming, bestial and ghastly, was echoing through the great hall. On the steps writhed four black-robed figures, twisting in convulsions, froth dripping from their livid mouths. Then with one frenzied crescendo of inhuman ululation they stiffened and lay still, and Conan knew that they were dead. He stared down at the altar and the crystal shards. Four headless golden serpents still coiled about the altar, but no alien life now animated the dully gleaming metal.

Kerim Shah was rising slowly from his knees, whither he had been dashed by some unseen force. He shook his head to clear the ringing from his ears.

"Did you hear that crash when you struck? It was as if a thousand crystal panels shattered all over the castle as that globe burst. Were the souls of the wizards imprisoned in those golden balls?—Ha!"

Conan wheeled as Kerim Shah drew his sword and pointed.

Another figure stood at the head of the stair. His robe, too, was black, but of richly embroidered velvet, and there was a velvet cap on his head. His face was calm, and not unhandsome.

"Who the devil are you?" demanded Conan, staring up at him, knife in hand.

"I am the Master of Yimsha!" His voice was like the chime of a temple bell, but a note of cruel mirth ran through it.

"Where is Yasmina?" demanded Kerim Shah.

The Master laughed down at him.

"What is that to you, dead man? Have you so quickly forgotten my strength, once lent to you, that you come armed against me, you poor fool? I think I will take your heart, Kerim Shah!"

He held out his hand as if to receive something, and the Turanian cried out sharply like a man in mortal agony. He reeled drunkenly, and then, with a splintering of bones, a rending of flesh and muscle, and a snapping of mail-links, his breast burst outward with a shower of blood, and through the ghastly aperture something red and dripping shot through the air into the Master's outstretched hand, as a bit of steel leaps to the magnet. The Turanian slumped to the floor and lay motionless, and the Master laughed and hurled the object to fall before Conan's feet—a still-quivering human heart.

With a roar and a curse Conan charged the stair. From Khemsa's girdle he felt strength and deathless hate flow into him to combat the terrible emanation of power that met him on the steps. The air filled with a shimmering steely haze through which he plunged like a swimmer, head lowered, left arm bent about his face, knife gripped low in his right hand. His half-blinded eyes, glaring over the crook of his elbow, made out the hated shape of the Seer before and above him, the outline wavering as a reflection wavers in disturbed water.

He was racked and torn by forces beyond his comprehension, but he felt a driving power outside and beyond his own lifting him inexorably upward and onward, despite the wizard's strength and his own agony.

Now he had reached the head of the stairs, and the Master's face floated in the steely haze before him, and a strange fear shadowed the inscrutable eyes. Conan waded through the mist as through a surf, and his knife lunged upward like a live thing. The keen point ripped the Master's robe as he sprang back with a low cry. Then before Conan's gaze, the wizard vanished—simply disappeared like a burst bubble, and something long and undulating darted up one of the smaller stairs that led up to left and right from the landing.

Conan charged after it, up the left-hand stair, uncertain as to just what he had seen whip up those steps, but in a berserk mood that drowned the nausea and horror whispering at the back of his consciousness.

He plunged out into a broad corridor whose uncarpeted floor and untapestried walls were of polished jade, and something long and swift whisked down the corridor ahead of him, and into a curtained door. From within the chamber rose a scream of urgent terror. The sound lent wings to Conan's flying feet, and he hurtled through the curtains and headlong into the chamber within.

A frightful scene met his glare. Yasmina cowered on the farther edge of a velvet-covered dais, screaming her loathing and horror, an arm lifted as if to ward off attack, while before her swayed the hideous head of a giant serpent, shining neck arching up from dark-gleaming coils. With a choked cry Conan threw his knife.

Instantly the monster whirled and was upon him like the rush of wind through tall grass. The long knife quivered in its neck, point and a foot of blade showing on one side, and the hilt and a hand's-breadth of steel on the other, but it only seemed to madden the giant reptile. The great head towered above the man who faced it, and then darted down, the venom-dripping jaws gaping wide. But Conan had plucked a dagger from his girdle and he stabbed upward as the head dipped down. The point tore through the lower jaw and transfixed the upper, pinning them together. The next instant, the great trunk had looped itself about the Cimmerian as the snake, unable to use its fangs, employed its remaining form of attack.

Conan's left arm was pinioned among the bone-crushing folds, but his right was free. Bracing his feet to keep upright, he stretched forth his hand, gripped the hilt of the long knife jutting from the serpent's neck, and tore it free in a shower of blood. As if divining his purpose with more than bestial intelligence, the snake writhed and knotted, seeking to cast its loops about his right arm. But with the speed of light the long knife rose and fell, shearing half-way through the reptile's giant trunk.

Before he could strike again, the great, pliant loops fell from him and the monster dragged itself across the floor, gushing blood from its ghastly wounds. Conan sprang after it, knife lifted, but his vicious swipe cut empty air as the serpent writhed away from him and struck its blunt nose against a paneled screen of sandalwood. One of the panels gave inward and the long, bleeding barrel whipped through it and was gone.

Conan instantly attacked the screen. A few blows rent it apart and he glared into the dim alcove beyond. No horrific shape coiled there; there was blood on the marble floor, and bloody tracks led to a cryptic arched door. Those tracks were of a man's bare feet. . . .

"*Conan!*" He wheeled back into the chamber just in time to catch the Devi of Vendhya in his arms as she rushed across the room and threw herself upon him, catching him about the neck with a frantic clasp, half hysterical with terror and gratitude and relief.

His wild blood had been stirred to its uttermost by all that had passed. He caught her to him in a grasp that would have made her wince at another time, and crushed her lips with his. She made no resistance; the Devi was drowned in the elemental woman. She closed her eyes and drank in his fierce, hot, lawless kisses with all the abandon of passionate thirst. She was panting with his violence when he ceased for breath, and glared down at her lying limp in his mighty arms.

"I knew you'd come for me," she murmured. "You would not leave me in this den of devils."

At her words, recollection of their environment came to him suddenly. He lifted his head and listened intently.

Silence reigned over the castle of Yimsha, but it was a silence impregnated with menace. Peril crouched in every corner, leered invisibly from every hanging.

"We'd better go while we can," he muttered. "Those cuts were enough to kill any common beast—or *man*—but a wizard has a dozen lives. Wound one, and he writhes away like a crippled snake to soak up fresh venom from some source of sorcery."

He picked up the girl and, carrying her in his arms like a child, he strode out into the gleaming jade corridor and down the stairs, nerves tautly alert for any sign or sound.

"I met the Master," she whispered, clinging to him and shuddering. "He worked his spells on me to break my will. The most awful was a moldering corpse which seized me in its arms—I fainted then and lay as one dead, I do not know how long. Shortly after I regained consciousness I heard sounds of strife below, and cries, and then that snake came slithering through the curtains—ah!" She shook at the memory of that horror. "I knew somehow that it was not an illusion, but a real serpent that sought my life."

"It was not a shadow, at least," answered Conan cryptically. "He knew he was beaten, and chose to slay you rather than let you be rescued."

"What do you mean, *he?*" she asked uneasily, and then shrank against him, crying out, and forgetting her question. She had seen the corpses at the foot of the stairs. Those of the Seers were not good to look at; as they lay twisted and contorted, their hands and feet exposed to view, and at the sight Yasmina went livid and hid her face against Conan's powerful shoulder.

10. *Yasmina and Conan*

Conan passed through the hall quickly enough, traversed the outer chamber, and approached the door that let upon the gallery. Then he saw the floor sprinkled with tiny, glittering shards. The crystal sheet that had covered the doorway had been shivered to bits, and he remembered the crash that had accompanied the shattering of the crystal globe. He believed that every piece of crystal in the castle had broken at that instant, and some dim instinct or memory of esoteric lore vaguely suggested the truth of the monstrous connection between the Lords of the Black Circle and the golden pomegranates. He felt the short hair bristle chilly at the back of his neck and put the matter hastily out of his mind.

He breathed a deep sigh of relief as he stepped out upon the green jade gallery. There was still the gorge to cross, but at least he could see the white peaks glistening in the sun, and the long slopes falling away into the distant blue hazes.

The Irakzai lay where he had fallen, an ugly blotch on the glassy smoothness. As Conan strode down the winding path, he was surprised to note the position of the sun. It had not yet passed its zenith; and yet it seemed to him that hours had passed since he plunged into the castle of the Black Seers.

He felt an urge to hasten, not a mere blind panic, but an instinct of peril growing behind his back. He said nothing to Yasmina, and she seemed content to nestle her dark head against his arching breast and find security in the clasp of his iron arms. He paused an instant on the brink of the chasm, frowning down. The haze which danced in the gorge was no longer rose-hued and sparkling. It was smoky, dim, ghostly, like the life-tide that flickered thinly in a wounded man. The thought came vaguely to Conan that the spells of magicians were more closely bound to their personal beings than were the actions of common men to the actors.

But far below, the floor shone like tarnished silver, and the gold thread sparkled undimmed. Conan shifted Yasmina across his shoulder, where she lay docilely, and began the descent. Hurriedly he descended the ramp, and hurriedly he fled across the echoing floor. He had a conviction that they were racing with time, that their chances of survival depended upon crossing that gorge of horrors before the wounded Master of the castle should regain enough power to loose some other doom upon them.

When he toiled up the farther ramp and came out upon the crest, he breathed a gusty sigh of relief and stood Yasmina upon her feet.

"You walk from here," he told her; "it's downhill all the way."

She stole a glance at the gleaming pyramid across the chasm; it reared up against the snowy slope like the citadel of silence and immemorial evil.

"Are you a magician, that you have conquered the Black Seers of Yimsha, Conan of Ghor?" she asked, as they went down the path, with his heavy arm about her supple waist.

"It was a girdle Khemsa gave me before he died," Conan answered. "Yes, I found him on the trail. It is a curious one, which I'll show you when I have time. Against some spells it was weak, but against others it was strong, and a good knife is always a hearty incantation."

"But if the girdle aided you in conquering the Master," she argued, "why did it not aid Khemsa?"

He shook his head. "Who knows? But Khemsa had been the Master's slave; perhaps that weakened its magic. He had no hold on me as he had on Khemsa. Yet I can't say that I conquered him. He retreated, but I have a feeling that we haven't seen the last of him. I want to put as many miles between us and his lair as we can."

He was further relieved to find horses tethered among the tamarisks as he had left them. He loosed them swiftly and mounted the black stallion, swinging the girl up before him. The others followed, freshened by their rest.

"And what now?" she asked. "To Afghulistan?"

"Not just now!" He grinned hardly. "Somebody—maybe the governor—killed my seven headmen. My idiotic followers think I had something to do with it, and unless I am able to convince them otherwise, they'll hunt me like a wounded jackal."

"Then what of me? If the headmen are dead, I am useless to you as a hostage. Will you slay me to avenge them?"

He looked down at her, with eyes fiercely aglow, and laughed at the suggestion.

"Then let us ride to the border," she said. "You'll be safe from the Afghulis there——"

"Yes, on a Vindhyan gibbet."

"I am queen of Vendhya," she reminded him with a touch of her old imperiousness. "You have saved my life. You shall be rewarded."

She did not intend it as it sounded, but he growled in his throat, ill pleased.

"Keep your bounty for your city-bred dogs, princess! If you're a queen of the plains, I'm chief of the hills, and not one foot toward the border will I take you!"

"But you would be safe——" she began bewilderedly.

"And you'd be the Devi again," he broke in. "No, girl; I prefer you as you are now—a woman of flesh and blood, riding on my saddle bow."

"But you can't *keep* me!" she cried. "You can't——"

"Watch and see!" he advised grimly.

"But I will pay you a vast ransom——"

"Devil take your ransom!" he answered roughly, his arms hardening about her supple figure. "The kingdom of Vendhya could give me nothing I desire half so much as I desire you. I took you at the risk of my neck; if your courtiers want you back, let them come up the Zhaibar and fight for you."

"But you have no followers now!" she protested. "You are hunted! How can you preserve your own life, much less mine?"

"I still have friends in the hills," he answered. "There is a chief of the Khurakzai who will keep you safely while I bicker with the Afghulis. If they will have none of me, by Crom! I will ride northward with you to the steppes of the *kozaki*. I was a hetman among the Free Companions before I rode southward. I'll make you a queen on the Zaporoska River!"

"But I can not!" she objected. "You must not hold me——"

"If the idea's so repulsive," he demanded, "why did you yield your lips to me so willingly?"

"Even a queen is human," she answered, coloring. "But because I am a queen, I must consider my kingdom. Do not carry me away into some foreign country. Come back to Vendhya with me!"

"Would you make me your king?" he asked sardonically.

"Well, there are customs——" she stammered, and he interrupted her with a hard laugh.

"Yes, civilized customs that won't let you do as you wish. You'll marry some withered old king of the plains, and I can go my way with only the memory of a few kisses snatched from your lips. Ha!"

"But I must return to my kingdom!" she repeated helplessly.

"Why?" he demanded angrily. "To chafe your rump on gold thrones, and listen to the plaudits of smirking, velvet-skirted fools? Where is the gain? Listen: I was born in the Cimmerian hills where the people are all barbarians. I have been a mercenary soldier, a corsair, a *kozak*, and a hundred other things. What king has roamed the countries, fought the battles, loved the women, and won the plunder that I have?

"I came into Ghulistan to raise a horde and plunder the kingdoms to the south—your own among them. Being chief of the Afghulis was only a start. If I can conciliate them, I'll have a dozen tribes following me within a year. But if I can't, I'll ride back to the steppes and loot the Turanian borders with the *kozaki*. And you'll go with me. To the devil with your kingdom; they fended for themselves before you were born."

She lay in his arms looking up at him, and she felt a tug at her spirit, a lawless, reckless urge that matched his own and was by it called into being. But a thousand generations of sovereignship rode heavy upon her.

"I can't! I can't!" she repeated helplessly.

"You haven't any choice," he assured her. "You—what the devil!"

They had left Yimsha some miles behind them, and were riding along a high ridge that separated two deep valleys. They had just topped a steep crest where they could gaze down into the valley on their right hand. And there a running fight was in progress. A strong wind was blowing away from them, carrying the sound from their ears, but even so the clashing of steel and thunder of hoofs welled up from far below.

They saw the glint of the sun on lancetip and spired helmet. Three thousand mailed horsemen were driving before them a ragged band of turbaned riders, who fled snarling and striking like fleeing wolves.

"Turanians!" muttered Conan. "Squadrons from Secunderam. What the devil are they doing here?"

"Who are the men they pursue?" asked Yasmina. "And why do they fall back so stubbornly? They can not stand against such odds."

"Five hundred of my mad Afghulis," he growled, scowling down into the vale. "They're in a trap, and they know it."

The valley was indeed a cul-de-sac at the end. It narrowed to a high-walled gorge, opening out further into a round bowl, completely rimmed with lofty, unscalable walls.

The turbaned riders were being forced into this gorge, because there was nowhere else for them to go, and they went reluctantly, in a shower of arrows and a whirl of swords. The helmeted riders harried them, but did not press in too rashly. They knew the desperate fury of the hill tribes, and they knew too that they had their prey in a trap from which there was no escape. They had recognized the hillmen as Afghulis, and they wished to hem them in and force a surrender. They needed hostages for the purpose they had in mind.

Their emir was a man of decision and initiative. When he reached Gurashah valley, and found neither guides nor emissary waiting for him, he pushed on, trusting to his

97

own knowledge of the country. All the way from Secunderam there had been fighting, and tribesmen were licking their wounds in many a crag-perched village. He knew there was a good chance that neither he nor any of his helmeted spearmen would ever ride through the gates of Secunderam again, for the tribes would all be up behind him now, but he was determined to carry out his orders—which were to take Yasmina Devi from the Afghulis at all costs, and to bring her captive to Secunderam or, if confronted by impossibility, to strike off her head before he himself died.

Of all this, of course, the watchers on the ridge were not aware. But Conan fidgeted with nervousness.

"Why the devil did they get themselves trapped?" he demanded of the universe at large. "I know what they're doing in these parts—they were hunting me, the dogs! Poking into every valley—and found themselves penned in before they knew it. The poor fools! They're making a stand in the gorge, but they can't hold out for long. When the Turanians have pushed them back into the bowl, they'll slaughter them at their leisure."

The din welling up from below increased in volume and intensity. In the strait of the narrow gut, the Afghulis, fighting desperately, were for the time holding their own against the mailed riders, who could not throw their whole weight against them.

Conan scowled darkly, moved restlessly, fingering his hilt, and finally spoke bluntly: "Devi, I must go down to them. I'll find a place for you to hide until I come back to you. You spoke of your kingdom—well, I don't pretend to look on those hairy devils as my children, but after all, such as they are, they're my henchmen. A chief should never desert his followers, even if they desert him first. They think they were right in kicking me out—Hell, I won't be cast off! I'm still chief of the Afghulis, and I'll prove it! I can climb down on foot into the gorge."

"But what of me?" she queried. "You carried me away forcibly from *my* people; now will you leave me to die in

98

the hills alone while you go down and sacrifice yourself uselessly?"

His veins swelled with the conflict of his emotions.

"That's right," he muttered helplessly. "Crom knows what I *can* do."

She turned her head slightly, a curious expression dawning on her beautiful face. Then:

"Listen!" she cried. "Listen!"

A distant fanfare of trumpets was borne faintly to their ears. They stared into the deep valley on the left, and caught a glint of steel on the farther side. A long line of lances and polished helmets moved along the vale, gleaming in the sunlight.

"The riders of Vendhya!" she cried exultingly.

"There are thousands of them!" muttered Conan. "It has been long since a Kshatriya host has ridden this far into the hills."

"They are searching for me!" she exclaimed. "Give me your horse! I will ride to my warriors! The ridge is not so precipitous on the left, and I can reach the valley floor. Go to your men and make them hold out a little longer. I will lead my horsemen into the valley at the upper end and fall upon the Turanians! We will crush them in the vise! Quick, Conan! Will you sacrifice your men to your own desire?"

The burning hunger of the steppes and the wintry forests glared out of his eyes, but he shook his head and swung off the stallion, placing the reins in her hands.

"You win!" he grunted. "Ride like the devil!"

She wheeled away down the left-hand slope, and he ran swiftly along the ridge until he reached the long ragged cleft that was the defile in which the fight raged. Down the rugged wall he scrambled like an ape, clinging to projections and crevices, to fall at last, feet first, into the mêlée that raged in the mouth of the gorge. Blades were whickering and clanging about him, horses rearing and stamping, helmet plumes nodding among turbans that were stained crimson.

As he hit, he yelled like a wolf, caught a gold-worked rein, and dodging the sweep of a scimitar, drove his long knife upward through the rider's vitals. In another instant he was in the saddle, yelling ferocious orders to the Afghulis. They stared at him stupidly for an instant; then as they saw the havoc his steel was wreaking among their enemies, they fell to their work again, accepting him without comment. In that inferno of licking blades and spurting blood there was no time to ask or answer questions.

The riders in their spired helmets and gold-worked hauberks swarmed about the gorge mouth, thrusting and slashing, and the narrow defile was packed and jammed with horses and men, the warriors crushed breast to breast, stabbing with shortened blades, slashing murderously when there was an instant's room to swing a sword. When a man went down he did not get up from beneath the stamping, swirling hoofs. Weight and sheer strength counted heavily there, and the chief of the Afghulis did the work of ten. At such times accustomed habits sway men strongly, and the warriors, who were used to seeing Conan in their vanguard, were heartened mightily, despite their distrust of him.

But superior numbers counted too. The pressure of the men behind forced the horsemen of Turan deeper and deeper into the gorge, in the teeth of the flickering tulwars. Foot by foot the Afghulis were shoved back, leaving the defile-floor carpeted with dead, on which the riders trampled. As he hacked and smote like a man possessed, Conan had time for some chilling doubts—would Yasmina keep her word? She had but to join her warriors, turn southward, and leave him and his band to perish.

But at last, what seemed centuries of desperate battling, in the valley outside there rose another sound above the clash of steel and yells of slaughter. And then with a burst of trumpets that shook the walls, and rushing thunder of hoofs, five thousand riders of Vendhya smote the hosts of Secunderam.

That stroke split the Turanian squadrons asunder, shattered, tore, and rent them and scattered their fragments all over the valley. In an instant the surge had ebbed back out of the gorge; there was a chaotic, confused swirl of fighting, horsemen wheeling and smiting singly and in clusters, and then the emir went down with a Kshatriya lance through his breast, and the riders in their spired helmets turned their horses down the valley, spurring like mad and seeking to slash a way through the swarms which had come upon them from the rear. As they scattered in flight, the conquerors scattered in pursuit, and all across the valley floor, and up on the slopes near the mouth and over the crests streamed the fugitives and the pursuers. The Afghulis, those left to ride, rushed out of the gorge and joined in the harrying of their foes, accepting the unexpected alliance as unquestionably as they had accepted the return of their repudiated chief.

The sun was sinking toward the distant crags when Conan, his garments hacked to tatters and the mail under them reeking and clotted with blood, his knife dripping and crusted to the hilt, strode over the corpses to where Yasmina Devi sat her horse among her nobles on the crest of the ridge, near a lofty precipice.

"You kept your word, Devi!" he roared. "By Crom, though, I had some bad seconds down in that gorge—*look out!*"

Down from the sky swooped a vulture of tremendous size with a thunder of wings that knocked men sprawling from their horses.

The scimitar-like beak was slashing for the Devi's soft neck, but Conan was quicker—a short run, a tigerish leap, the savage thrust of a dripping knife, and the vulture voiced a horribly human cry, pitched sideways and went tumbling down the cliffs to the rocks and river a thousand feet below. As it dropped, its black wings thrashing the air, it took on the semblance, not of a bird, but of a black-robed human body that fell, arms in wide black sleeves thrown abroad.

Conan turned to Yasmina, his red knife still in his hand, his blue eyes smoldering, blood oozing from wounds on his thickly-muscled arms and thighs.

"You are the Devi again," he said, grinning fiercely at the gold-clasped gossamer robe she had donned over her hill-girl attire, and awed not at all by the imposing array of chivalry about him. "I have you to thank for the lives of some three hundred and fifty of my rogues, who are at least convinced that I didn't betray them. You have put my hands on the reins of conquest again."

"I still owe you my ransom," she said, her dark eyes glowing as they swept over him. "Ten thousand pieces of gold I will pay you——"

He made a savage, impatient gesture, shook the blood from his knife and thrust it back in its scabbard, wiping his hands on his mail.

"I will collect your ransom in my own way, at my own time," he said. "I will collect it in your palace at Ayodhya, and I will come with fifty thousand men to see that the scales are fair."

She laughed, gathering her reins into her hands. "And I will meet you on the shores of the Jhumda with a hundred thousand!"

His eyes shone with fierce appreciation and admiration as, stepping back, he lifted his hand with a gesture that was like the assumption of kingship, indicating that her road was clear before her.

The Slithering Shadow

When his plans for welding the hill tribes into a single army fail, Conan rides back through Hyrkania and Turan, avoiding King Yezdigerd's patrols and sharing the tents of his former kozak companions. Big wars rage in the West and, scenting greener pastures and larger loot, Conan returns to the Hyborian kingdoms. Almuric, prince of Koth, has rebelled against the hated King Strabonus. He has raised a formidable army from far and wide, and Conan signs up with him. Strabonus' neighbors, however, come to his aid. The rebel cause fails, and Almuric's motley army is driven south. They cut their way through the lands of Shem, the borders of Stygia, and into the grasslands of Kush. Here they are run down and wiped out by the combined black and Stygian forces at the edge of the southern desert. Conan is one of the few survivors.

1.

THE DESERT shimmered in the heat waves. Conan the Cimmerian stared out over the aching desolation and involuntarily drew the back of his powerful hand over his blackened lips. He stood like a bronze image in the sand, apparently impervious to the murderous sun, though his only garment was a silk loin-cloth, girdled by a wide gold-buckled belt from which hung a saber and a broad-bladed poniard. On his cleancut limbs were evidences of scarcely healed wounds.

At his feet rested a girl, one white arm clasping his knee, against which her blond head drooped. Her white skin contrasted with his hard, bronzed limbs; her short silken tunic, low-necked and sleeveless, girdled at the waist, emphasized rather than concealed her lithe figure.

Conan shook his head, blinking. The sun's glare half blinded him. He lifted a small canteen from his belt and shook it, scowling at the faint splashing within.

The girl moved wearily, whimpering.

"Oh, Conan, we shall die here! I am so thirsty!"

The Cimmerian growled wordlessly, glaring truculently at the surrounding waste, with outthrust jaw, and blue eyes smoldering savagely from under his black tousled mane, as if the desert were a tangible enemy.

He stooped and put the canteen to the girl's lips.

"Drink till I tell you to stop, Natala," he commanded.

She drank with little panting gasps, and he did not check her. Only when the canteen was empty did she realize that he had deliberately allowed her to drink all their water supply, little enough that it was.

Tears sprang to her eyes. "Oh, Conan," she wailed, wringing her hands, "why did you let me drink it all? I did not know—now there is none for you!"

"Hush," he growled. "Don't waste your strength in weeping."

Straightening, he threw the canteen from him.

"Why did you do that?" she whispered.

He did not reply, standing motionless, his fingers closing slowly about the hilt of his saber. He was not looking at the girl; his fierce eyes seemed to plumb the mysterious purple hazes of the distance.

Endowed with all the barbarian's ferocious love of life and instinct to live, Conan the Cimmerian yet knew that he had reached the end of his trail. He had not come to the limits of his endurance, but he knew another day under the merciless sun in those waterless wastes would bring him down. As for the girl, she had suffered enough. Better a quick, painless sword-stroke than the lingering agony that faced him. Her thirst was temporarily quenched; it was a false mercy to let her suffer until delirium and death brought relief. Slowly he slid the saber from its sheath.

He halted suddenly, stiffening. Far out on the desert to the south, something glimmered through the heat waves.

At first he thought it a phantom, one of the mirages which had mocked and maddened him in that accursed desert. Shading his sun-dazzled eyes, he made out spires and minarets, and gleaming walls. He watched it grimly, waiting for it to fade and vanish. Natala had ceased to sob; she struggled to her knees and followed his gaze.

"Is it a city, Conan?" she whispered, too fearful to hope: "Or is it but a shadow?"

The Cimmerian did not reply for a space. He closed and opened his eyes several times; he looked away, then back. The city remained where he had first seen it.

"The devil knows," he grunted. "It's worth a try, though."

He thrust the saber back in its sheath. Stooping, he lifted Natala in his mighty arms as though she had been an infant. She resisted weakly.

"Don't waste your strength carrying me, Conan," she pleaded. "I can walk."

"The ground gets rockier here," he answered. "You would soon wear your sandals to shreds," glancing at her soft green footwear. "Besides, if we are to reach that city at all, we must do it quickly, and I can make better time this way."

The chance for life had lent fresh vigor and resilience to the Cimmerian's steely thews. He strode out across the sandy waste as if he had just begun the journey. A barbarian of barbarians, the vitality and endurance of the wild were his, granting him survival where civilized men would have perished.

He and the girl were, so far as he knew, the sole survivors of Prince Almuric's army, that mad motley horde which, following the defeated rebel prince of Koth, swept through the lands of Shem like a devastating sandstorm and drenched the outlands of Stygia with blood. With a Stygian host on its heels, it had cut its way through the black kingdom of Kush, only to be annihilated on the edge of the southern desert. Conan likened it in his mind to a great torrent, dwindling gradually as it rushed southward, to run dry at last in the sands of the naked desert. The bones of its members—mercenaries, outcasts, broken men, outlaws—lay strewn from the Kothic uplands to the dunes of the wilderness.

From that final slaughter, when the Stygians and the Kushites closed in on the trapped remnants, Conan had cut his way clear and fled on a camel with the girl. Behind them the land swarmed with enemies; the only way open to them was the desert to the south. Into those menacing depths they had plunged.

The girl was a Brythunian, whom Conan had found in the slave-market of a stormed Shemite city, and appropriated. She had had nothing to say in the matter, but her new position was so far superior to the lot of any Hyborian woman in the Shemitish seraglio, that she accepted it thankfully. So she had shared in the adventures of Almuric's damned horde.

For days they had fled into the desert, pursued so far by Stygian horsemen that when they shook off the pursuit, they dared not turn back. They pushed on, seeking water, until the camel died. Then they went on foot. For the past few days their suffering had been intense. Conan had shielded Natala all he could, and the rough life of the camp had given her more stamina and strength than the average woman possesses; but even so, she was not far from collapse.

The sun beat fiercely on Conan's tangled black mane. Waves of dizziness and nausea rose in his brain, but he set his teeth and strode on unwaveringly. He was convinced that the city was a reality and not a mirage. What they would find there he had no idea. The inhabitants might be hostile. Nevertheless it was a fighting chance, and that was as much as he had ever asked.

106

The sun was nigh to setting when they halted in front of the massive gate, grateful for the shade. Conan stood Natala on her feet, and stretched his aching arms. Above them the walls towered some thirty feet in height, composed of a smooth, greenish substance that shone almost like glass. Conan scanned the parapets, expecting to be challenged, but saw no one. Impatiently he shouted, and banged on the gate with his saber-hilt, but only the hollow echoes mocked him. Natala cringed close to him, frightened by the silence. Conan tried the portal, and stepped back, drawing his saber, as it swung silently inward. Natala stifled a cry.

"Oh, look, Conan!"

Just inside the gate lay a human body. Conan glared at it narrowly, then looked beyond it. He saw a wide open expanse, like a court, bordered by the arched doorways of houses composed of the same greenish material as the outer walls. These edifices were lofty and imposing, pinnacled with shining domes and minarets. There was no sign of life among them. In the center of the court rose the square curb of a well, and the sight stung Conan, whose mouth felt caked with dry dust. Taking Natala's wrist he drew her through the gate, and closed it behind them.

"Is he dead?" she whispered, shrinkingly indicating the man who lay limply before the gate. The body was that of a tall powerful individual, apparently in his prime; the skin was yellow, the eyes slightly slanted; otherwise the man differed little from the Hyborian type. He was clad in high-strapped sandals and a tunic of purple silk, and a short sword in a cloth-of-gold scabbard hung from his girdle. Conan felt his flesh. It was cold. There was no sign of life in the body.

"Not a wound on him," grunted the Cimmerian, "but he's dead as Almuric with forty Stygian arrows in him. In Crom's name, let's see to the well! If there's water in it, we'll drink, dead men or no."

There was water in the well, but they did not drink of

107

it. Its level was a good fifty feet below the curb, and there was nothing to draw it up with. Conan cursed blackly, maddened by the sight of the stuff just out of his reach, and turned to look for some means of obtaining it. Then a scream from Natala brought him about.

The supposedly dead man was rushing upon him, eyes blazing with indisputable life, his short sword gleaming in his hand. Conan cursed amazedly, but wasted no time in conjecture. He met the hurtling attacker with a slashing cut of his saber that sheared through flesh and bone. The fellow's head thudded on the flags; the body staggered drunkenly, an arch of blood jetting from the severed jugular; then it fell heavily.

Conan glared down, swearing softly.

"This fellow is no deader now than he was a few minutes agone. Into what madhouse have we strayed?"

Natala, who had covered her eyes with her hands at the sight, peeked between her fingers and shook with fear.

"Oh, Conan, will the people of the city not kill us, because of this?"

"Well," he growled, "this creature would have killed us if I hadn't lopped off his head."

He glanced at the archways that gaped blankly from the green walls above them. He saw no hint of movement, heard no sound.

"I don't think any one saw us," he muttered. "I'll hide the evidence——"

He lifted the limp carcass by its swordbelt with one hand, and, grasping the head by its long hair in the other, he half carried, half dragged the ghastly remnants over to the well.

"Since we can't drink this water," he gritted vindictively, "I'll see that nobody else enjoys drinking it. Curse such a well, anyway!" He heaved the body over the curb and let it drop, tossing the head after it. A dull splash sounded far beneath.

"There's blood on the stones," whispered Natala.

"There'll be more unless I find water soon," growled

the Cimmerian, his short store of patience about exhausted. The girl had almost forgotten her thirst and hunger in her fear, but not Conan.

"We'll go into one of these doors," he said. "Surely we'll find people after awhile."

"Oh, Conan!" she wailed, snuggling up as close to him as she could. "I'm afraid! This is a city of ghosts and dead men! Let's go back into the desert! Better to die there, than to face these terrors!"

"We'll go into the desert when they throw us off the walls," he snarled. "There's water somewhere in this city, and I'll find it, if I have to kill every man in it."

"But what if they come to life again?" she whispered.

"Then I'll keep killing them until they stay dead!" he snapped. "Come on! That doorway is as good as another! Stay behind me, but don't run unless I tell you to."

She murmured a faint assent and followed him so closely that she stepped on his heels, to his irritation. Dusk had fallen, filling the strange city with purple shadows. They entered the open doorway, and found themselves in a wide chamber, the walls of which were hung with velvet tapestries, worked in curious designs. Floor, walls and ceiling were of the green, glassy stone, the walls decorated with gold frieze-work. Furs and satin cushions littered the floor. Several doorways let into other rooms. They passed through, and traversed several chambers, counterparts of the first. They saw no one, but the Cimmerian grunted suspiciously.

"Some one was here not long ago. This couch is still warm from contact with human body. That silk cushion bears the imprint of some one's hips. Then there's a faint scent of perfume lingering in the air."

A weird, unreal atmosphere hung over all. Traversing this dim, silent palace was like an opium dream. Some of the chambers were unlighted, and these they avoided. Others were bathed in a soft, weird light that seemed to emanate from jewels set in the walls in fantastic designs. Suddenly, as they passed into one of these illumined

109

chambers, Natala cried out and clutched her companion's arm. With a curse he wheeled, glaring for an enemy, bewildered because he saw none.

"What's the matter?" he snarled. "If you ever grab my sword-arm again, I'll skin you. Do you want me to get my throat cut? What were you yelling about?"

"Look there," she quavered, pointing.

Conan grunted. On a table of polished ebony stood golden vessels, apparently containing food and drink. The room was unoccupied.

"Well, whoever this feast is prepared for," he growled, "he'll have to look elsewhere tonight."

"Dare we eat it, Conan?" ventured the girl nervously. "The people might come upon us, and——"

"*Lir an mannanam mac lir!*" he swore, grabbing her by the nape of her neck and thrusting her into a gilded chair at the end of the table with no great ceremony. "We starve and you make objections! Eat!"

He took the chair at the other end and, seizing a jade goblet, emptied it at a gulp. It contained a crimson wine-like liquor of a peculiar tang, unfamiliar to him, but it was like nectar to his parched gullet. His thirst allayed, he attacked the food before him with rare gusto. It too was strange to him; exotic fruits and unknown meats. The vessels were of exquisite workmanship, and there were golden knives and forks as well. These Conan ignored, grasping the meat-joints in his fingers and tearing them with his strong teeth. The Cimmerian's table manners were rather wolfish at any time. His civilized companion ate more daintily, but just as ravenously. It occurred to Conan that the food might be poisoned, but the thought did not lessen his appetite; he preferred to die of poisoning rather than starvation.

His hunger satisfied, he leaned back with a deep sigh of relief. That there were humans in that silent city was evidenced by the fresh food, and perhaps every dark corner concealed a lurking enemy. But he felt no apprehension on that score, having a large confidence in

110

his own fighting ability. He began to feel sleepy, and considered the idea of stretching himself on a nearby couch for a nap.

Not so Natala. She was no longer hungry and thirsty, but she felt no desire to sleep. Her lovely eyes were very wide indeed as she timidly glanced at the doorways, boundaries of the unknown. The silence and mystery of the strange place preyed on her. The chamber seemed larger, the table longer than she had first noticed, and she realized that she was farther from her grim protector than she wished to be. Rising quickly, she went around the table and seated herself on his knee, glancing nervously at the arched doorways. Some were lighted and some were not, and it was at the unlighted ones she gazed longest.

"We have eaten, drunk, and rested," she urged. "Let us leave this place, Conan. It's evil. I can feel it."

"Well, we haven't been harmed so far," he began, when a soft but sinister rustling brought him about. Thrusting the girl off his knee he rose with the quick ease of a panther, drawing his saber, facing the doorway from which the sound had seemed to come. It was not repeated, and he stole forward noiselessly, Natala following with her heart in her mouth. She knew he suspected peril. His outthrust head was sunk between his giant shoulders, he glided forward in a half crouch, like a stalking tiger. He made no more noise than a tiger would have made.

At the doorway he halted, Natala peering fearfully from behind him. There was no light in the room, but it was partially illuminated by the radiance behind them, which streamed across it into yet another chamber. And in this chamber a man lay on a raised dais. The soft light bathed him, and they saw he was a counterpart of the man Conan had killed before the outer gate, except that his garments were richer, and ornamented with jewels which twinkled in the uncanny light. Was he dead, or merely sleeping? Again came that faint sinister sound, as if some one had thrust aside a hanging. Conan drew back,

111

drawing the clinging Natala with him. He clapped his hand over her mouth just in time to check her shriek.

From where they now stood, they could no longer see the dais, but they could see the shadow it cast on the wall behind it. And now another shadow moved across the wall: a huge shapeless black blot. Conan felt his hair prickle curiously as he watched. Distorted though it might be, he felt that he had never seen a man or beast which cast such a shadow. He was consumed with curiosity, but some instinct held him frozen in his tracks. He heard Natala's quick panting gasps as she stared with dilated eyes. No other sound disturbed the tense stillness. The great shadow engulfed that of the dais. For a long instant only its black bulk was thrown on the smooth wall. Then slowly it receded, and once more the dais was etched darkly against the wall. But the sleeper was no longer upon it.

An hysterical gurgle rose in Natala's throat, and Conan gave her an admonitory shake. He was aware of an iciness in his own veins. Human foes he did not fear; anything understandable, however grisly, caused no tremors in his broad breast. But this was beyond his ken.

After awhile, however, his curiosity conquered his uneasiness, and he moved out into the unlighted chamber again, ready for anything. Looking into the other room, he saw it was empty. The dais stood as he had first seen it, except that no bejeweled human lay thereon. Only on its silken covering shone a single drop of blood, like a great crimson gem. Natala saw it and gave a low choking cry, for which Conan did not punish her. Again he felt the icy hand of fear. On that dais a man had lain; *something* had crept into the chamber and carried him away. What that something was, Conan had no idea, but an aura of unnatural horror hung over those dim-lit chambers.

He was ready to depart. Taking Natala's hand, he turned back, then hesitated. Somewhere back among the chambers they had traversed, he heard the sound of a footfall. A human foot, bare or softly shod, had made that sound, and Conan, with the wariness of a wolf, turned quickly aside. He believed he could come again into the outer court, and yet avoid the room from which the sound had appeared to come.

But they had not crossed the first chamber on their new route, when the rustle of a silken hanging brought them about suddenly. Before a curtained alcove stood a man eyeing them intently.

He was exactly like the others they had encountered: tall, well-made, clad in purple garments, with a jeweled girdle. There was neither surprise nor hostility in his amber eyes. They were dreamy as a lotus-eater's. He did not draw the short sword at his side. After a tense moment he spoke, in a far-away detached tone, and a language his hearers did not understand.

On a venture Conan replied in Stygian, and the stranger answered in the same tongue: "Who are you?"

"I am Conan, a Cimmerian," answered the barbarian. "This is Natala, of Brythunia. What city is this?"

The man did not at once reply. His dreamy, sensuous gaze rested on Natala, and he drawled, "Of all my rich visions, this is the strangest! O, girl of the golden locks, from what far dreamland do you come? From Andarra, or Tothra, or Kuth of the star-girdle?"

"What madness is this?" growled the Cimmerian harshly, not relishing the man's words or manner.

The other did not heed him.

"I have dreamed more gorgeous beauties," he murmured; "lithe women with hair dusky as night, and dark eyes of unfathomed mystery. But your skin is white as milk, your eyes are clear as dawn, and there is about you a freshness and daintiness alluring as honey. Come to my couch, little dream-girl!"

He advanced and reached for her, and Conan struck aside his hand with a force that might have broken his arm. The man reeled back, clutching the numbed member, his eyes clouding.

"What rebellion of ghosts is this?" he muttered. "Barbarian, I command ye—begone! Fade! Dissipate! Fade! Vanish!"

113

"I vanish your head from your shoulders!" snarled the infuriated Cimmerian, his saber gleaming in his hand. "Is this the welcome you give strangers? By Crom, I'll drench these hangings in blood!"

The dreaminess had faded from the other's eyes, to be replaced by a look of bewilderment.

"Thog!" he ejaculated. "You are real! Whence come you? Who are you? What do you in Xuthal?"

"We came from the desert," Conan growled. "We wandered into the city at dusk, famishing. We found a feast set for some one, and we ate. I have no money to pay for it. In my country no starving man is denied food, but you civilized people must have your recompense— if you are like all I ever met. We have done no harm and we were just leaving. By Crom, I do not like this place where dead men rise and sleeping men vanish into the bellies of shadows!"

The man started violently at the last comment, his yellow face turning ashy.

"What do you say? Shadows? Into the bellies of shadows?"

"Well," answered the Cimmerian cautiously, "whatever it is that takes a man from a sleeping-dais and leaves only a spot of blood."

"You have seen? You have *seen*?" The man was shaking like a leaf; his voice cracked on the high-pitched note.

"Only a man sleeping on a dais, and a shadow that engulfed him," answered Conan.

The effect of his words on the other was horrifying. With an awful scream the man turned and rushed from the chamber. In his blind haste he caromed from the side of the door, righted himself, and fled through the adjoining chambers, still screaming at the top of his voice. Amazed, Conan stared after him, the girl trembling as she clutched the giant's arm. They could no longer see the flying figure, but they still heard his frightful screams, dwindling in the distance, and echoing as from vaulted roofs. Suddenly one cry, louder than the others, rose and broke short, followed by blank silence.

114

"Crom!"

Conan wiped the perspiration from his forehead with a hand that was not entirely steady.

"Surely this is a city of the mad! Let's get out of here, before we meet other madmen!"

"It is all a nightmare!" whimpered Natala. "We are dead and damned! We died out on the desert and are in Hell! We are disembodied spirits—*ow!*" Her yelp was induced by a resounding spank from Conan's open hand.

"You're no spirit when a pat makes you yell like that," he commented, with the grim humor which frequently manifested itself at inopportune times. "We are alive, though we may not be if we loiter in this devil-haunted pile. Come!"

They had traversed but a single chamber when again they stopped short. Some one or something was approaching. They faced the doorway whence the sounds came, waiting for they knew not what. Conan's nostrils widened, and his eyes narrowed. He caught the faint scent of the perfume he had noticed earlier in the night. A figure framed itself in the doorway. Conan swore under his breath; Natala's red lips opened wide.

It was a woman who stood there staring at them in wonder. She was tall, lithe, shaped like a goddess; clad in a narrow girdle crusted with jewels. A burnished mass of night-black hair set off the whiteness of her ivory body. Her dark eyes, shaded by long dusky lashes, were deep with sensuous mystery. Conan caught his breath at her beauty, and Natala stared with dilated eyes. The Cimmerian had never seen such a woman; her facial outline was Stygian, but she was not dusky-skinned like the Stygian women he had known; her limbs were like alabaster.

But when she spoke, in a deep rich musical voice, it was in the Stygian tongue.

"Who are you? What do you in Xuthal? Who is that girl?"

115

"Who are you?" bluntly countered Conan, who quickly wearied of answering questions.

"I am Thalis the Stygian," she replied. "Are you mad, to come here?"

"I've been thinking I must be," he growled. "By Crom, if I am sane, I'm out of place here, because these people are all maniacs. We stagger in from the desert, dying of thirst and hunger, and we come upon a dead man who tries to stab me me in the back. We enter a palace, rich and luxuriant, yet apparently empty. We find a meal set, but with no feasters. Then we see a shadow devour a sleeping man——" he watched her narrowly and saw her change color slightly. "Well?"

"Well what?" she demanded, apparently regaining control of herself.

"I was just waiting for you to run through the rooms howling like a wild woman," he answered. "The man I told about the shadow did."

She shrugged her slim ivory shoulders. "That was the screams I heard, then. Well, to every man his fate, and it's foolish to squeal like a rat in a trap. When Thog wants me, he will come for me."

"Who is Thog?" demanded Conan suspiciously.

She gave him a long appraising stare that brought color to Natala's face and made her bite her small red lip.

"Sit down on that divan and I will tell you," she said. "But first tell me your names."

"I am Conan, a Cimmerian, and this is Natala, a daughter of Brythunia," he answered. "We are refugees of an army destroyed on the borders of Kush. But I am not desirous of sitting down, where black shadows might steal up on my back."

With a lithe musical laugh, she seated herself, stretching out her supple limbs with studied abandon.

"Be at ease," she advised. "If Thog wishes you, he will take you, wherever you are. The man you mentioned, who screamed and ran—did you not hear him give one great cry, and then fall silent? In his frenzy, he must

116

have run full into that which he sought to escape. No man can avoid his fate."

Conan grunted noncommittally, but he sat down on the edge of a couch, his saber across his knees, his eyes wandering suspiciously about the chamber. Natala nestled against him, clutching him jealously, her legs tucked up under her. She eyed the stranger woman with suspicion and resentment. She felt small and dust-stained and insignificant before this glamorous beauty, and she could not mistake the look in the dark eyes which feasted on every detail of the bronzed giant's physique.

"What is this place, and who are these people?" demanded Conan.

"This city is called Xuthal; it is very ancient. It is built over an oasis, which the founders of Xuthal found in their wanderings. They came from the east, so long ago that not even their descendants remember the age."

"Surely there are not many of them; these palaces seem empty."

"No; and yet more than you might think. The city is really one great palace, with every building inside the walls closely connected with the others. You might walk among these chambers for hours and see no one. At other times, you would meet hundreds of the inhabitants."

"How is that?" Conan inquired uneasily; this savored too strongly of sorcery for comfort.

"Much of the time these people lie in sleep. Their dream-life is as important—and to them as real—as their waking life. You have heard of the black lotus? In certain pits of the city it grows. Through the ages they have cultivated it, until, instead of death, its juice induces dreams, gorgeous and fantastic. In these dreams they spend most of their time. Their lives are vague, erratic, and without plan. They dream, they wake, drink, love, eat, and dream again. They seldom finish anything they begin, but leave it half completed and sink back again into the slumber of the black lotus. That meal you found —doubtless one awoke, felt the urge of hunger, prepared

117

the meal for himself, then forgot about it and wandered away to dream again."

"Where do they get their food?" interrupted Conan. "I saw no fields or vineyards outside the city. Have they orchards and cattle-pens within the walls?"

She shook her head. "They manufacture their own food out of the primal elements. They are wonderful scientists, when they are not drugged with their dream-flower. Their ancestors were mental giants, who built this marvelous city in the desert, and though the race became slaves to their curious passions, some of their wonderful knowledge still remains. Have you wondered about these lights? They are jewels, fused with radium. You rub them with your thumb to make them glow, and rub them again, the opposite way, to extinguish them. That is but a single example of their science. But much they have forgotten. They take little interest in waking life, choosing to lie most of the time in death-like sleep."

"Then the dead man at the gate——" began Conan.

"Was doubtless slumbering. Sleepers of the lotus are like the dead. Animation is apparently suspended. It is impossible to detect the slightest sign of life. The spirit has left the body and is roaming at will through other, exotic worlds. The man at the gate was a good example of the irresponsibility of these peoples' lives. He was guarding the gate, where custom decrees a watch be kept, though no enemy has ever advanced across the desert. In other parts of the city you would find other guards, generally sleeping as soundly as the man at the gate."

Conan mulled over this for a space.

"Where are the people now?"

"Scattered in different parts of the city; lying on couches, on silken divans, in cushion-littered alcoves, on fur-covered daisies; all wrapped in the shining veil of dreams."

Conan felt the skin twitch between his massive shoulders. It was not soothing to think of hundreds of people lying cold and still throughout the tapestried palaces, their glassy eyes turned unseeingly upward. He remembered something else.

"What of the thing that stole through the chambers and carried away the man on the dais?"

A shudder twitched her ivory limbs.

"That was Thog, the Ancient, the god of Xuthal, who dwells in the sunken dome in the center of the city. He has always dwelt in Xuthal. Whether he came here with the ancient founders, or was here when they built the city, none knows. But the people of Xuthal worship him. Mostly he sleeps below the city, but sometimes at irregular intervals he grows hungry, and then he steals through the secret corridors and the dim-lit chambers, seeking prey. Then none is safe."

Natala moaned with terror and clasped Conan's mighty neck as if to resist an effort to drag her from her protector's side.

"Crom!" he ejaculated, aghast. "You mean to tell me these people lie down calmly and sleep, with this demon crawling among them?"

"It is only occasionally that he is hungry," she repeated. "A god must have his sacrifices. When I was a child in Stygia the people lived under the shadow of a priest. None ever knew when he or she would be seized and dragged to the altar. What difference whether the priests give a victim to the gods, or the god comes for his own victim?"

"Such is not the custom of my people," Conan growled, "nor of Natala's either. The Hyborians do not sacrifice humans to their god, Mitra, and as for my people—by Crom, I'd like to see a priest try to drag a Cimmerian to the altar! There'd be blood spilt, but not as the priest intended."

"You are a barbarian," laughed Thalis, but with a glow in her luminous eyes. "Thog is very ancient and very terrible."

"These folk must be either fools or heroes," grunted Conan, "to lie down and dream their idiotic dreams, knowing they might awaken in his belly."

119

She laughed. "They know nothing else. For untold generations Thog has preyed on them. He has been one of the factors which have reduced their numbers from thousands to hundreds. A few more generations and they will be extinct, and Thog must either fare forth into the world for new prey, or retire to the underworld whence he came so long ago.

"They realize their ultimate doom, but they are fatalists, incapable of resistance or escape. Not one of the present generation has been out of sight of these walls. There is an oasis a day's march to the south—I have seen it on the old maps their ancestors drew on parchment— but no man of Xuthal has visited it for three generations, much less made any attempt to explore the fertile grasslands which the maps show lying another day's march beyond it. They are a fast-fading race, drowned in lotus-dreams, stimulating their waking hours by means of the golden wine which heals wounds, prolongs life, and invigorates the most sated debauchee.

"Yet they cling to life, and fear the deity they worship. You saw how one went mad at the knowledge that Thog was roving the palaces. I have seen the whole city screaming and tearing its hair, and running frenziedly out of the gates, to cower outside the walls and draw lots to see which would be bound and flung back through the arched doorways to satisfy Thog's lust and hunger. Were they not all slumbering now, the word of his coming would send them raving and shrieking again through the outer gates.

"Oh, Conan!" begged Natala hysterically. "Let us flee!"

"In good time," muttered Conan, his eyes burning on Thalis' ivory limbs. "What are you, a Stygian woman, doing here?"

"I came here when a young girl," she answered, leaning lithely back against the velvet divan, and intertwining slender fingers behind her dusky head. "I am the daughter of a king, no common woman, as you can see by my skin, which is as white as that of your little blonde there. I was abducted by a rebel prince, who, with an

120

army of Kushite bowmen, pushed southward into the wilderness, searching for a land he could make his own. He and all his warriors perished in the desert, but one, before he died, placed me on a camel and walked beside it until he dropped and died in his tracks. The beast wandered on, and I finally passed into delirium from thirst and hunger, and awakened in this city. They told me I had been seen from the walls, early in the dawn, lying senseless beside a dead camel. They went forth and brought me in and revived me with their wonderful golden wine. And only the sight of a woman would have led them to have ventured that far from their walls.

"They were naturally much interested in one, especially the men. As I could not speak their language, they learned to speak mine. They are very quick and able of intellect; they learned my language long before I learned theirs. But they were more interested in me than in my language. I have been, and am, the only thing for which a man of them will forego his lotus-dreams for a space."

She laughed wickedly, flashing her audacious eyes meaningly at Conan.

"Of course the women are jealous of me," she continued tranquilly. "They are handsome enough in their yellow-skinned way, but they are dreamy and uncertain as the men, and these latter like me not only for my beauty, but for my reality. I am no dream! Though I have dreamed the dreams of the lotus, I am a normal woman, with earthly emotions and desires. With such these moon-eyed yellow women can not compare.

"That is why it would be better for you to cut that girl's throat with your saber, before the men of Xuthal waken and catch her. They will put her through paces she never dreamed of! She is too soft to endure what I have thrived on. I am a daughter of Luxur, and before I had known fifteen summers I had been led through the temples of Derketo, the dusky goddess, and had been initiated into the mysteries. Not that my first years in Xuthal were years of unmodified pleasure! The people of Xuthal have forgotten more than the priestesses of Derketo ever dreamed.

They live only for sensual joys. Dreaming or waking, their lives are filled with exotic ecstasies, beyond the ken of ordinary men."

"Damned degenerates!" growled Conan.

"It is all in the point of view," smiled Thalis lazily.

"Well," he decided, "we're merely wasting time. I can see this is no place for ordinary mortals. We'll be gone before your morons awake, or Thog comes to devour us. I think the desert would be kinder."

Natala, whose blood had curdled in her veins at Thalis' words, fervently agreed. She could speak Stygian only brokenly, but she understood it well enough. Conan stood up, drawing her up beside him.

"If you'll show us the nearest way out of this city," he grunted, "we'll take ourselves off." But his gaze lingered on the Stygian's sleek limbs and ivory breasts.

She did not miss his look, and she smiled enigmatically as she rose with the lithe ease of a great lazy cat.

"Follow me," she directed and led the way, conscious of Conan's eyes fixed on her supple figure and perfectly poised carriage. She did not go the way they had come, but before Conan's suspicions could be roused, she halted in a wide ivory-chased chamber, and pointed to a tiny fountain which gurgled in the center of the ivory floor.

"Don't you want to wash your face, child?" she asked Natala. "It is stained with dust, and there is dust in your hair."

Natala colored resentfully at the suggestion of malice in the Stygian's faintly mocking tone, but she complied, wondering miserably just how much havoc the desert sun and wind had wrought on her complexion—a feature for which women of her race were justly noted. She knelt beside the fountain, shook back her hair, slipped her tunic down to her waist, and began to lave not only her face, but her white arms and shoulders as well.

"By Crom!" grumbled Conan, "a woman will stop to consider her beauty, if the devil himself were on her heels. Haste, girl; you'll be dusty again before we've got out of

122

sight of this city. And Thalis, I'd take it kindly if you'd furnish us with a bit of food and drink."

For answer Thalis leaned herself against him, slipping one white arm about his bronzed shoulders. Her sleek naked flank pressed against his thigh and the perfume of her foamy hair was in his nostrils.

"Why dare the desert?" she whispered urgently. "Stay here! I will teach you the ways of Xuthal. I will protect you. I will love you! You are a real man: I am sick of these moon-calves who sigh and dream and wake, and dream again. I am hungry for the hard, clean passion of a man from the earth. The blaze of your dynamic eyes makes my heart pound in my bosom, and the touch of your iron-thewed arm maddens me.

"Stay here! I will make you king of Xuthal! I will show you all the ancient mysteries, and the exotic ways of pleasure! I——" She had thrown both arms about his neck and was standing on tiptoe, her vibrant body shivering against his. Over her ivory shoulder he saw Natala, throwing back her damp tousled hair, stop short, her lovely eyes dilating, her red lips parting in a shocked O. With an embarrassed grunt, Conan disengaged Thalis' clinging arms and put her aside with one massive arm. She threw a swift glance at the Brythunian girl and smiled enigmatically, seeming to nod her splendid head in mysterious cogitation.

Natala rose and jerked up her tunic, her eyes blazing, her lips pouting sulkily. Conan swore under his breath. He was no more monogamous in his nature than the average soldier of fortune, but there was an innate decency about him that was Natala's best protection.

Thalis did not press her suit. Beckoning them with her slender hand to follow, she turned and walked across the chamber. There, close to the tapestried wall, she halted suddenly. Conan, watching her, wondered if she had heard the sounds that might be made by a nameless monster stealing through the midnight chambers, and his skin crawled at the thought.

"What do you hear?" he demanded.

"Watch that doorway," she replied, pointing.

He wheeled, sword ready. Only the empty arch of the entrance met his gaze. Then behind him sounded a quick faint scuffling noise, a half-choked gasp. He whirled. Thalis and Natala had vanished. The tapestry was settling back in place, as if it had been lifted away from the wall. As he gaped bewilderedly, from behind that tapestried wall rang a muffled scream in the voice of the Brythunian girl.

2.

When Conan turned, in compliance with Thalis' request, to glare at the doorway opposite, Natala had been standing just behind him, close to the side of the Stygian. The instant the Cimmerian's back was turned, Thalis, with a pantherish quickness almost incredible, clapped her hand over Natala's mouth, stifling the cry she tried to give. Simultaneously the Stygian's other arm was passed about the blond girl's supple waist, and she was jerked back against the wall, which seemed to give way as Thalis' shoulder pressed against it. A section of the wall swung inward, and through a slit that opened in the tapestry Thalis slid with her captive, just as Conan wheeled back.

Inside was utter blackness as the secret door swung to again. Thalis paused to fumble at it for an instant, apparently sliding home a bolt, and as she took her hand from Natala's mouth to perform this act, the Byrthunian girl began to scream at the top of her voice. Thalis' laugh was like poisoned honey in the darkness.

"Scream if you will, little fool. It will only shorten your life."

At that Natala ceased suddenly, and cowered shaking in every limb.

"Why did you do this?" she begged. "What are you going to do?"

"I am going to take you down this corridor for a short distance," answered Thalis, "and leave you for one who will sooner or later come for you."

"Ohhhhhh!" Natala's voice broke in a sob of terror. "Why should you harm me? I have never injured you!"

"I want your warrior. You stand in my way. He desires me—I could read the look in his eyes. But for you, he would be willing to stay here and be my king. When you are out of the way, he will follow me."

"He will cut your throat," answered Natala with conviction, knowing Conan better than Thalis did.

"We shall see," answered the Stygian coolly from the confidence of her power over men. "At any rate, you will not know whether he stabs or kisses me, because you will be the bride of him who dwells in darkness. Come!"

Half mad with terror, Natala fought like a wild thing, but it availed her nothing. With a lithe strength she would not have believed possible in a woman, Thalis picked her up and carried her down the black corridor as if she had been a child. Natala did not scream again, remembering the Stygian's sinister words; the only sounds were her desperate quick panting and Thalis' soft taunting lascivious laughter. Then the Brythunian's fluttering hand closed on something in the dark—a jeweled dagger-hilt jutting from Thalis' gem-crusted girdle. Natala jerked it forth and struck blindly and with all her girlish power.

A scream burst from Thalis' lips, feline in its pain and fury. She reeled, and Natala slipped from her relaxing grasp, to bruise her tender limbs on the smooth stone floor. Rising, she scurried to the nearest wall and stood there panting and trembling, flattening herself against the stones. She could not see Thalis, but she could hear her. The Stygian was quite certainly not dead. She was cursing in a steady stream, and her fury was so concentrated and deadly that Natala felt her bones turn to wax, her blood to ice.

"Where are you, you little she-devil?" gasped Thalis. "Let me get my fingers on you again, and I'll——" Natala grew physically sick as Thalis described the bodily injuries she intended to inflict on her rival. The Stygian's choice

125

of language would have shamed the toughest courtezan in Aquilonia.

Natala heard her groping in the dark, and then a light sprang up. Evidently whatever fear Thalis felt of this black corridor was submerged in her anger. The light came from one of the radium gems which adorned the walls of Xuthal. This Thalis had rubbed, and now she stood bathed in its reddish glow: a light different from that which the others had emitted. One hand was pressed to her side and blood trickled between the fingers. But she did not seem weakened or badly hurt, and her eyes blazed fiendishly. What little courage remained to Natala ebbed away at sight of the Stygian standing limned in that weird glow, her beautiful face contorted with a passion that was no less than hellish. She now advanced with a pantherish tread, drawing her hand away from her wounded side, and shaking the blood drops impatiently from her fingers. Natala saw that she had not badly harmed her rival. The blade had glanced from the jewels of Thalis' girdle and inflicted a very superficial flesh-wound, only enough to rouse the Stygian's unbridled fury. "Give me that dagger, you fool!" she gritted, striding up to the cowering girl.

Natala knew that she ought to fight while she had the chance, but she simply could not summon up the courage. Never much of a fighter, the darkness, violence, and horror of her adventure had left her limp, mentally and physically. Thalis snatched the dagger from her lax fingers and threw it contemptuously aside.

"You little slut!" she ground between her teeth, slapping the girl viciously with either hand. "Before I drag you down the corridor and throw you into Thog's jaws, I'll have a little of your blood myself! You would dare to knife me—well, for that audacity you shall pay!"

Seizing her by the hair, Thalis dragged her down the corridor a short distance, to the edge of the circle of light. A metal ring showed in the wall, above the level of a man's head. From it depended a silken cord. As in a nightmare Natala felt her tunic being stripped from her, and the next instant Thalis had jerked up her wrists and bound them to the ring, where she hung, naked as the day she was born, her feet barely touching the floor. Twisting her head, Natala saw Thalis unhook a jewel-handled whip from where it hung on the wall, near the ring. The lashes consisted of seven round silk cords, harder yet more pliant than leather thongs.

With a hiss of vindictive gratification, Thalis drew back her arm, and Natala shrieked as the cords curled across her loins. The tortured girl writhed, twisted and tore agonizedly at the thongs which imprisoned her wrists. She had forgotten the lurking menace her cries might summon, and so apparently had Thalis. Every stroke evoked screams of anguish. The whippings Natala had received in the Shemite slave-markets paled to insignificance before this. She had never guessed the punishing power of hard-woven silk cords. Their caress was more exquisitely painful than any birch twigs or leather thongs. They whistled venomously as they cut the air.

Then, as Natala twisted her tear-stained face over her shoulder to shriek for mercy, something froze her cries. Agony gave place to paralyzing horror in her beautiful eyes.

Struck by her expression, Thalis checked her lifted hand and whirled quick as a cat. Too late! An awful cry rang from her lips as she swayed back, her arms upflung. Natala saw her for an instant, a white figure of fear etched against a great black shapeless mass that towered over her; then the white figure was whipped off its feet, the shadow receded with it, and in the circle of dim light Natala hung alone, half fainting with terror.

From the black shadows came sounds, incomprehensible and blood-freezing. She heard Thalis' voice pleading frenziedly, but no voice answered. There was no sound except the Stygian's panting voice, which suddenly rose to screams of agony, and then broke in hysterical laughter, mingled with sobs. This dwindled to a convulsive panting, and presently this too ceased, and a silence more terrible hovered over the secret corridor.

Nauseated with horror, Natala twisted about and dared to look fearfully in the direction the black shape had carried Thalis. She saw nothing, but she sensed an unseen peril, more grisly than she could understand. She fought against a rising tide of hysteria. Her bruised wrists, her smarting body were forgotten in the teeth of this menace which she dimly felt threatened not only her body, but her soul as well.

She strained her eyes into the blackness beyond the rim of the dim light, tense with fear of what she might see. A whimpering gasp escaped her lips. The darkness was taking form. Something huge and bulky grew up out of the void. She saw a giant misshapen head emerging into the light. At least she took it for a head, though it was not the member of any sane or normal creature. She saw a great toad-like face, the features of which were as dim and unstable as those of a specter seen in a mirror of nightmare. Great pools of light that might have been eyes blinked at her, and she shook at the cosmic lust reflected there. She could tell nothing about the creature's body. Its outline seemed to waver and alter subtly even as she looked at it; yet its substance was apparently solid enough. There was nothing misty or ghostly about it.

As it came toward her, she could not tell whether it walked, wriggled, flew, or crept. Its method of locomotion was absolutely beyond her comprehension. When it had emerged from the shadows she was still uncertain as to its nature. The light from the radium gem did not illumine it as it would have illumined an ordinary creature. Impossible as it seemed, the being seemed almost impervious to the light. Its details were still obscure and indistinct, even when it halted so near that it almost touched her shrinking flesh. Only the blinding,- toad-like face stood out with any distinctness. The thing was a blur in the sight, a black blot of shadow that normal radiance would neither dissipate nor illuminate.

She decided she was mad, because she could not tell whether the being looked up at her or towered above her. She was unable to say whether the dim, repulsive face blinked up at her from the shadows at her feet, or looked down at her from an immense height. But if her sight convinced her that whatever its mutable qualities, it was yet composed of solid substance, her sense of feel further assured her of that fact. A dark tentacle-like member slid about her body, and she screamed at the touch of it on her naked flesh. It was neither warm nor cold, rough nor smooth; it was like nothing that had ever touched her before, and at its caress she knew such fear and shame as she had never dreamed of. All the obscenity and salacious infamy spawned in the muck of the abysmal pits of Life seemed to drown her in seas of cosmic filth. And in that instant she knew that whatever form of life this thing represented, it was not a beast.

She began to scream uncontrollably, the monster tugged at her as if to tear her from the ring by sheer brutality; then something crashed above their heads, and a form hurtled down through the air to strike the stone floor.

3.

When Conan wheeled to see the tapestry settling back in place and to hear Natala's muffled cry, he hurled himself against the wall with a maddened roar. Rebounding from the impact that would have splintered the bones of a lesser man, he ripped away the tapestry, revealing what appeared to be a blank wall. Beside himself with fury he lifted his saber as though to hew through the marble, when a sudden sound brought him about, eyes blazing.

A score of figures faced him, yellow men in purple tunics, with short swords in their hands. As he turned, they surged in on him with hostile cries. He made no attempt to conciliate them. Maddened at the disappearance of his sweetheart, the barbarian reverted to type.

A snarl of bloodthirsty gratification hummed in his bull-throat as he leaped, and the first attacker, his short sword overreached by the whistling saber, went down with his brains gushing from his split skull. Wheeling like a cat, Conan caught a descending wrist on his edge, and the hand gripping the short sword flew into the air scattering a shower of red drops. But Conan had not paused or hesitated. A pantherish twist and shift of his body avoided the blundering rush of two yellow swordsmen, and the blade of one, missing its objective, was sheathed in the breast of the other.

A yell of dismay went up at this mischance, and Conan allowed himself a short bark of laughter as he bounded aside from a whistling cut and slashed under the guard of yet another man of Xuthal. A long spurt of crimson followed his singing edge and the man crumpled screaming, his belly-muscles cut through.

The warriors of Xuthal howled like mad wolves. Unaccustomed to battle, they were ridiculously slow and clumsy compared to the tigerish barbarian whose motions were blurs of quickness possible only to steel thews knit to a perfect fighting brain. They floundered and stumbled, hindered by their own numbers; they struck too quick or too soon, and cut only empty air. He was never motionless or in the same place an instant; springing, sidestepping, whirling, twisting, he offered a constantly shifting target for their swords, while his own curved blade sang death about their ears.

But whatever their faults, the men of Xuthal did not lack courage. They swarmed about him yelling and hacking, and through the arched doorways rushed others, awakened from their slumbers by the unwonted clamor.

Conan, bleeding from a cut on the temple, cleared a space for an instant with a devastating sweep of his dripping saber, and cast a quick glance about for an avenue of escape. At that instant he saw the tapestry on one of the walls drawn aside, disclosing a narrow stairway. On this stood a man in rich robes, vague-eyed and blinking, as if he had just awakened and had not yet shaken the dusts of slumber from his brain. Conan's sight and action were simultaneous.

A tigerish leap carried him untouched through the hemming ring of swords, and he bounded toward the stair with the pack giving tongue behind him. Three men

130

confronted him at the foot of the marble steps, and he struck them with a deafening crash of steel. There was a frenzied instant when the blades flamed like summer lightning; then the group fell apart and Conan sprang up the stair. The oncoming horde tripped over three writhing forms at its foot: one lay face-down in a sickening welter of blood and brains; another propped himself on his hands, blood spurting blackly from his severed throat veins; the other howled like a dying dog as he clawed at the crimson stump that had been an arm.

As Conan rushed up the marble stair, the man above shook himself from his stupor and drew a sword that sparkled frostily in the radium light. He thrust downward as the barbarian surged upon him. But as the point sang toward his throat, Conan ducked deeply. The blade slit the skin of his back, and Conan straightened, driving his saber upward as a man might wield a butcher-knife, with all the power of his mighty shoulders.

So terrific was his headlong drive that the sinking of the saber to the hilt into the belly of his enemy did not check him. He caromed against the wretch's body, knocking it sidewise. The impact sent Conan crashing against the wall; the other, the saber torn through his body, fell headlong down the stair, ripped open to the spine from groin to broken breastbone. In a ghastly mess of streaming entrails the body tumbled against the men rushing up the stairs, bearing them back with it.

Half stunned, Conan leaned against the wall an instant, glaring down upon them; then with a defiant shake of his dripping saber, he bounded up the steps.

Coming into an upper chamber, he halted only long enough to see that it was empty. Behind him the horde was yelling with such intensified horror and rage, that he knew he had killed some notable man there on the stair, probably the king of that fantastic city.

He ran at random, without plan. He desperately wished to find and succor Natala, who he was sure needed aid badly; but harried as he was by all the warriors in

Xuthal, he could only run on, trusting to luck to elude them and find her. Among those dark or dimly lighted upper chambers he quickly lost all sense of direction, and it was not strange that he eventually blundered into a chamber into which his foes were just pouring.

They yelled vengefully and rushed for him, and with a snarl of disgust he turned and fled back the way he had come. At least he thought it was the way he had come. But presently, racing into a particularly ornate chamber, he was aware of his mistake. All the chambers he had traversed since mounting the stair had been empty. This chamber had an occupant, who rose up with a cry as he charged in.

Conan saw a yellow-skinned woman, loaded with jeweled ornaments but otherwise nude, staring at him with wide eyes. So much he glimpsed as she raised her hand and jerked a silken rope hanging from the wall. Then the floor dropped from under him, and all his steel-trap co-ordination could not save him from the plunge into the black depths that opened beneath him.

He did not fall any great distance, though it was far enough to have snapped the leg bones of a man not built of steel springs and whalebone.

He hit cat-like on his feet and one hand, instinctively retaining his grasp on his saber hilt. A familiar cry rang in his ears as he rebounded on his feet as a lynx rebounds with snarling bared fangs. So Conan, glaring from under his tousled mane, saw the white naked figure of Natala writhing in the lustful grasp of a black nightmare shape that could have only been bred in the lost pits of hell.

The sight of that awful shape alone might have frozen the Cimmerian with fear. In juxtaposition to his girl, the sight sent a red wave of murderous fury through Conan's brain. In a crimson mist he smote the monster.

It dropped the girl, wheeling toward its attacker, and the maddened Cimmerian's saber, shrilling through the air, sheared clear through the black viscous bulk and rang on the stone floor, showering blue sparks. Conan went to his knees from the fury of the blow; the edge had not encountered the resistance he had expected. As he bounded up, the thing was upon him.

It towered above him like a clinging black cloud. It seemed to flow about him in almost liquid waves, to envelop and engulf him. His madly slashing saber sheared through it again and again, his ripping poniard tore and rent it; he was deluged with a slimy liquid that must have been its sluggish blood. Yet its fury was nowise abated.

He could not tell whether he was slashing off its members or whether he was cleaving its bulk, which knit behind the slicing blade. He was tossed to and fro in the violence of that awful battle, and had a dazed feeling that he was fighting not one, but an aggregation of lethal creatures. The thing seemed to be biting, clawing, crushing and clubbing him all at the same time. He felt fangs and talons rend his flesh; flabby cables that were yet hard as iron encircled his limbs and body, and worse than all, something like a whip of scorpions fell again and again across his shoulders, back and breast, tearing the skin and filling his veins with a poison that was like liquid fire.

They had rolled beyond the circle of light, and it was in utter blackness that the Cimmerian battled. Once he sank his teeth, beast-like, into the flabby substance of his foe, revolting as the stuff writhed and squirmed like living rubber from between his iron jaws.

In that hurricane of battle they were rolling over and over, farther and father down the tunnel. Conan's brain reeled with the punishment he was taking. His breath came in whistling gasps between his teeth. High above him he saw a great toad-like face, dimly limned in an eery glow that seemed to emanate from it. And with a panting cry that was half curse, half gasp of straining agony, he lunged toward it, thrusting with all his waning power. Hilt-deep the saber sank, somewhere below the grisly face, and a convulsive shudder heaved the vast bulk that half enveloped the Cimmerian. With a volcanic burst of contraction and expansion, it tumbled backward, rolling now with frantic haste down the corridor. Conan went with it, bruised, battered, invincible, hanging on like a bulldog to the hilt of his saber which he could not withdraw, tearing and ripping at the shuddering bulk with the poniard in his left hand, goring it to ribbons.

The thing glowed all over now with a weird phosphorous radiance, and this glow was in Conan's eyes, blinding him, as suddenly the heaving, billowing mass fell away from beneath him, the saber tearing loose and remaining in his locked hand. This hand and arm hung down into space, and far below him the glowing body of the monster was rushing downward like a meteor. Conan dazedly realized that he lay on the brink of a great round well, the edge of which was slimy stone. He lay there watching the hurtling glow dwindling and dwindling until it vanished into a dark shining surface that seemed to surge upward to meet it. For an instant a dimming witchfire glimmered in those dusky depths; then it disappeared, and Conan lay staring down into the blackness of the ultimate abyss from which no sound came.

4.

Straining vainly at the silk cords which cut into her wrists, Natala sought to pierce the darkness beyond the radiant circle. Her tongue seemed frozen to the roof of her mouth. Into that blackness she had seen Conan vanish, locked in mortal combat with the unknown demon, and the only sounds that had come to her straining ears had been the panting gasps of the barbarian, the impact of struggling bodies, and the thud and rip of savage blows. These ceased and Natala swayed dizzily on her cords, half fainting.

A footstep roused her out of her apathy of horror, to see Conan emerging from the darkness. At the sight she found her voice in a shriek which echoed down the vaulted tunnel. The manhandling the Cimmerian had received was appalling to behold. At every step he dripped blood. His face was skinned and bruised as if he had been beaten with a bludgeon. His lips were pulped, and blood oozed down his face from a wound in his scalp,

There were deep gashes in his thighs, calves and forearms, and great bruises showed on his limbs and body from impacts against the stone floor. But his shoulders, back and upper-breast muscles had suffered most. The flesh was bruised, swollen and lacerated, the skin hanging in loose strips, as if he had been lashed with wire whips.

"Oh, Conan!" she sobbed. "What has happened to you?"

He had no breath for conversation, but his smashed lips writhed in what might have been grim humor as he approached her. His hairy breast, glistening with sweat and blood, heaved with his panting. Slowly and laboriously he reached up and cut her cords, then fell back against the wall and leaned there, his trembling legs braced wide. She scrambled up from where she had fallen and caught him in a frenzied embrace, sobbing hysterically.

"Oh, Conan, you are wounded unto death! Oh, what shall we do?"

"Well," he panted, "you can't fight a devil out of Hell and come off with a whole skin!"

"Where is It?" she whispered. "Did you kill it?"

"I don't know. It fell into a pit. It was hanging in bloody shreds, but whether it can be killed by steel I know not."

"Oh, your poor back!" she wailed, wringing her hands.

"It lashed me with a tentacle," he grimaced, swearing as he moved. "It cut like wire and burned like poison. But it was its damnable squeezing that got my wind. It was worse than a python. If half my guts are not mashed out of place, I'm much mistaken."

"What shall we do?" she whimpered.

He glanced up. The trap was closed. No sound came from above.

"We can't go back through the secret door," he muttered. "That room is full of dead men, and doubtless warriors keep watch there. They must have thought my doom sealed when I plunged through the floor above, or else they dare not follow me into this tunnel.—Twist that

135

radium gem off the wall.—As I groped my way back up the corridor I felt arches opening into other tunnels. We'll follow the first we come to. It may lead to another pit, or to the open air. We must chance it. We can't stay here and rot."

Natala obeyed, and holding the tiny point of light in his left hand and his bloody saber in his right, Conan started down the corridor. He went slowly, stiffly, only his animal vitality keeping him on his feet. There was a blank glare in his bloodshot eyes, and Natala saw him involuntarily lick his battered lips from time to time. She knew his suffering was ghastly, but with the stoicism of the wilds he made no complaint.

Presently the dim light shone on a black arch, and into this Conan turned. Natala cringed at what she might see, but the light revealed only a tunnel similar to that they had just left.

How far they went she had no idea, before they mounted a long stair and came upon a stone door, fastened with a golden bolt.

She hesitated, glancing at Conan. The barbarian was swaying on his feet, the light in his unsteady hand flinging fantastic shadows back and forth along the wall.

"Open the door, girl," he muttered thickly. "The men of Xuthal will be waiting for us, and I would not disappoint them. By Crom, the city has not seen such a sacrifice as I will make!"

She knew he was half delirious. No sound came from beyond the door. Taking the radium gem from his bloodstained hand, she threw the bolt and drew the panel inward. The inner side of a cloth-of-gold tapestry met her gaze and she drew it aside and peeked through, her heart in her mouth. She was looking into an empty chamber in the center of which a silvery fountain tinkled.

Conan's hand fell heavily on her naked shoulder.

"Stand aside, girl," he mumbled. "Now is the feasting of swords."

"There is no one in the chamber," she answered. "But there is water——"

"I hear it." He licked his blackened lips. "We will drink before we die."

He seemed blinded. She took his darkly stained hand and led him through the stone door. She went on tiptoe, expecting a rush of yellow figures through the arches at any instant.

"Drink while I keep watch," he muttered.

"No, I am not thirsty. Lie down beside the fountain and I will bathe your wounds."

"What of the swords of Xuthal?" He continually raked his arm across his eyes as if to clear his blurred sight.

"I hear no one. All is silent."

He sank down gropingly and plunged his face into the crystal jet, drinking as if he could not get enough. When he raised his head there was sanity in his bloodshot eyes and he stretched his massive limbs out on the marble floor as she requested, though he kept his saber in his hand, and his eyes continually roved toward the archways. She bathed his torn flesh and bandaged the deeper wounds with strips torn from a silk hanging. She shuddered at the appearance of his back; the flesh was discolored, mottled and spotted black and blue and a sickly yellow, where it was not raw. As she worked she sought frantically for a solution to their problem. If they stayed where they were, they would eventually be discovered. Whether the men of Xuthal were searching the palaces for them, or had returned to their dreams, she could not know.

As she finished her task, she froze. Under the hanging that partly concealed an alcove, she saw a hand's breadth of yellow flesh.

Saying nothing to Conan, she rose and crossed the chamber softly, grasping his poniard. Her heart pounded suffocatingly as she cautiously drew aside the hanging. On the dais lay a young yellow woman, naked and apparently lifeless. At her hand stood a jade jar nearly full of peculiar golden-colored liquid. Natala believed it to be the elixir described by Thalis, which lent vigor and vitality to the degenerate Xuthal. She leaned across the

137

supine form and grasped the vessel, her poniard poised over the girl's bosom. The latter did not wake.

With the jar in her possession, Natala hesitated, realizing it would be the safer course to put the sleeping girl beyond the power of waking and raising an alarm. But she could not bring herself to plunge the Cimmerian poniard into that still bosom, and at last she drew back the hanging and returned to Conan, who lay where she had left him, seemingly only partly conscious.

She bent and placed the jar to his lips. He drank, mechanically at first, then with a suddenly aroused interest. To her amazement he sat up and took the vessel from her hands. When he lifted his face, his eyes were clear and normal. Much of the drawn haggard look had gone from his features, and his voice was not the mumble of delirium.

"Crom! Where did you get this?"

She pointed. "From that alcove, where a yellow hussy is sleeping."

He thrust his muzzle again into the golden liquid.

"By Crom," he said with a deep sigh, "I feel new life and power rush like wildfire through my veins. Surely this is the very elixir of Life!"

He rose, picking up his saber.

"We had best go back into the corridor," Natala ventured nervously. "We shall be discovered if we stay here long. We can hide there until your wounds heal——"

"Not I!" he grunted. "We are not rats, to hide in dark burrows. We leave this devil-city now, and let none seek to stop us."

"But your wounds!" she wailed.

"I do not feel them," he answered, "It may be a false strength this liquor has given me, but I swear I am aware of neither pain nor weakness."

With sudden purpose he crossed the chamber to a window she had not noticed. Over his shoulder she looked out. A cool breeze tossed her tousled locks. Above was the dark velvet sky, clustered with stars. Below them stretched a vague expanse of sand.

"Thalis said the city was one great palace," said Conan. "Evidently some of the chambers are built like towers on the wall. This one is. Chance has led us well."

"What do you mean?" she asked, glancing apprehensively over her shoulder.

"There is a crystal jar on that ivory table," he answered. "Fill it with water and tie a strip of that torn hanging about its neck for a handle while I rip up this tapestry."

She obeyed without question, and when she turned from her task she saw Conan rapidly tying together the long tough strips of silk to make a rope, one end of which he fastened to the leg of the massive ivory table.

"We'll take our chance with the desert," said he. "Thalis spoke of an oasis a day's march to the south, and grasslands beyond that. If we reach the oasis we can rest until my wounds heal. This wine is like sorcery. A little while ago I was little more than a dead man; now I am ready for anything. Here is enough silk left for you to make a garment of."

Natala had forgotten her nudity. The mere fact caused her no qualms, but her delicate skin would need protection from the desert sun. As she knotted the silk length about her supple body, Conan turned to the window and with a contemptuous wrench tore away the soft gold bars that guarded it. Then, looping the loose end of the silk rope about Natala's hips, and cautioning her to hold on with both hands, he lifted her through the window and lowered her the thirty-odd feet to the earth. She stepped out of the loop and, drawing it back up, he made fast the vessels of water and wine, and lowered them to her. He followed them, sliding down swiftly, hand over hand.

As he reached her side, Natala gave a sigh of relief. They stood alone at the foot of the great wall, the paling stars overhead and the naked desert about them. What perils yet confronted them she could not know, but her heart sang with joy because they were out of that ghostly, unreal city.

"They may find the rope," grunted Conan, slinging the precious jars across his shoulders, wincing at the contact with his mangled flesh. "They may even pursue us, but from what Thalis said, I doubt it. That way is south," a bronze muscular arm indicated their course; "so somewhere in that direction lies the oasis. Come!"

Taking her hand with a thoughtfulness unusual for him, Conan strode out across the sands, suiting his stride to the shorter legs of his companion. He did not glance back at the silent city, brooding dreamily and ghostily behind them.

"Conan," Natala ventured finally, "when you fought the monster, and later, as you came up the corridor, did you see anything of—of Thalis?"

He shook his head. "It was dark in the corridor; but it was empty."

She shuddered. "She tortured me—yet I pity her."

"It was a hot welcome we got in that accursed city," he snarled. Then his grim humor returned. "Well, they'll remember our visit long enough, I'll wager. There are brains and guts and blood to be cleaned off the marble tiles, and if their god still lives, he carries more wounds than I. We got off light, after all: we have wine and water and a good chance of reaching a habitable country, though I look as if I'd gone through a meat-grinder, and you have a sore——"

"It's all your fault," she interrupted. "If you had not looked so long and admiringly at that Stygian cat——"

"Crom and his devils!" he swore. "When the oceans drown the world, women will take time for jealousy. Devil take their conceit! Did I tell the Stygian to fall in love with me? After all, she was only human!"

Drums of Tombalku

Eventually, Conan beats his way back to the Hyborian lands. Seeking further employment as a condottiere, he joins a mercenary army that a Zingaran, Prince Zapayo da Kova, is raising for Argos. Argos and Koth are at war with Stygia. The plan is that Koth shall invade Stygia from the north, while the Argossean army enters Stygia from the south by sea. Koth, however, makes a separate peace with Stygia, and the mercenary army is trapped in southern Stygia between two hostile forces. Again, Conan is among the few survivors. Fleeing through the desert with a young Aquilonian soldier, Amalric, he is captured by desert nomads while Amalric escapes.

1.

THREE MEN squatted beside the water hole, beneath a sunset sky that painted the desert umber and red. One was white, and his name was Amalric; the other two were Ghanatas, their tatters scarcely concealing their wiry black frames. Men called them Gobir and Saidu; they looked like vultures as they crouched beside the water hole.

Nearby, a camel noisily ground its cud and a pair of weary horses vainly nuzzled the bare sand. The men cheerlessly munched dried dates. The black men were intent only on the working of their jaws, while the white man occasionally glanced at the dull-red sky or out across the monotonous level, where shadows were gathering and deepening. He was the first to see the horseman who rode up and drew rein with a jerk that set the steed to rearing.

The rider was a giant whose skin, blacker than that of the other two, as well as his thick lips and flaring nostrils, told of a heavy predominance of Negro blood. His wide silk pantaloons, gathered in about his bare ankles, were supported by a broad girdle wrapped repeatedly about his huge belly. That girdle also supported a flaring-tipped scimitar, which few men could have wielded with one hand. With that scimitar, the man was famed wherever the dark-skinned sons of the desert rode. He was Tilutan, the pride of the Ghanata.

Across his saddle a limp shape lay, or rather hung. Breath hissed through the teeth of the Ghanatas as they caught the gleam of pale limbs. It was a white girl who hung face-down across Tilutan's saddle bow, her loose hair flowing over his stirrup in a rippling black wave.

The black giant grinned with a glint of white teeth as he casually cast his captive into the sand, where she lay laxly, unconscious. Instinctively, Gobir and Saidu turned toward Amalric, while Tilutan watched him from his saddle: three black men against one white. The entrance of a white woman into the scene had wrought a subtle change in the atmosphere.

Amalric was the only one apparently oblivious to the tension. He absently raked back his yellow locks and glanced indifferently at the girl's limp figure. If there was a momentary gleam in his gray eyes, the others did not catch it.

Tilutan swung down from his saddle, contemptuously tossing the rein to Amalric.

"Tend my horse," he said. "By Jhil, I did not find a desert antelope, but I did find this little filly. She was reeling through the sands and fell just as I approached. I think she fainted from weariness and thirst. Get away from there, you jackals, and let me give her a drink."

The big black stretched the girl out beside the water hole and began laving her face and wrists and trickling a few drops between her parched lips. Presently, she moaned and stirred. Gobir and Saidu crouched with their hands on their knees, staring at her over Tilutan's burly shoulder. Amalric stood a little apart, his interest seeming only casual.

"She is coming to," announced Gobir.

Saidu said nothing but licked his thick lips.

Amalric's gaze traveled impersonally over the prostrate form, from the torn sandals to the loose crown of glossy black hair. The girl's only garment was a silken kirtle, girdled at the waist. It left her arms, her neck, and part of her bosom bare, and the skirt ended several inches above her knees. On the parts revealed, the gaze of the Ghanatas rested with devouring intensity, taking in the soft contours, childish in their white softness, yet rounded with budding womanhood.

Amalric shrugged. "After Tilutan, who?" he carelessly asked.

A pair of lean heads turned toward him; bloodshot eyes rolled at the question. Then the black men turned and stared at each other. Sudden rivalry crackled electrically between them.

"Don't fight," urged Amalric. "Cast the dice." His hand came out from under his worn tunic, and he threw down a pair of dice before them. A clawlike hand seized them.

"Aye!" agreed Gobir. "We cast—after Tilutan, the winner!"

Amalric threw a glance toward the giant black, who still bent above his captive, bringing life back into her exhausted body. As Amalric looked, her long-lashed lids parted. Deep violet eyes stared bewilderedly up into the leering face of the black man. An explosive exclamation of pleasure escaped the thick lips of Tilutan. Wrenching a flask from his girdle, he put it to her mouth. Mechanically, she drank the wine. Amalric avoided her wandering gaze; he was one white man to three blacks—any one of them his match.

Gobir and Saidu bent above the dice; Saidu cupped them in his palm, breathed on them for luck, shook, and threw. Two vulturelike heads bent over the cubes, which spun in the dim light. And with the same motion, Amalric drew and struck. The edge sliced through a lean neck, severing the windpipe. Gobir, his head hanging by a thread, fell across the dice, spurting blood.

Simultaneously Saidu, with the desperate quickness of a desert man, shot to his feet, drew, and hacked ferociously at the slayer's head. Amalric barely had time to catch the stroke on his lifted sword. The whistling scimitar beat the straight blade down on the white man's head, staggering him so that he dropped his sword. Recovering, he threw both arms about Saidu, dragging him into close quarters where his scimitar was useless. Under the desert man's rags, the wiry frame was like steel and rawhide.

Tilutan, instantly comprehending the matter, had cast the girl down and risen with a roar. He rushed toward the strugglers like a charging bull, his great scimitar flaming in his hand. Amalric saw him coming, and his flesh turned cold. Saidu jerked and wrenched, handicapped by the scimitar he was still futilely seeking to turn against his antagonist. Their feet twisted and stamped in the sand; their bodies ground against each other. Amalric smashed his sandaled heel down on the Ghanata's bare instep, feeling bones give way. Saidu howled and plunged convulsively. They lurched drunkenly about, just as Tilutan struck with a rolling drive of his broad shoulders. Amalric felt the steel rasp the under part of his arm and chug deep into Saidu's body. The smaller Ghanata gave an agonized scream, and his convulsive start tore him free of Amalric's grasp.

Tilutan roared a furious oath and, wrenching his steel free, hurled the dying man aside. Before he could strike again, Amalric, his skin crawling with the fear of that great curved blade, had grappled with him.

Despair swept over Amalric as he felt the strength of

144

the Negro. Tilutan was wiser than Saidu. He dropped the scimitar and, with a bellow, caught Amalric's throat with both hands. The great black fingers locked like iron. Amalric, vainly striving to break their grip, was borne down with the Ghanata's great weight pinning him to the earth. The smaller man was shaken like a rat in the jaws of a dog. His head was savagely smashed against the sand. As in a red mist he saw the furious face of the Negro, the thick lips writhed back in a ferocious grin of hate, the teeth glistening.

"You want her, you white dog!" the Ghanata snarled, mad with rage and lust. "Arrgh! I break your neck! I tear out your throat! I—my scimitar! I cut off your head and make her kiss it!"

With a final ferocious smash of Amalric's head against the hard-packed sand, Tilutan, in an excess of murderous passion, half-lifted his antagonist and hurled him down. Rising, the black ran, stooping, and caught up his scimitar from where it lay, a broad crescent of steel in the sand. Yelling in ferocious exaltation, he turned and charged back, brandishing the blade on high. Amalric— dazed, shaken, and sick from the manhandling he had received—rose to meet him.

Tilutan's girdle had become unwound in the fight, and now the end dangled about his feet. He tripped, stumbled, and fell headlong, throwing out his arms to save himself. The scimitar flew from his hand.

Amalric, galvanized, caught up the scimitar with both hands and took a reeling step forward. The desert swam darkly to his gaze. In the dusk before him, he saw Tilutan's face go slack with a premonition of doom. The wide mouth gaped; the whites of the eyeballs rolled up. The black froze on one knee and one hand, as if incapable of further motion. Then the scimitar fell, cleaving the round head to the chin. Amalric had a dim impression of a black face, divided by a widening red line, fading in the thickening shadows. Then darkness caught him with a rush.

Something cool and soft was touching Amalric's face with gentle persistence. He groped blindly, and his hand closed on something warm, firm, and resilient. As his sight cleared, he looked into a soft, oval face, framed in lustrous black hair. As in a trance, he gazed unspeaking, hungrily dwelling on each detail of the full, red lips, the dark, violet eyes, and the alabaster throat. With a start, he realized that the vision was speaking in a soft, musical voice. The words were strange, yet possessed of an elusive familiarity. A small, white hand, holding a dripping bunch of silk, was passed gently over his throbbing head and his face. Dizzily, he sat up.

It was night, under star-splashed skies. The camel still munched its cud; a horse whinnied restlessly. Not far away lay a hulking figure with its cleft head in a horrible puddle of blood and brains.

Amalric looked up at the girl who knelt beside him, talking in her gentle, unknown tongue. As the mists cleared from his brain, he began to understand her. Harking back into half-forgotten tongues he had learned and spoken in the past, he remembered a language used by a scholarly class in a southern province of Koth.

"Who—are—you, girl?" he asked in slow and stumbling speech, imprisoning a small hand in his own hardened fingers.

"I am Lissa." The name was spoken with almost the suggestion of a lisp. It was like the rippling of a slender stream. "I am glad you are conscious. I feared you were not alive."

"A little more and I shouldn't have been," he muttered, glancing at the grisly sprawl that had been Tilutan. The girl, shuddering, refused to follow his glance. Her hand trembled and, in their nearness, Amalric thought he could feel the quick throb of her heart.

"It was horrible," she faltered. "Like an awful dream. Anger—and blows—and blood—"

"It might have been worse," he growled.

She seemed sensitive to every changing inflection of voice or mood. Her free hand stole timidly to his own.

146

"I did not mean to offend you. It was very brave for you to risk your life for a stranger. You are noble as the northern knights about which I have read."

He cast a quick glance at her. Her wide clear eyes met his, reflecting only the thought that she had spoken. He started to speak, then changed his mind and said another thing.

"What are you doing in the desert?"

"I came from Gazal," she answered. "I—I was running away. I could not stand it any longer. But it was hot and lonely and wearying, and I saw only sand, sand—and the blazing blue sky. The sands burned by feet, and my sandals were quickly worn out. I was so thirsty; my canteen was soon empty. And then I wished to return to Gazel, but one direction looked like another. I did not know which way to go. I was terribly afraid and started running in the direction in which I thought Gazal to be. I do not remember much after that; I ran until I could run no further.

"I must have lain in the burning sand for a while. I remember rising and staggering on; and, toward the last, I thought I heard someone shouting and saw a black man on a black horse riding toward me. Then I knew no more until I awoke and found myself lying with my head in that man's lap, while he gave me wine to drink. Then there were shouting and fighting—" She shuddered. "When it was all over, I crept to where you lay like a dead man and tried to bring you to."

"Why?" he demanded.

She seemed at a loss. "Why?" she floundered, "why—you were hurt—and—it is what anyone would do. Besides, I realized that you were fighting to protect me from these black men. The people of Gazal have always said that the black people are wicked and would harm the helpless."

"That's no exclusive characteristic of the blacks," muttered Amalric. "Where is this Gazal?"

"It cannot be far," she answered. "I walked a whole day—and then I do not know how far the black man

147

carried me after he found me. But he must have discov-ered me about sunset, so he could not have come far."

"In which direction?" he demanded.

"I do not know. I traveled eastward when I left the city."

"City?" he muttered. "A day's travel from this spot? I had thought there was only desert for a thousand miles."

"Gazal is in the desert," she answered. "It is built amidst the palms of an oasis."

Putting the girl aside, he got to his feet, swearing softly as he fingered his throat, the skin of which was bruised and lacerated. He examined the three blacks in turn, finding no life in any of them. Then, one by one, he dragged them a short distance out into the desert. Somewhere, the jackals began yelping. Returning to the water hole, where the girl patiently squatted, he cursed to find only the black stallion of Tilutan with the camel. The other horses had broken their tethers and bolted during the fight.

Amalric returned to the girl and proffered her a handful of dried dates. She nibbled at them eagerly, while the other sat and watched her, an increasing im-patience throbbing in his veins.

"Why did you run away?" he asked abruptly. "Are you a slave?"

"We have no slaves in Gazal," she answered. "Oh, I was weary—so weary of the eternal monotony. I wished to see something of the outer world. Tell me, from what land do you come?"

"I was born in the western hills of Aquilonia," he an-swered.

She clapped her hands like a delighted child. "I know where that is! I have seen it on the maps. It is the wes-ternmost country of the Hyborians, and its king is Epeus the Sword-wielder."

Amalric experienced a distinct shock. His head jerked up, and he stared at his companion.

148

"Epeus? Why, Epeus has been dead for nine hundred years. The king's name is Vilerus."

"Oh, of course," she said with embarrassment. "I am foolish. Of course Epeus was king nine centuries ago, as you say. But tell me—tell me all about the world!"

"Why, that's a big order!" he answered, nonplussed. "You have not traveled?"

"This is the first time I have ever been out of sight of the walls of Gazal," she declared.

His gaze was fixed on the curve of her white bosom. He was not, at the moment, interested in her adventures; Gazal might have been Hell for all he cared.

He started to speak; then, changing his mind, caught her roughly in his arms, his muscles tensed for the struggle he expected. But he encountered no resistance. Her soft, yielding body lay across his knees, and she looked up at him somewhat in surprise but without fear or embarrassment. She might have been a child, submitting to a new kind of play. Something about her direct gaze confused him. If she had screamed, wept, fought, or smiled knowingly, he would have known how to deal with her.

"Who in Mitra's name are you, girl?" he asked roughly. "You are neither touched with the sun nor playing a game with me. Your speech shows you to be no simple country lass, innocent in her ignorance. Yet you seem to know nothing of the world and its ways."

"I am a daughter of Gazal," she answered helplessly. "If you saw Gazal, perhaps you would understand."

He lifted her and set her down in the sand. Rising, he brought a saddle blanket and spread it out for her.

"Sleep, Lissa," he said, his voice harsh with conflicting emotions. "Tomorrow I mean to see Gazal."

At dawn they started westward. Amalric had placed Lissa on the camel, showing her how to maintain her balance. She clung to the seat with both hands, displaying no knowledge whatever of camels. This again surprised the young Aquilonian. A girl raised in the desert, who

149

had never before been on a camel; nor, until the preceding night, had she ever ridden or been carried on a horse.

Amalric had manufactured a sort of cloak for her. She wore it without question, not asking whence it came—accepting it as she accepted all the things he did for her, gratefully but blindly, without asking the reason. Amalric did not tell her that the silk that shielded her from the sun once covered the black hide of her abductor.

As they rode, she again begged him to tell her something of the world, like a child asking for a story.

"I know Aquilonia is far from this desert," she said. "Stygia lies between, and the lands of Shem, and other countries. How is it that you are here, so far from your homeland?"

He rode for a space in silence, his hand on the camel's guide rope.

"Argos and Stygia are at war," he said abruptly. "Koth became embroiled. The Kothians urged a simultaneous invasion of Stygia. Argos raised an army of mercenaries, which went into ships and sailed southward along the coast. At the same time, a Kothic army was to invade Stygia by land. I was one of that mercenary army of Argos. We met the Stygian fleet and defeated it, driving it back into Khemi. We should have landed, looted the city, and advanced along the course of the Styx, but our admiral was cautious. Our leader was Prince Zapayo da Kova, a Zingaran.

"We cruised southward until we reached the jungle-clad coasts of Kush. There we landed, and the ships anchored while the army pushed eastward, along the Stygian frontier, burning and pillaging as we went. It was our intention to turn northward at a certain point and strike into the heart of Stygia, to join the Kothic host pushing down from the north.

"Then word came that we were betrayed. Koth had concluded a separate peace with the Stygians. A Stygian army was pushing southward to intercept us, while another had already cut us off from the coast.

"Prince Zapayo, in desperation, conceived the mad idea of marching eastward, hoping to skirt the Stygian border and eventually to reach the eastern lands of Shem. But the army from the north overtook us. We turned and fought.

"All day we fought, and we drove them back in rout to their camp. But, the next day, the pursuing army came up from the west. Crushed between the hosts, our army ceased to be. We were broken, annihilated, destroyed. There were few left to flee. When night fell, I broke away with my companion, a Cimmerian named Conan —a brute of a man with the strength of a bull.

"We rode southward into the desert, because there was no other direction in which we might go. Conan had been in this part of the world before and believed we had a chance to survive. Far to the south we found an oasis, but Stygian riders harried us. We fled again, from oasis to oasis, starving and thirsting until we found ourselves in a barren, unknown land of blazing sun and empty sand. We rode until our horses were reeling and we were half delirious.

"Then, one night, we saw fires and rode up to them, taking a desperate chance that we might make friends with them. As soon as we came within range, a shower of arrows greeted us. Conan's horse was hit and reared, throwing its rider. His neck must have broken like a twig, for he never moved. Somehow I got away in the darkness, although my horse died under me. I had only a glimpse of the attackers—tall, lean, brown men, wearing strange barbaric garments.

"I wandered on foot through the desert and fell in with those three vultures you saw yesterday. They were jackals —Ghanatas, members of a robber tribe of mixed blood: Negro and Mitra knows what else. The only reason they didn't murder me was that I had nothing they wished. For a month I have been wandering and thieving with them, because there was nothing else I could do."

"I did not know it was like that," she murmured. "They said there were wars and cruelty out in the world,

151

but it seemed like a dream and far away. Hearing you speak of treachery and battle seems almost like seeing it."

"Do no enemies ever come against Gazal?" he demanded.

She shook her head. "Men ride wide of Gazal. Sometimes I have seen black dots moving in lines along the horizon, and the old men said they were armies moving to war; but they never come near Gazal."

Amalric felt a dim stirring of uneasiness. This desert, seemingly empty of life, nevertheless contained some of the fiercest tribes on earth: the Ghanatas, who ranged far to the east; the masked Tibu, who he believed dwelt further to the south; and, somewhere off to the southwest, the semi-mythical empire of Tombalku, ruled by a wild and barbaric race. It was strange that a city in the midst of this savage land should be left so completely alone that one of its inhabitants did not even know the meaning of war.

When he turned his gaze elsewhere, strange thoughts assailed him. Was the girl touched by the sun? Was she a demon in womanly form, come out of the desert to lure him to some cryptic doom? A glance at her, clinging childishly to the high peak of the camel's saddle, was sufficient to dispel these broodings. Then again, doubt assailed him. Was he bewitched? Had she cast a spell on him?

Westward they steadily forged, halting only to nibble dates and drink water at midday. To shield her from the burning sun, Amalric fashioned a frail shelter out of his sword and sheath and the saddle blankets. Weary and stiff from the tossing, bucking gait of the camel, she had to be lifted down in his arms. As he felt again the voluptuous sweetness of her soft body, a hot throb of passion seared through him. He stood momentarily motionless, intoxicated with her nearness, before he laid her down in the shade of a makeshift tent.

He felt a touch almost of anger at the clear gaze with which she met his, at the docility with which she yielded her young body to his hands. It was as if she were un-

152

aware of things that might harm her; her innocent trust shamed him and pent a helpless wrath within him.

As they ate, he did not taste the dates he munched; his eyes burned on her, avidly drinking in every detail of her lithe young figure. She seemed as unaware of his intentness as a child. When he lifted her to place her again on her camel, and her arms went instinctively about his neck, he shuddered. But he lifted her up on her mount, and they took up the journey once more.

2

It was just before sundown when Lissa pointed and cried out: "Look! The towers of Gazal!"

On the desert rim he saw them—spires and minarets, rising in a jade-green cluster against the blue sky. But for the girl, he would have thought it the phantom city of a mirage. He glanced at Lissa curiously; she showed no signs of eager joy at her homecoming. She sighed, and her slim shoulders seemed to droop.

As they approached, the details swam more plainly into view. Sheer from the desert sands rose the wall that inclosed the towers. And Amalric saw that the wall was crumbling in many places. The towers, too, were much in disrepair. Roofs sagged; broken battlements gaped; spires leaned drunkenly. Panic assailed him; was it a city of the dead to which he rode, guided by a vampire? A quick glance at the girl reassured him. No demon could lurk in that divinely molded form. She glanced at him with a strange, wistful questioning in her deep eyes, turned irresolutely toward the desert, and then, with a deep sigh, set her face toward the city, as if gripped by a subtle and fatalistic despair.

Now, through the gaps in the jade-green wall, Amalric saw figures moving within the city. No one hailed them as they rode through a broad breach in the wall and came out into a wide street. Close at hand, limned in the sinking sun, the decay was more apparent. Grass grew rank

153

in the streets, pushing through shattered paving; grass grew rank in the small plazas. Streets and courts were likewise littered with a rubbish of fallen stones. Here and there, the ruins of a house had been cleared away and the space given over to vegetable gardening.

Domes rose, cracked and discolored. Portals gaped, vacant of doors. Everywhere, ruin had laid its hand. Then Amalric saw one spire untouched: a shining, red, cylindrical tower, which rose in the extreme southeastern corner of the city. It gleamed among the ruins. Amalric indicated it.

"Why is that tower less ruined than the others?" he asked. Lissa turned pale, trembled, and convulsively caught his hand.

"Do not speak of it!" she whispered. "Do not look toward it—do not even *think* of it!"

Amalric scowled; the nameless implication of her words had somehow changed the aspect of the mysterious tower. Now it seemed like a serpent's head, rearing amid ruin and desolation. A stream of black specks—bats on the wing—poured from its high black apertures.

The young Aquilonian looked warily about him. After all, he had no assurance that the people of Gazal would receive him in a friendly manner. He saw people moving leisurely about the streets. When they halted and stared at him, his flesh for some reason crawled. They were men and women with kindly features, and their looks were mild. But their interest seemed so slight—so vague and impersonal. They made no move to approach or speak to him. It might have been the commonest thing in the world for an armed horseman to ride into their city from the desert; yet Amalric knew that this was not the case, and the casual manner with which the people of Gazal received him caused a faint uneasiness in his bosom.

Lissa spoke to them, indicating Amalric, whose hand she lifted like an affectionate child. "This is Amalric of Aquilonia, who rescued me from the black people and has brought me home."

A polite murmur of welcome rose from the people, and

several of them approached to extend their hands. Amalric thought he had never seen such vague, kindly faces; their eyes were soft and mild, without fear and without wonder. Yet they were not the eyes of stupid oxen; rather, they were the eyes of people wrapped in dreams.

Their stare gave him a feeling of unreality; he hardly knew what was said to him. His mind was occupied by the strangeness of it all: these quiet, dreamy people, in their silken tunics and soft sandals, moving with aimless vagueness among the discolored ruins. A lotus paradise of illusion? Somehow that sinister red tower struck a discordant note.

One of the men, with a smooth, unlined face but hair of silver, said: "Aquilonia? There was an invasion—we heard by King Bragorus of Nemedia. How went the war?"

"He was driven back," answered Amalric briefly, resisting a shudder. Nine hundred years had passed since Bragorus had led his spearmen across the marches of Aquilonia.

His questioner did not press him further; the people drifted away, and Lissa tugged at his hand. He turned and feasted his eyes upon her. In a realm of illusion and dream, her soft, firm body anchored his wandering conjectures. She was no dream; she was real; her body was sweet and tangible as cream and honey.

"Come," she said, "let us go to rest and eat."

"What of the people?" he demurred. "Will you not tell them of your experiences?"

"They would not heed, except for a few moments," she answered. "They would listen a little, then drift away. They hardly know I have been gone. Come!"

Amalric led the horse and the camel into an enclosed court, where the grass grew high and water seeped from a broken fountain into a marble trough. There he tethered them; then he followed Lissa. Taking his hand, she led him across the court into an arched doorway. Night had fallen. In the open space above the court, the stars clustered, etching the jagged pinnacles.

Through a series of dark chambers Lissa went, moving with the sureness of long practice. Amalric groped after her, guided by her little hand in his. He found it no pleasant adventure. The scent of dust and decay hung in the thick darkness. Under his feet were sometimes broken tiles and sometimes worn carpets. His free hand touched the fretted arches of doorways. Then the stars gleamed through a broken roof, showing him a dim winding hallway, hung with rotting tapestries. They rustled in a faint breeze; their noise was like the whispering of witches, causing the hair of his scalp to stir.

Then they came into a chamber dimly lighted by starshine streaming through open windows, and Lissa released his hand. She fumbled for an instant and produced a faint light. It was a glassy knob, which glowed with a golden radiance. She set it on a marble table and indicated that Amalric should recline on a couch thickly littered with silks. Groping into some hidden recess, she produced a golden vessel of wine and others containing food unfamiliar to Amalric. There were dates; but the other fruits and vegetables, pallid and insipid to his taste, he did not recognize. The wine was pleasant to the palate but no more heady than dishwater.

Seated on a marble seat facing him, Lissa nibbled daintily.

"What sort of place is this?" he demanded. "You are like these people, yet strangely unlike them."

"They say I am like our ancestors," answered Lissa. "Long ago, they came into the desert and built this city amid a great oasis, which contained a series of springs. The stone they took from the ruins of a much older city—only the Red Tower—" (her voice dropped, and she glanced nervously at the star-framing windows) "—only the red tower stood there. It was empty—then.

"Our ancestors, who were called Gazali, once dwelt in southern Koth. They were noted for their scholarly wisdom. But they sought to revive the worship of Mitra, which the Kothians had long since abandoned, and the king drove them from his kingdom. They came southward, many of them: priests, scholars, teachers, and scientists, with their Shemitish slaves.

"They reared Gazal in the desert; but the slaves revolted almost as soon as the city was built and, fleeing, mixed with the wild tribes of the desert. They were not ill-treated; but word came to them in the night—a word that sent them fleeing madly from the city into the desert.

"My people dwelt here, learning to produce their food and drink from such material as was at hand. Their learning was a marvel. When the slaves fled, they took with them every camel, horse, and ass in the city. Thenceforth, there was no communication with the outer world. There are whole chambers in Gazal filled with maps and books and chronicles, but they are all nine hundred years old at the least; for it was nine hundred years ago that my people fled from Koth. Since then, no man of the outside world has set foot in Gazal. And the people are slowly vanishing. They have become so dreamy and introspective that they have neither human passions nor human appetites. The city falls into ruins and none moves a hand to repair it. Horror—" (she choked and shuddered) "—when horror came upon them, they could neither flee nor fight."

"What do you mean?" he whispered, a cold wind blowing on his spine. The rustling of rotten hangings down nameless black corridors stirred dim fears in his soul.

She shook her head. She rose, came around the marble table, and laid hands on his shoulders. Her eyes were wet and shone with horror and a desperate yearning that caught at his throat. Instinctively his arm went around her lithe form, and he felt her tremble.

"Hold me!" she begged. "I am afraid! Oh, I have dreamed of such a man as you. I am not like my people; they are dead men walking forgotten streets; but I am alive. I am warm and sentient. I hunger and thirst and yearn for life. I cannot abide the silent streets and ruined halls and dim people of Gazal, although I have never known anything else. That is why I ran away; I yearned for life—"

She was sobbing uncontrollably in his arms. Her hair streamed over his face; her fragrance made him dizzy. Her firm body strained against his. She was lying across his knees, her arms locked about his neck. Straining her to his breast, he crushed her lips with his. Eyes, lips, cheeks, hair, throat, breasts—he showered her with hot kisses, until her sobs changed to panting gasps. His passion was not the violence of a ravisher. The passion that slumbered in her woke in one overpowering wave. The glowing golden ball, struck by his groping fingers, tumbled to the floor and was extinguished. Only the starshine gleamed through the windows.

Lying in Amalric's arms on the silk-heaped couch, Lissa opened her heart and whispered her dreams and hopes and aspirations—childish, pathetic, terrible.

"I'll take you away," he muttered. "Tomorrow. You are right; Gazal is a city of the dead. We will seek life in the outer world. It is violent, rough, and cruel, but better than this living death—"

The night was broken by a shuddering cry of agony, horror, and despair. Its timbre brought out cold sweat on Amalric's skin. He started upright from the couch, but Lissa desperately clung to him.

"No, no!" she begged in a frantic whisper. "Do not go! Stay!"

"But murder is being done!" he exclaimed, fumbling for his sword. The cries seemed to come from across an outer court. Mingled with them was an indescribable, tearing, rending sound. They rose higher and thinner, unbearable in their hopeless agony, then sank away in a long, shuddering sob.

"I have heard men dying on the rack cry out like that!" muttered Amalric, shaking with horror. "What devil's work is this?"

Lissa was trembling violently in a frenzy of terror. He felt the wild pounding of her heart.

"It is the horror of which I spoke!" she whispered. "The horror that dwells in the Red Tower. Long ago it

158

came; some say it dwelt there in the lost years and returned after the building of Gazal. It devours human beings. What it is, no one knows, since none has seen it and lived to tell of it. It is a god or a devil. That is why the slaves fled; why the desert people shun Gazal. Many of us have gone into its awful belly. Eventually, all will have gone, and it will rule over an empty city, as men say it ruled over the ruins from which Gazal was reared."

"Why have the people stayed to be devoured?" he demanded.

"I do not know," she whimpered. "They dream . . ."

"Hypnosis," muttered Amalric; "hypnosis coupled with decay. I saw it in their eyes. This devil has them mesmerized. Mitra, what a foul secret!"

Lissa pressed her face against his bosom and clung to him.

"But what are we to do?" he asked uneasily.

"There is nothing to do," she whispered. "Your sword would be useless. Perhaps it will not harm us. It has taken a victim tonight. We must wait like sheep for the butcher."

"I'll be damned if I will—" Amalric exclaimed, galvanized. "We will not wait for morning. We'll go tonight. Make a bundle of food and drink. I'll get the horse and the camel and bring them to the court outside. Meet me there!"

Since the unknown monster had already struck, Amalric felt that he was safe in leaving the girl alone for a few minutes. But his flesh crawled as he groped his way down the winding corridor and through the black chambers, where the swinging tapestries whispered. He found the beasts huddled nervously together in the court where he had left them. The stallion whinnied and nuzzled him, as if sensing peril in the breathless night.

Amalric saddled and bridled the animals and led them through the narrow opening into the street. A few minutes later, he was standing in the starlit court. Even as he reached it, he was electrified by an awful scream,

159

which rang shudderingly upon the air. It came from the chamber where he had left Lissa.

He answered that piteous cry with a wild yell. Drawing his sword, he rushed across the court and hurled himself through the window. The golden ball was glowing again, carving out black shadows in the shrinking corners. Silks lay scattered on the floor. The marble seat was upset; but the chamber was empty.

A sick weakness overcame Amalric, and he staggered against the marble table, the dim light wavering dizzily to his sight. Then he was swept by a mad rage. The Red Tower! There the fiend would bear its victim!

He darted back across the court, sought the streets, and raced toward the tower, which glowed with an unholy light under the stars. The streets did not run straight. He cut through silent black buildings and crossed courts whose rank grass waved in the night wind.

Ahead of him, clustered about the crimson tower, rose a heap of ruins, where decay had eaten more savagely than at the rest of the city. Apparently none dwelt among them. They reeled and tumbled, a crumbling mass of quaking masonry, with the red tower rearing up among them like a poisonous red flower from charnel-house ruin.

To reach the tower, he would be forced to traverse the ruins. Recklessly he plunged into the black mass, groping for a door. He found one and entered, thrusting his sword ahead of him. Then he saw such a vista as men sometimes see in fantastic dreams.

Ahead of him stretched a long corridor, visible in a faint, unhallowed glow, its black walls hung with strange, shuddersome tapestries. Far down it he saw a receding figure—a white, naked, stooped figure, lurching along, dragging something the sight of which filled him with sweating horror. Then the apparition vanished from his sight, and with it vanished the eerie glow. Amalric stood in the soundless dark, seeing nothing, hearing nothing; thinking only of a stooped, white figure, which dragged a limp human form down a long black corridor.

As he groped onward, a vague memory stirred in his brain: the memory of a grisly tale mumbled to him over a dying fire in the skull-shaped devil-devil hut of a black witch-man—a tale of a god that dwelt in a crimson house in a ruined city—a god worshipped by darksome cults in dank jungles and along sullen, dusky rivers. And there stirred, too, in his mind, an incantation whispered in his ear in awed and shuddering tones, while the night held its breath, the lions had ceased to roar along the river, and the very fronds had ceased their scraping, one against the other.

Ollam-onga, whispered a dark wind down the sightless corridor. *Ollam-onga,* whispered the dust that ground beneath his stealthy feet. Sweat stood on his skin, and the sword shook in his hand. He stole through the house of a god, and fear held him in its bony fist. *The house of the god*—the full horror of the phrase filled his mind. All the ancestral fears and the fears that reached beyond ancestry and primordial race memory crowded upon him; horror cosmic and unhuman sickened him. The realization of his weak humanity crushed him as he went through the house of darkness, which was the house of a god.

About him shimmered a glow so faint that it was scarcely discernable. He knew that he was approaching the tower itself. Another instant, and he groped his way through an arched door and stumbled upon strangely-spaced steps. Up and up he went; and, as he climbed, that blind fury, which is mankind's last defense against diabolism and all the hostile forces of the universe, surged in him. He forgot his fear. Burning with terrible eagerness, he climbed up and up through the thick, evil darkness, until he came into a chamber lit by a weird, golden glow.

At the far end of the chamber, a short flight of broad steps led upward to a kind of dais or platform, on which stood articles of stone furniture. The mangled remains of the victim lay sprawled on the dais, an arm dangling limply down the steps. The marble steps were stained with a pattern of trickles of blood, like the stalactites that form around the lip of a hot spring. Most of these streaks were old, dried, and dark brown; but a few were still red, moist, and shiny.

Before Amalric, at the foot of these steps, stood a white, naked figure. Amalric halted, his tongue cleaving to his palate. It was to all appearance a naked white man that stood gazing at him, its mighty arms folded on an alabaster breast. The eyes, however, were balls of luminous fire, such as had never looked from any human head. In those eyes, Amalric glimpsed the frozen fires of the ultimate hells, touched by awful shadows.

Then, before him, the form began to grow dim in outline—to waver. With a terrible effort, the Aquilonian burst the bonds of silence and spoke a cryptic and awful incantation. And, as the frightful words cut the silence, the white giant halted—froze. Again his outlines stood out clear and bold against the golden background.

"Now fall on, damn you!" cried Amalric hysterically. "I have bound you into your human shape! The black wizard spoke truly! It was the master word he gave me! Fall on, Ollam-onga! Till you break the spell by feasting on my heart, you are no more than a man like me!"

With a roar like the gust of a black wind, the creature charged. Amalric sprang aside from the clutch of those hands, whose strength was more than that of a whirlwind. A single, taloned finger, spread wide and catching in his tunic, ripped the garment from him like a rotten rag as the monster plunged by. But Amalric, nerved to more than human quickness by the horror of the fight, wheeled and drove his sword through the thing's back, so that the point stood out a foot from the broad breast.

A fiendish howl of agony shook the tower. The monster whirled and rushed at Amalric, but the youth sprang aside and raced up the stairs to the dais. There he wheeled and, catching up a marble seat, hurled it down upon the horror lumbering up the stairs. Full in the face the massive missile struck, carrying the fiend back down the steps.

162

It rose, an awful sight, streaming blood, and again essayed the stairs. In desperation, Amalric lifted a bench of jade, whose weight wrenched a groan of effort from him, and hurled it.

Beneath the impact of the hurtling bulk, Ollam-onga pitched back down the stair and lay among the marble shards, which were flooded with its blood. With a last, desperate effort, it heaved itself up on its hands, eyes glazing. Throwing back its bloody head, it voiced an awful cry.

Amalric shuddered and recoiled from the abysmal horror of that scream, *which was answered*. From somewhere in the air above the tower, a faint medley of fiendish cries came back like an echo. Then the mangled white figure went limp among the bloodstained shards. And Amalric knew that one of the gods of Kush was no more. With the thought came blind, unreasoning horror.

In a fog of terror, he rushed down the steps from the dais, shrinking from the thing that lay staring on the floor. The night seemed to cry out against him, aghast at the sacrilege. Reason, exultant over his triumph, was submerged in a flood of cosmic fear.

As he put foot on the head of the stair, he halted short. Up from the darkness, Lissa came to him, her white arms outstretched, her eyes pools of horror.

"Amalric!" It was a haunting cry. He crushed her in his arms.

"I saw *it*," she whispered, "dragging a dead man through the corridor. I screamed and fled; then, when I returned, I heard you cry out and knew you had gone to search for me in the Red Tower—"

"And you came to share my fate." His voice was almost inarticulate.

Then, as she tried to peer in trembling fascination past him, he covered her eyes and turned her about. Better that she should not see what lay on the crimson floor. He snatched up his torn tunic but did not dare to touch his sword. As he half led, half carried Lissa down the shadowed stairs, a glance over his shoulder showed him that a naked white figure no longer lay amid the broken marble. The incantation had bound Ollam-onga into his human form in life but not in death. Blindness momentarily assailed Amalric; then, stimulated into frantic haste, he hurried Lissa down the stairs and through the dark ruins.

He did not slacken pace until they reached the street, where the camel and the stallion huddled against each other. Quickly he mounted the girl on the camel and swung up on the stallion. Taking the lead line, he headed straight for the broken wall. A few minutes later, he breathed gustily. The open air of the desert cooled his blood; it was free of the scent of decay and hideous antiquity.

There was a small water pouch hanging from his saddle bow. They had no food, and his sword was in the chamber of the Red Tower. Without food and unarmed, they faced the desert; but its peril seemed less grim than the horror of the city behind them.

Without speaking, they rode. Amalric headed south; somewhere in that direction was a water hole. Just at dawn, as they mounted a crest of sand, he looked back toward Gazal, unreal in the pink light. He stiffened, and Lissa cried out. Out of a breach in the wall rode seven horsemen. Their steeds were black, and the riders were cloaked in black from head to foot. There had been no horses in Gazal. Horror swept over Amalric and, turning, he urged their mounts on.

The sun rose red, and then gold, and then a ball of white beaten flame. On and on the fugitives pressed, reeling with heat and fatigue, blinded by the glare. From time to time, they moistened their lips with water. And behind them, at an even pace, rode seven black dots.

Evening began to fall, and the sun reddened and lurched toward the desert's rim. A cold hand clutched Amalric's heart. The riders were closing in.

As darkness came on, so came the black riders. Amalric glanced at Lissa, and a groan burst from him. His stallion stumbled and fell. The sun had gone down; the moon was suddenly blotted out by a bat-shaped shadow. In the utter darkness, the stars glowed red, and behind him Amalric heard a rising rush, as of an approaching wind. A black, speeding clump bulked against the night, in which glinted sparks of awful light.

"Ride, girl!" he cried despairingly. "Go on—save yourself; it is I they want!"

For answer, she slid down from the camel and threw her arms about him. "I will die with you!"

Seven black shapes loomed against the stars, racing like the wind. Under the hoods shone balls of evil fire; fleshless jawbones seemed to clack together.

Then there was an interruption; a horse swept past Amalric, a vague bulk in the unnatural darkness. There was the sound of an impact as the unknown steed caromed among the oncoming shapes. A horse screamed frenziedly, and a bull-like voice bellowed in a strange tongue. From somewhere in the night, a clamor of yells replied.

Some sort of violent action was taking place. Horses' hoofs stamped and clattered; there was the impact of savage blows; and the same stentorian voice cursed lustily. Then the moon came abruptly out and lit a fantastic scene.

A man on a giant horse whirled, slashed, and smote, apparently at thin air. From another direction swept a wild horde of riders, their curved swords flashing in the moonlight. Away over the crest of a rise, seven black figures were vanishing, their cloaks floating out like the wings of bats.

Amalric was swamped by wild men, who leaped from their horses and swarmed around him. Sinewy arms pinioned him; fierce brown hawklike faces snarled at him. Lissa screamed.

Then the attackers were thrust right and left as the man on the great horse reined through the crowd. He bent from his saddle and glared closely at Amalric.

"The devil!" he roared. "Amalric the Aquilonian!"

"Conan!" Amalric exclaimed in bewilderment. "Conan! Alive!"

"More alive than you seem to be," answered the other. "By Crom, man, you look as if all the devils of this desert had been hunting you through the night. What things were those pursuing you? I was riding around the camp my men had pitched, to make sure no enemies were in hiding, when the moon went out like a candle, and then I heard sounds of flight. I rode toward the sounds; and by Macha, I was among those devils before I knew what was happening. I had my sword in my hand and I laid about me—by Crom, their eyes blazed like fire in the dark! I know my edge bit them; but, when the moon came out, they were gone like a puff of wind. Were they men or devils?"

"Fiends sent up from Hell," shuddered Amalric. "Ask me not; some things are not to be discussed."

Conan did not press the matter; nor did he look incredulous. His beliefs included night fiends, ghosts, hobgoblins, and dwarfs.

"Trust you to find a woman, even in a desert," he said, glancing at Lissa. The girl had crept to Amalric and was clinging close to him, glancing fearfully at the wild figures that hemmed them in.

"Wine!" roared Conan. "Bring flasks! Here!" He seized a leather flask from those thrust out at him and placed it in Amalric's hand. "Give the girl a swig and drink some yourself," he advised. "Then we'll put you on horses and take you to the camp. You need food, rest, and sleep. I can see that."

A richly caparisoned horse was brought, rearing and prancing, and willing hands helped Amalric into the saddle. The girl was handed up to him, and they moved off southward, surrounded by the wiry brown riders in their picturesque tatters. Many wore face cloths, which concealed their faces below the eyes.

"Who is he?" whispered Lissa, her arms about her

166

lover's neck. He was holding her on the saddle in front of him.

"Conan the Cimmerian," muttered Amalric. "The man I wandered with in the desert after the defeat of the mercenaries. These are the men who struck him down. I left him lying under their spears, apparently dead. Now we meet him, obviously in command of them and respected by them."

"He is a terrible man," she whispered.

He smiled. "You have never seen a white-skinned barbarian before. He is a wanderer, a plunderer, and a slayer; but he has his own code of morals. I don't think we have anything to fear from him."

In his heart, Amalric was not so sure. In a way, it might be said that he had forfeited Conan's comradeship when he had ridden away into the desert, leaving the Cimmerian senseless on the ground. But he had not known that Conan was alive. Doubt haunted Amalric. Savagely loyal to his companions, the Cimmerian's wild nature saw no reason why the rest of the world should not be plundered. He lived by the sword. And Amalric suppressed a shudder as he thought of what might chance, did Conan desire Lissa.

Later on, having eaten and drunk in the camp of the riders, Amalric sat by a small fire in front of Conan's tent; Lissa, covered with a silken cloak, slumbered with her curly head on his knees. And across from him the firelight played on Conan's face, interchanging lights and shadows.

"Who are these men?" asked the young Aquilonian.

"The riders of Tombalku," answered the Cimmerian.

"Tombalku!" exclaimed Amalric. "Then it is no myth!"

"Far from it!" agreed Conan. "When my accursed steed fell with me, I was knocked senseless; and, when I recovered consciousness, the devils had me bound hand and foot. This angered me, so I snapped several of the cords they had tied me with; but they rebound them as fast as I could break them—never did I get a hand entirely free. Still, to them my strength seemed remarkable . . ."

Amalric gazed at Conan unspeakingly. The man was as tall and broad as Tilutan had been, without the black man's surplus flesh. He could have broken the Ghanata's neck with his naked hands.

"They decided to carry me to their city instead of killing me out of hand," Conan went on. "They thought a man like me should be a long time in dying by torture and so give them sport. Well, they bound me on a horse without a saddle, and we went to Tombalku.

"There are two kings of Tombalku. They took me before them—a lean, brown-skinned devil named Zehbeh, and a big fat Negro, who dozed on his ivory-tusk throne. Zehbeh asked a brown priest, Daura, what should be done with me, and Daura cast dice made of sheep bone and said I should be flayed alive before the altar of Jhil. Everyone cheered, and that woke the Negro king.

"I spat on Daura and cursed him roundly, and the kings as well. I told them that, if I was to be skinned, by Crom, I demanded a good bellyfull of wine before they began, and I damned them for thieves and cowards and sons of harlots.

"At this, the black king roused and sat up and stared at me. Then he rose and shouted: 'Amra!' and I knew him—Sakumbe, a Suba from the Black Coast, a fat adventurer I had known well in the days when I was a corsair along that coast. He trafficked in ivory, gold dust, and slaves and would cheat the devil out of his eye teeth. Well, when he knew me the smelly old devil descended from his throne and embraced me for joy and took my cords off me with his own hands. Then he announced that I was Amra, the Lion, and his friend, and no harm should come to me.

"Then followed much discusson, because Zehbeh and Daura wanted my hide. But Sakumbe yelled for his witch finder, Askia, and he came—all feathers and bells and snake skins—a wizard of the Black Coast and a son of the Devil if ever there was one.

"Askia pranced and made incantations and announced

168

that Sakumbe was the chosen of Ajujo, the Dark One, and what he said, went. All the black people of Tombalku shouted, and Zehbeh backed down.

"For the blacks in Tombalku are the real power. Several centuries ago, the Aphaki, a Shemitish race, pushed into the southern desert and established the kingdom of Tombalku. They mixed with the desert blacks, and the result was a brown, straight-haired race, which is still more white than black. They are the dominant caste in Tombalku. But they are in the minority, and a pure black king always sits on the throne beside the Aphaki ruler.

"The Aphaki conquered the nomads of the southwestern desert and the Negro tribes of the steppes that lie to the south of them. Most of these riders, for instance, are Tibu, of mixed Stygian and Negro blood. Others are the Bigharma, the Mindanga, and the Borni.

"Well, Sakumbe, through Askia, is the real ruler of Tombalku. The Aphaki worship Jhil, but the blacks worship Ajujo the Dark One and his kin. Askia came to Tombalku with Sakumbe and revived the worship of Ajujo, which was crumbling because of the Aphaki priests. He also has a private cult of his own, worshiping the gods know what sort of abominations. Askia made black magic, which defeated the wizardry of the Aphaki, and the blacks hailed him as a prophet sent by the dark gods. Sakumbe and Askia wax as Zehbeh and Daura wane.

"Since I am Sakumbe's friend, and Askia spoke for me, the blacks received me with great applause. Sakumbe had Kordofo, the general of the horsemen, poisoned and gave me his place, which delighted the blacks and exasperated the Aphaki.

"You will like Tombalku! It was made for men like us to loot! There are half a dozen powerful factions plotting and intriguing against one another. There are continual brawls in the taverns and streets, secret murders, mutilations, and executions. And there are women, gold, wine— all that a mercenary wants! And I am high in favor and power! By Crom, Amalric, you could not come at a better time! Why, what's the matter? You do not seem so enthusiastic as I remember your once having been in such matters."

"I crave your pardon, Conan," said Amalric. "I do not lack interest, but weariness and want of sleep overcome me."

However, it was not of gold, women, and intrigue that the Aquilonian was thinking, but of the girl who slumbered in his lap. There was no joy in the thought of taking her into such a welter of intrigue and blood as Conan had described. A subtle change had come over Amalric, almost without his knowledge. Carefully, he said:

"You saved our lives just now, for which I shall always be grateful. But I have no real claim on your generosity, since I rode off and left you lying for the Aphaki to capture. True, I thought you surely dead, but . . ."

Conan threw back his head and laughed a deep, rumbling laugh. Then he slapped the younger man on the back with a force that almost knocked him sprawling. "Forget it! I ought to have been dead, by all reasonable chances; and they've had speared you like a frog if you'd tried to rescue me. Come on to Tombalku with us and make yourself useful! You commanded a troop of horse for Zapayo, didn't you?"

"Aye, that I did."

"Well, I need an adjutant to help drill my lads. They fight like fiends but without order, each man for himself. Between us, we can make real soldiers of them. More wine!" he roared.

3.

It was the third day after Amalric's meeting with Conan that the riders of Tombalku neared the capital. Amalric rode at the head of the column beside Conan, and Lissa followed closely behind Amalric on a mare. Behind them trotted the company, strung out in a double line. Loose white garments fluttered in the breeze; bridles jingled; saddle leather creaked; the setting sun shone redly

170

on the points of lances. Most of the riders were Tibu, but there were also contingents from the lesser desert tribes.

All, besides their local languages, spoke the simplified dialect of Shemitish that served as a common tongue for the dark-skinned folk from Kush to Zembabwei and from Stygia to the half-mythical black kingdom of the Atlaians, far to south. Many centuries before, Shemitish traders had stitched this vast area with their trade routes and had brought to it their language along with their trade goods. And Amalric knew enough Shemitish to communicate with these fierce warriors of the arid lands.

As the sun, like a vast drop of blood, sank toward the horizon, points of light appeared ahead. The ground fell away in a gentle slope before the riders, then leveled out again. On this level sprawled a large city of low dwellings. All these houses were made of dun-colored mud brick, so that Amalric's first impression was of a natural formation of earth and rock—a tumbled mass of bluffs, ravines, and boulders—rather than a city.

At the foot of the slope rose a stout brick wall, over which appeared the upper parts of the houses. Lights glowed from an open space at the center of the city, whence came a roaring sound, faint with distance.

"Tombalku," said Conan briefly, then cocked his head to listen. "Crom! Something's up. We'd better hurry." He touched spurs to his horse. The column cantered down the slope, jingling, behind him.

Tombalku stood on a low, wedge-shaped escarpment amid widespread groves of palms and spiny mimosas. The escarpment overlooked a bend in a sluggish river, which reflected the deepening blue of the evening sky. Beyond the river, the land rolled away in grassy savannas.

"What river is that?" asked Amalric.

"The Jeluba," replied Conan. "It flows east from here. Some say it flows on across Darfar and Keshan to join the Styx; some, that it swings south to pour into the Zarkheba. Perhaps some day I'll follow it down to see."

The massive wooden gates stood open as the column cantered through. Inside the gate, white-clad forms moved through the narrow, crooked streets. Behind the white men, the riders shouted hails to acquaintances and boasts of their prowess.

Turning in his saddle, Conan snapped out an order to a brown-skinned warrior, who led the column off toward the barracks. The Cimmerian, followed by Amalric and Lissa, trotted purposefully toward the central square.

Tombalku was awakening from its afternoon doze. Everywhere white-clad, dark-skinned figures trudged through the soft sand of the streets. Amalric was struck by the unexpected size of this desert metropolis and by the incongruous mixtures of barbarism and civilization to be seen on every hand. In spacious temple courtyards, within a few yards of each other, painted and feathered witch-doctors pranced and shook their sacred bones, dusky priests intoned the myths of their race, and dusky philosophers argued the nature of man and the gods.

As the three riders neared the central square, they fell in with more of the people of the city, all hurrying in the same direction. When the street became crowded, Conan's bellowing voice cleared a path for the horses.

They dismounted on the edge of the square, and Conan tossed the bridles of the horses to a man he picked out of the crowd. Then the Cimmerian shouldered his way toward the thrones on the far side of the square. Lissa clung to Amalric's arm as he pushed through the crowd in Conan's wake.

Around the plaza, regiments of black spearmen were drawn up to form a vast hollow square. The light of fires, blazing at the corners of the square, lit up the warriors' great oval shields of elephant hide, the long blades of their spearheads, the ostrich plumes and lions' manes of their headdresses, and white eyeballs and teeth against shiny black skins.

In the center of the hollow square, a man was tied to a post. This man, stripped to a loin cloth, was stocky, muscular, and brown-skinned, with heavy features. He strained at his bonds, while in front of him pranced a lean, fantastic figure. This man was black, but most of his skin was covered with painted designs. His shaven head was painted to resemble a skull. His regalia of plumes and monkey fur whipped this way and that as he danced in front of a small tripod, under which a fire smouldered and from which a thin spire of colored smoke ascended.

Beyond the stake, at one side of the hollow square, rose two thrones of stuccoed and painted brick, ornamented with bits of colored glass, with arms made from whole elephants' tusks. These thrones stood on a single dais, to which several steps led up. On the throne to Amalric's right, a huge, fat, black figure lounged. This man wore a long white gown and, on his head, an elaborate headdress, which included the skull of a lion and several ostrich plumes.

The other throne was empty, but the man who would have occupied it stood beside the other throne. This was a thin, hawk-faced, brown man, who wore a white robe like the other but, on his head, a jeweled turban instead of the first man's headgear of bones and feathers. The lean man was shaking a fist at the fat one and shouting, while a group of throne guards uneasily watched their kings quarrel. As Amalric, following Conan, came closer, he made out the lean one's words:

"You lie! Askia himself sent this sending of serpents, as you call it, to give him an excuse to murder Daura! If you do not stop this buffoonery, there will be war! We shall slay you, you black savage, little by little!" The thin man's voice rose to a scream. "Do as I say! Stop Askia, or else, by Jhil the Merciless . . ."

He reached for his scimitar; the guards about the throne shifted their spears. The fat black merely laughed up at the furious face above him.

Conan, having pushed through the lines of spearmen, bounded up the brick steps of the dais and thrust himself between the two monarchs.

"Better take your hand off that sword, Zehbeh," he growled, and turned to the other. "What's going on, Sakumbe?"

The black king chuckled. "Daura thought to get rid of me by a sending of serpents. Ugh! Vipers in my bedding, asps among my robes, mambas dripping from the roof beams. Three of my women have died of their bites, besides several slaves and attendants. Askia learned by divination that Daura was the culprit, and my men surprised him with the evidence in the midst of his incantations. Look yonder, General Conan: Askia has just slain the goat. His demons will arrive any time, now."

Following Conan's gaze, Amalric looked down into the hollow square towards the stake with its bound victim, in front of which the goat was expiring. Askia was nearing the climax of his incantation. His voice rose to a shriek as he leaped and capered and rattled his bones. The smoke from the tripod thickened, writhed, and glowed with a ghastly radiance of its own.

Overhead, night had fallen. The stars, which had begun to shine out brightly in the clear desert air, turned dim and red; a crimson veil seemed to be drawn across the face of the rising moon. The fires sank and smouldered redly. A crackle of speech, in no human tongue, wafted down from the upper air. There was a sound like the beating of leathery wings.

Askia stood straight and still, with arms outstretched, plumed head thrown back, mouthing a long incantation of strange names. Amalric's hair rose; for, among the rush of meaningless syllables, he caught the name "Ollam-onga," repeated thrice.

Then Daura shrieked so loudly as to drown out Askia's incantation. In the flickering firelight, with the weird glow from the tripod blurring the sight, Amalric could not be quite sure of what he saw. Something seemed to be happening to Daura, who struggled and screamed.

Around the base of the stake to which the wizard was tied, a pool of blood grew and widened. Ghastly wounds appeared all over the man, although nothing could be seen

174

to deal such injuries. His screams sank to a faint sob and ceased, although his body continued to move in its bindings, as if some invisible presence were tugging at it. A faint gleam of white appeared amidst the dark mass that had been Daura; then another and another. Amalric realized with a start of horror that these white things were bones . . .

The moon returned to its normal silvery radiance; the stars shone out again like jewels; the fires in the hollow square blazed up. The waxing light showed a skeleton, still bound to the stake and slumped in a pool of blood. King Sakumbe spoke in his high, musical voice:

"So much for that scoundrel Daura. Now, as for Zehbeh—By Ajujo's nose, where is the villain?"

Zehbeh had disappeared while all other eyes had been focused on the drama at the stake.

"Conan," said Sakumbe, "you had better call up the regiments; for I do not think my brother king will let this night's work pass without taking a hand in it."

Conan dragged Amalric forward. "King Sakumbe, this is Amalric the Aquilonian, a sometime comrade in arms of mine. I need him for an adjutant. Amalric, you and your girl had better stay with the king, since you don't know your way around the city and would only get yourselves killed if you tried to mix in the fight that's coming."

"I am pleased to meet a friend of the mighty Amra," said Sakumbe. "Put him on the payroll, Conan, and muster the warriors—Derketo, the rascal has not lost any time! Look yonder!"

An uproar arose at the far side of the plaza. Conan sprang from the dais in a flying leap and began shouting orders to the commanders of the black regiments. Messengers dashed off. Somewhere, deep-voiced drums, beaten with the light-brown palms of black hands, began to mutter and mumble.

At the far side of the plaza, a troop of white-clad horsemen burst into view, thrusting with lances and smiting with scimitars at the black masses in front of them. Before their onslaught, the lines of black spearmen crumbled into shapeless masses. Man after man went down before their flashing steel. King Sakumbe's bodyguard closed up around the dais with the two thrones, one empty and the other occupied by the ponderous bulk of Sakumbe.

Lissa, trembling, clung to Amalric's arm. "Who fights whom?" she whispered.

"That would be Zehbeh's Aphaki," replied Amalric, "trying to slay the black king, here, to make Zehbeh sole ruler."

"Will they break through to the throne?" she said, pointing to the struggling mass of dark figures across the plaza.

Amalric shrugged and glanced at Sakumbe. The Negro king lolled in his throne, apparently unconcerned. He raised a golden cup to his lips and took a swig of wine. Then he handed a similar cup to Amalric.

"You must be thirsty, white man, after coming in from a long patrol without time to wash or rest," he said. "Have a drink!"

Amalric shared his drink with Lissa. Across the plaza, the trampling and neighing of horses, the clash of arms, the screams of wounded men merged in an unholy din. Raising his voice to be heard, Amalric said:

"Your Majesty must be very brave, to show so little concern; or else very . . ." Amalric bit off the end of the sentence.

"Or else very stupid, you mean?" The king laughed musically. "No; I am only realistic. I am much too fat to outrun an active man on foot, let alone a mounted man. So, if I run, my people will cry that all is lost and flee, leaving me to be caught by the pursuers. Whereas, if I stay here, there is a good chance that—ah, there they come!"

More black warriors were pouring into the square and adding their weight to the battle. And now the Aphaki mounted force began to give way. Horses, speared, reared and fell on their riders; riders were pulled from their horses by strong black arms or struck from the saddle by javelins. Soon a trumpet sounded harshly; the remaining Aphaki wheeled their mounts and galloped out of the square. The din diminished.

Silence fell, save for the moans of the wounded who littered the paving of the plaza. Black women came out of the side streets to look for their men among the fallen, to tend them if alive and to wail for them if dead.

Sakumbe sat placidly on his throne, drinking, until Conan, bloody sword in hand and followed by a knot of befeathered black officers, strode across the plaza.

"Zehbeh and most of his Aphaki got away," he said. "I had to dent a few of your boys' skulls to stop them from massacring the Aphaki women and children. We may need them for hostages."

"It is well," said Sakumbe. "Have a drink."

"A good idea," said Conan, quaffing deeply. Then he glanced at the empty throne beside that of Sakumbe. The black king followed his glance and grinned.

"Well?" said Conan. "How about it? Do I get it?"

Sakumbe gave a giggle. "Trust you to strike while the iron is hot, Conan! You have not changed."

Then the king spoke in a language that Amalric did not know. Conan grunted a reply, and there was an exchange in this unknown tongue. Askia climbed the stairs of the dais and joined the talk. He spoke vehemently, shooting suspicious, scowling glances at Conan and at Amalric.

At last, Sakumbe silenced the wizard with one sharp word and heaved his huge bulk up out of his throne. "People of Tombalku!" he cried.

All over the plaza, eyes turned towards the dais. Sakumbe continued: "Since the false traitor Zehbeh has fled the city, one of the two thrones of Tombalku is empty. You have seen what a mighty warrior Conan is. Will you have him for your other king?"

After a moment of silence, a few shouts of approval were heard. Amalric noted that the men shouting seemed to be Tibu riders, whom Conan had led in person. The shouts swelled to a roar of approval. Sakumbe pushed Conan into the vacant throne. A mighty yell went up. In the plaza, which had now been cleared of corpses and wounded, the fires were rekindled. Drums began to beat again, this time not for war but for a wild all-night celebration.

Hours later, dizzy with drink and weariness, Amalric dragged himself and Lissa along the streets of Tombalku, under Conan's guidance, to the modest house he had found for them. Before they parted, Amalric asked Conan:

"What was that speech with Sakumbe, in some tongue I do not know, just before you were enthroned?"

A laugh rumbled deep in Conan's throat. "We spoke a coastal dialect, which these people don't understand. Sakumbe was telling me that we should get along fine as co-kings, provided I remembered the color of my skin."

"What did he mean by that?"

"That it would do me no good to scheme to steal his power, because the pure blacks are now in the overwhelming majority here, and they would never obey a white king."

"Why not?"

"Because they have been too often massacred and plundered and enslaved by marauding bands of white men from Stygia and Shem, I suppose."

"What about the wizard, Askia? What was he haranguing Sakumbe about?"

"He was warning the king against us. He claimed his spooks have told him that we shall be the cause of woe and destruction to Tombalku. But Sakumbe shut him up, saying he knew me better than that; that he trusted me farther than he trusted any medicine man." Conan yawned like a sleepy lion. "Get your little girl to bed before she falls asleep on her feet."

"How about you?"

"Me? I'm going back. The party has hardly started!"

4.

A month later, Amalric, covered with sweat and dust, reined in his horse as his squadrons thundered past in a last, grand charge. All morning, and for many earlier mornings, he had drilled them over and over in the elements of civilized cavalry tactics: "Forward, walk!" "Forward, trot!" "Forward, canter!" "Charge!" "Wheel!" "Retreat!" "Rally!" "Forward, walk!" And so on, over and over.

Although their evolutions were still ragged, the brown desert hawks seemed to be learning at last. At the start there had been much grumbling and sour looks at these strange foreign methods of fighting. But Amalric, backed up by Conan, had overcome resistance by a combination of even-handed justice and tough discipline. Now he was building a formidable fighting force.

"Give them, 'form column,'" he said to the trumpeter at his side. At the blast of the trumpet, the riders reined in and, with much jostling and cursing, sorted themselves out in a column. They trotted back toward the walls of Tombalku, past fields where half-naked black peasant women stopped work to lean on their hoes and watch.

Back in Tombalku, Amalric turned in his horse at the cavalry stables and sought his home. As he neared the house, he was surprised to see Askia, the wizard, standing in the street in front of the house and talking with Lissa. The latter's servant, a Suba woman, stood in the doorway, listening.

"How now, Askia?" said Amalric in no very friendly tone as he came up. "What are you doing here?"

"I watch over the welfare of Tombalku. To do that, I must needs ask questions."

"I do not like strange men to question my wife in my absence."

Askia smiled a crooked, malevolent grin. "The fate of the city is more important than your likes and dislikes, white man. Fare you well until next time!"

179

The wizard walked off, his plumes nodding. Amalric, frowning, followed Lissa into the house. "What was he asking you about?" he asked.

"Oh, about my life in Gazal, and how I had come to meet you."

"What did you tell him?"

"I told him what a hero you are, and how you slew the god of the Red Tower."

Amalric frowned in thought. "I wish you had not revealed that. I do not know why, but I am sure he means to make trouble for us. I ought to go to Conan about it, right now . . . Why, Lissa, you're weeping!"

"I—I'm so happy!"

"About what?"

"You acknowledged me as your wife!" Her arms were around his neck as she poured out endearments.

"There, there," he said. "I should have thought of it before."

"We must have a wedding feast, tonight!"

"Of course! But meantime, I ought to see Conan—"

"Oh, let that wait! Besides, you are dirty and tired. Eat, drink, and rest first, before your face these fearful men!"

Amalric's better judgment told him that he ought to go to Conan at once. But he was apprehensive about the meeting. While he was sure that Askia harbored some nefarious plan against him, he had no definite charge to bring against the wizard. In the end, he allowed Lissa to persuade him. What with eating and drinking and washing and love-making and sleeping, the afternoon slipped away. The sun was low when Amalric set out for the palace.

King Sakumbe's palace was a large compound—like all the rest of Tombalku, of dun-colored mud brick—just off the central plaza. Sakumbe's bodyguards, knowing Amalric, quickly passed him into the interior, where thin sheets of beaten gold covered the brick walls and dazzlingly reflected the ruddy glare of the setting sun. He

180

crossed a wide courtyard swarming with the king's wives and children and entered the king's private apartment.

He found the two kings of Tombalku, the white and the black, sprawled on mounds of cushions on a large Bakhariot rug, which in turn covered a mosaic floor. In front of each was a pile of golden coins from many lands, and at the elbow of each stood a large winecup. A slave stood ready with a pitcher to refill each cup.

Both men were bloodshot of eye. Evidently, they had been drinking heavily for many hours. A pair of dice lay on the rug between them.

Amalric bowed formally. "My lords—"

Conan looked blearily up; he wore a bejeweled turban like that which Zehbeh had worn. "Amalric! Flop down on a cushion and take a few throws with us. "Your luck can't be any worse than mine tonight!"

"My lord, I really cannot afford—"

"Oh, to hell with that! Here's a stake for you." Conan scooped a fistful of coins from his pile and slammed it down on the rug. As Amalric lowered himself to the floor, Conan, as if struck by a sudden thought, looked sharply at Sakumbe.

"I'll tell you, brother King," he said. "We'll make one throw each. If I win, you'll order the army to march against the king of Kush."

"And if I win?" said Sakumbe.

"Then they don't, as you prefer."

Sakumbe shook his head with a chuckle. "No, brother King, I am not caught so easily. When we are ready, then we shall march, and no sooner."

Conan struck the rug with his fist. "What in Hell's the matter with you, Sakumbe? You're not the man you were in the old days. Then you were ready for any adventure; now, all you care about is your food, wine, and women. What's changed you?"

Sakumbe hiccupped. "In the old days, brother King, I wanted to be a king, with many men to obey my commands and plenty of wine, women, and food. Now I have these things. Why should I risk them in unnecessary adventures?"

"But we must extend our boundaries to the Western Ocean, to gain control of the trade routes that come up from the coast. You know as well as I that Tombalku's wealth derives from control of trade routes."

"And when we have conquered the king of Kush and reached the sea, what then?"

"Why, then we should turn our armies eastward, to bring the Ghanata tribes under our rule and stop their raiding."

"And then, no doubt, you'll want to strike north or south, and so on forever. Tell me, man, suppose we conquered every nation within a thousand miles of Tombalku and possessed wealth greater than that of the kings of Stygia. What should we do then?"

Conan yawned and stretched. "Why, enjoy life, I suppose: deck ourselves in gold, hunt and feast all day, and drink and wench all night. In between times, we could tell each other lies about our adventures."

Sakumbe laughed again. "If that is all you want, why, we are doing just those things now! If you want more gold, or food, or drink, or women, ask me and you shall have it."

Conan shook his head, grunting something inaudible and frowning in a puzzled way. Sakumbe turned to Amalric. "And you, my young friend, did you come here with something to tell us?"

"My lord, I came to ask the lord Conan to visit my house and confirm my marriage to my woman. Afterwards, I thought he might do me the favor to remain for a small repast."

"Small repast?" said Sakumbe. "Not so, by Ajujo's nose! We shall make a grand revel of it, with whole roast oxen, rivers of wine, and our drummers and dancers! What say you, brother King?"

Conan belched and grinned. "I'm with you, brother King. We'll give Amalric such a wedding feast that he won't wake up for three days afterwards!"

"There was another matter," said Amalric, a little appalled at the prospect of another celebration of the kind these barbarian kings preferred but not knowing how to refuse. He told about Askia's interrogation of Lissa.

The two kings frowned when he had finished. Sakumbe said: "Fear not Askia, Amalric. All wizards need to be watched, but this one is a valued servant of mine. Why, without his sorcery—" Sakumbe glanced toward the doorway and spoke: "What would you?"

A bodyguard, standing in the doorway, said: "O Kings, a scout of the Tibu riders would speak with you."

"Send him in," said Conan.

A lean black in ragged white garments entered and prostrated himself. As he flopped down on his belly, a cloud of dust arose from his garments.

"My lords!" he gasped. "Zehbeh and the Aphaki march against us! I sighted them yesterday at the oasis of Kidessa and rode all night to bring word."

Conan and Sakumbe, both suddenly sobered, lurched to their feet. Conan said: "Brother King, this means that Zehbeh could be here tomorrow. Order the drums beaten for the muster." While Sakumbe called in an officer and gave this command, Conan turned to Amalric. "Do you think you could surprise the Aphaki on the way here and smash them with your riders?"

"Perhaps I can," said Amalric cautiously. "They will outnumber us, but some ravines to the north would be suitable for an ambush . . ."

5.

An hour later, as the sun set behind the dun brick walls of Tombalku, Conan and Sakumbe mounted the thrones on the dais in the plaza. As the drums thundered the muster, black men of military age streamed into the square. Bonfires were lit. Plumed officers pushed warriors into line and thumbed the heads of the men's spears to assure themselves that these were sharp.

Amalric strode across the square to report to the kings

183

that his riders would be ready to move out by midnight. His mind teemed with schemes and stratagems: Whether, if the Aphaki refused to break at the first onslaught, he should break off the fight and retire, to attack again when the Aphaki were spread out and dismounted to attack the walls of Tombalku . . .

He mounted the steps to where the kings sat, surrounded by black officers to whom they were issuing orders. "My lords—" he began.

A screech interrupted him. Askia appeared beside the throne, pointing at Amalric and shouting at the kings.

"There he is!" screamed the wizard. "The man who slew a god! The man who slew one of *my* gods!"

The Negroes around the thrones turned startled faces toward Amalric. In the firelight, eyeballs gleamed whitely against dark skins. Their expressions had in them something of awe and fear. Clearly, it was inconceivable to them that a man should slay a god. One who did so must be, in some sort, a god himself.

"What punishment were cruel enough for such blasphemy?" continued Askia. "I demand that the slayer of Ollam-onga and his wench be turned over to me for torture! Gods, they shall suffer such pain as no mortal has ever suffered in all the aeons—"

"Shut up!" roared Conan. "If Amalric killed the spook of Gazal, the world is better for it. Now get out of here and stop bothering us; we have business."

"But, Conan—" said Sakumbe.

"These white-skinned devils always hang together!" yelled Askia. "Are you king any longer, Sakumbe? If you are, then order them seized and bound! If you do not know what to do with them—"

"Well—" said Sakumbe.

"Listen!" cried Conan. "If Gazal is no longer haunted by this so-called god, we can capture the place, put its people to work, and get them to teach us their sciences. But first get rid of this prancing he-witch, before I try my edge on him!"

"I demand—" screamed Askia.

"Get rid of him!" bellowed the Cimmerian, hand on his hilt. "By Crom, do you think I'd deliver an old comrade like Amalric to the mercy of a devil-worshiping cutthroat?"

Sakumbe at last roused himself and sat up straight on his throne. "Go, Askia!" he said. "Amalric is a good warrior, and you shall not have him. Rather, busy yourself with sorceries to defeat Zehbeh."

"But I—"

"Go!" The fat arm pointed.

Askia foamed with rage. "Very well, I go!" he shouted at last. "But you have not heard the last of me, you two!" And away rushed the witch doctor.

Amalric resumed his report on the Tibu riders. What with the constant coming and going of messengers, and of officers reporting on the strength of their commands, it was some time before he had laid his entire plan before the king. Conan made a few suggestions and then said:

"It looks good to me, eh, Sakumbe?"

"If you like it, brother King, it must be good. Go, Amalric, and muster our riders—*aieee!*" An awful scream suddenly broke from Sakumbe, whose eyes seemed to be starting from his head. He staggered up from his throne, clutching at his throat. "I burn! *I burn!* Save me!"

A terrible phenomenon was taking place on the body of Sakumbe. Although there was no sign of visible fire, no sensation of heat, it was plain to be seen that the man was in fact burning, as surely as if he had been tied to a stake over lighted faggots. His skin blistered, then charred and cracked, while the air was filled with the odor of burning flesh.

"Pour water on him!" shouted Amalric. "Or wine! Anything you have!"

Scream after scream from the tortured throat of the black king. Someone threw a bucketful of liquid over him; there was a hiss and a cloud of steam, but the screams continued.

"Crom and Ishtar!" swore Conan, glaring furiously

185

about, "I ought to have killed that dancing devil while he was in reach."

The screams died away and ceased. The remains of the king—a shriveled, shapeless object, not at all like the living Sakumbe—lay on the surface of the dais in a pool of melted human fat. Some of the plumed officers fled in panic; some prostrated themselves, calling upon their various gods.

Conan seized Amalric's wrist in a bone-crushing grip. "We must get out of here, quickly!" he said in a low, tense tone. "Come along!"

Amalric did not doubt the Cimmerian's knowledge of the dangers they faced. He followed Conan down the steps of the dais. In the plaza, all was confusion. Plumed warriors milled around, shouting and gesticulating. Fights had broken out here and there among them.

"Die, slayer of Kordofo!" screamed a voice above the din. Directly in front of Conan, a tall, brown man drew back his arm and hurled a javelin at point-blank range. Only the steel-trap quickness of the barbarian saved Conan. The Cimmerian whirled and crouched, so that the missile passed over him, missing Amalric's head by a finger's breadth and burying itself in the body of another warrior.

The attacker drew back his arm to hurl a second spear; but, before he could loose it, Conan's sword sang from its sheath, whirled in a scarlet arc in the firelight, and struck home. The Tombalkan sank to the ground, cloven from shoulder to breastbone.

"Run!" yelled Conan.

Amalric ran, dodging through the swirling crowds in the plaza. Men shouted and pointed at them; some ran after them.

Amalric, his legs pounding and his lungs laboring, raced down a side street after Conan. Behind them swelled the sounds of pursuit. The street narrowed and bent. Ahead of Amalric, Conan suddenly disappeared.

"In here, quickly!" came the voice of the Cimmerian,

who had dodged into a space a yard in width between two mud-brick houses.

Amalric squeezed into this alcove and stood silently, gasping for breath, as the pursuit raced past in the street.

"Some more of Kordofo's kin," muttered the Cimmerian in the darkness. "They've been sharpening their spears for me ever since Sakumbe got rid of Kordofo."

"What do we do now?" asked Amalric.

Conan turned his head up to the narrow, starlit strip of sky above them. "I think we can climb up to the roofs," he said.

"How?"

"The way I used to climb a cleft in the rocks, when I was a youth in Cimmeria. Here, hold this sticker for me."

Conan handed Amalric a javelin, and Amalric realized that the Cimmerian had taken it from the man he had slain. The weapon had a narrow head a full yard in length, of soft iron sharpened to a finely serrated edge. Below the hand grip, a slender iron shank balanced the weight of the head.

Conan grunted softly, braced his back against one wall and his feet against the other, and inched his way up. Soon he became a black silhouette against the stars, and then disappeared. A call came softly down: "Hand up that spear, and come on up."

Amalric handed up the javelin and, in his turn, inched his way up. The roofs were made of wooden beams, on which was laid down a thick layer of palm fronds and, over that, a layer of clay. Sometimes the clay gave a little as they walked on it, and the crackle of the fronds underneath could be heard.

Following Conan, Amalric crossed several roofs, leaping over the chasms between them. At length, they came to a building of good size, almost on the edge of the plaza.

"I must get Lissa out of here!" said Amalric, desperately anxious.

"One thing at a time," growled Conan. "We want to know what is happening."

The confusion in the plaza had somewhat died down. Officers were getting their men into orderly formations once more. On the dais with the two thrones, across the square, stood Askia in his wizard's regalia, speaking. Although Amalric could not hear all his words, the wizard was evidently telling the Tombalkans what a great and wise leader he would be to them.

A sound off to Amalric's left drew the Aquilonian's attention. At first a murmur, like the crowd noises in the square, it swelled to a roar. A man dashed into the square and shouted to Askia:

"The Aphaki attack the east wall!"

Then all was chaos again. The war drums thundered. Askia screamed orders right and left. A regiment of black spearmen began to file out of the square towards the disturbance. Conan said:

"We'd better get out of Tombalku. Whichever side wins, they'll have our hides. Sakumbe was right; these people will never obey a whiteskin. Go to your house and get your girl ready. Rub your faces and arms with soot from the hearth; that way you'll be less conspicuous in the dark. Grab whatever money you have. I'll meet you there with horses. If we hurry, we can get out the west gate before they close it or Zehbeh attacks it. Before I go, though, I have one little task."

Conan stared across the serried ranks of the black warriors at Askia, still shouting and orating on the dais. He hefted the javelin.

"A long cast, but I think I can do it," he muttered.

The Cimmerian walked deliberately back to the other side of the roof, then made a short run forward, towards the side facing the square. Just before he reached the edge of the roof, with a mighty whirl of arms and twist of torso, he hurled the weapon. The missile vanished from Amalric's sight into the darkness above. For three heartbeats he wondered whither it had gone.

Askia suddenly screamed and staggered about, the long shaft protruding from his chest and lashing back and forth with the wizard's convulsive movements. As the witch-man collapsed on the dais, Conan snarled:

"Let's go!"

Amalric ran, leaping from roof to roof. To the east, the din of battle rose in a medley of war cries, drumbeats, trumpet calls, screams, and clatter of weapons.

It was not yet midnight when Amalric, Lissa, and Conan reined in their horses on a sandy ridge a mile to the west of Tombalku. They looked back toward the city, now illumined by the lurid glare of a conflagration. Fires had sprung up here and there during the battle, when the Aphaki had swarmed over the eastern wall and fought the black spearmen in the streets. Although the latter were much more numerous, their lack of leaders put them at a disadvantage that all their barbaric valor might not be able to overcome. The Aphaki pressed further and further into the city, while the fires merged into a holocaust.

From the ridge, the hideous clamor of battle and massacre came as a murmur. Conan grunted:

"So much for Tombalku! Whoever wins, we shall have to seek our fortunes elsewhere. I'm for the coast of Kush, where I have friends—and also enemies—and where I can pick up a ship for Argos. What of you?"

"I had not thought," said Amalric.

"That's a shapely filly you have there," said Conan with a grin. The light of the rising moon gleamed on his strong white teeth, shining against his soot-blackened skin. "You can't drag her over the whole wide world."

Amalric felt himself bristle at the Cimmerian's tone. He drew closer to Lissa and slid an arm around her waist, meanwhile dropping his free hand toward his sword hilt. Conan's grin broadened.

"Fear not," he said. "I have never been so hard up for women that I've had to steal those of my friends. If you two come with me, you can beat your way back to Aquilonia."

"I cannot return to Aquilonia," said Amalric.

189

"Why not?"

"My father was slain in a broil with Count Terentius, who is in favor with King Vilerus. So all my father's kin had to flee the land, lest Terentius' agents hunt us down."

"Oh, had you not heard?" said Conan. "Vilerus died within a six-month; his nephew, Numedides, is now king. All the old king's hangers-on, they say, have been dismissed, and the exiles recalled. I got it from a Shemite trader. If I were you, I'd scurry home. The new king should find a worthy post for you. Take your little Lissa along and make her a countess or something. As for me, I'm for Kush and the blue sea."

Amalric glanced back toward the red blaze that had been Tombalku. "Conan," he said, "why did Askia destroy Sakumbe instead of us, with whom he had a more immediate quarrel?"

Conan shrugged his huge shoulders. "Perhaps he had fingernail parings and the like from Sakumbe but not from us. So he worked what spells he could. I have never understood wizardly minds."

"And why did you take the time to kill Askia?"

Conan stared. "Are you joking, Amalric? Me, leave a slain comrade unavenged? Sakumbe, damn his sweaty black hide, was a friend of mine. Even if he got fat and lazy in his late years, he was a better man than most of the white men I have known." The Cimmerian sighed gustily and shook his head, as a lion shakes his mane. "Well, he's dead, and we're alive. If we want to go on being alive, we had better move on before Zehbeh sends a patrol out to hunt for us. Let's go!"

The three horses plodded down the western slope of the sandy ridge and broke into a brisk trot to westward.

The Pool of the Black One

Conan makes his way across the southern grasslands of the black kingdoms. Here he is known of old, and Amra the Lion has no difficulty in making his way to the coast, which he had ravaged in his days with Bêlit. But Bêlit is now only a memory on the Black Coast. The ship that eventually heaves in sight off the headland where Conan sits whetting his sword is manned by pirates of the Baracha Isles, off the coast of Zingara. They, too, have heard of Conan and welcome his sword and experience. He is in his middle thirties when he joins the Barachan pirates, with whom he remains for a considerable time. To Conan, however, accustomed as he is to the tightly organized armies of the Hyborian kings, the organization of the Barachan bands appears so loose that there is small opportunity to rise to leadership and its rewards. Slipping out of an unusually tight spot in the pirate rendezvous at Tortage, he finds that the alternative to a slit throat lies in an attempt to swim the Western Ocean. This he does with complete confidence and perfect aplomb.

Into the west, unknown of man,
Ships have sailed since the world began.
Read, if you dare, what Skelos wrote,
With dead hands fumbling his silken coat;
And follow the ships through the wind-blown wrack—
Follow the ships that come not back.

1.

SANCHA, once of Kordava, yawned daintily, stretched her supple limbs luxuriously, and composed herself more comfortably on the ermine-fringed silk spread on the carack's poop-deck. That the crew watched her with burning interest from waist and forecastle she was lazily aware, just as she was also aware that her short silk kirtle veiled little of her voluptuous contours from their eager eyes. Wherefore she smiled insolently and prepared to snatch a few more winks before the sun, which was just thrusting his golden disk above the ocean, should dazzle her eyes.

But at that instant a sound reached her ears unlike the creaking of timbers, thrum of cordage, and lap of waves. She sat up, her gaze fixed on the rail, over which, to her amazement, a dripping figure clambered. Her dark eyes opened wide, her red lips parted in an O of surprise. The intruder was a stranger to her. Water ran in rivulets from his great shoulders and down his heavy arms. His single garment—a pair of bright crimson silk breeks— was soaking wet, as was his broad gold-buckled girdle and the sheathed sword it supported. As he stood at the rail, the rising sun etched him like a great bronze statue. He ran his fingers through his streaming black mane, and his blue eyes lit as they rested on the girl.

"Who are you?" she demanded. "Whence did you come?"

He made a gesture toward the sea that took in a whole quarter of the compass, while his eyes did not leave her supple figure.

"Are you a merman, that you rise up out of the sea?" she asked, confused by the candor of his gaze, though she was accustomed to admiration.

Before he could reply, a quick step sounded on the boards, and the master of the carack was glaring at the stranger, fingers twitching at a sword-hilt.

192

"Who the devil are you, sirrah?" this one demanded in no friendly tone.

"I am Conan," the other answered inperturbably. Sancha pricked up her ears anew; she had never heard Zingaran spoken with such an accent as the stranger spoke it.

"And how did you get aboard my ship?" The voice grated with suspicion.

"I swam."

"Swam!" exclaimed the master angrily. "Dog, would you jest with me? We are far beyond sight of land. Whence do you come?"

Conan pointed with a muscular brown arm toward the east, banded in dazzling gold by a lifting sun.

"I came from the Islands."

"Oh!" The other regarded him with increased interest. Black brows drew down over scowling eyes, and the thin lip lifted unpleasantly.

"So you are one of those dogs of the Barachans."

A faint smile touched Conan's lips.

"And do you know who I am?" his questioner demanded.

"This ship is the Wastrel; so you must be Zaporavo."

"Aye!" It touched the captain's grim vanity that the man should know him. He was a tall man, tall as Conan, though of leaner build. Framed in his steel morion, his face was dark, saturnine, and hawk-like, wherefore men called him the Hawk. His armor and garments were rich and ornate, after the fashion of a Zingaran grandee. His hand was never far from his sword-hilt.

There was little favor in the gaze he bent on Conan. Little love was lost between the Zingaran renegades and the outlaws who infested the Baracha Islands off the southern coast of Zingara. These men were mostly sailors from Argos, with a sprinkling of other nationalities. They raided the shipping, and harried the Zingaran coast towns, just as the Zingaran buccaneers did, but these dignified their profession by calling themselves Freebooters, while they dubbed the Barachans pirates. They were neither the first nor the last to gild the name of thief.

Some of these thoughts passed through Zaporavo's mind as he toyed with his sword-hilt and scowled at his uninvited guest. Conan gave no hint of what his own thoughts might be. He stood with folded arms as placidly as if upon his own deck; his lips smiled and his eyes were untroubled.

"What are you doing here?" the Freebooter demanded abruptly.

"I found it necessary to leave the rendezvous at Tortage before moonrise last night," answered Conan. "I departed in a leaky boat, and rowed and bailed all night. Just at dawn I saw your topsails, and left the miserable tub to sink, while I made better speed in the water."

"There are sharks in these waters," growled Zaporavo, and was vaguely irritated by the answering shrug of the mighty shoulders. A glance toward the waist showed a screen of eager faces staring upward. A word would send them leaping up on the poop in a storm of swords that would overwhelm even such a fighting-man as the stranger looked to be.

"Why should I burden myself with every nameless vagabond the sea casts up?" snarled Zaporavo, his look and manner more insulting than his words.

"A ship can always use another good sailor," answered the other without resentment. Zaporavo scowled, knowing the truth of that assertion. He hesitated, and doing so, lost his ship, his command, his girl, and his life. But of course he could not see into the future, and to him Conan was only another wastrel, cast up, as he put it, by the sea. He did not like the man; yet the fellow had given him no provocation. His manner was not insolent, though rather more confident than Zaporavo liked to see.

"You'll work for your keep," snarled the Hawk. "Get off the poop. And remember, the only law here is my will."

The smile seemed to broaden on Conan's thin lips. Without hesitation but without haste he turned and descended into the waist. He did not look again at Sancha, who, during the brief conversation, had watched eagerly, all eyes and ears.

As he came into the waist the crew thronged about him—Zingarans, all of them, half naked, their gaudy silk garments splashed with tar, jewels glinting in earrings and dagger-hilts. They were eager for the time-honored sport of baiting the stranger. Here he would be tested, and his future status in the crew decided. Up on the poop Zaporavo had apparently already forgotten the stranger's existence, but Sancha watched, tense with interest. She had become familiar with such scenes, and knew the baiting would be brutal and probably bloody.

But her familiarity with such matters was scanty compared to that of Conan. He smiled faintly as he came into the waist and saw the menacing figures pressing truculently about him. He paused and eyed the ring inscrutably, his composure unshaken. There was a certain code about these things. If he had attacked the captain, the whole crew would have been at this throat, but they would give him a fair chance against the one selected to push the brawl.

The man chosen for this duty thrust himself forward—a wiry brute, with a crimson sash knotted about his head like a turban. His lean chin jutted out, his scarred face was evil beyond belief. Every glance, each swaggering movement was an affront. His way of beginning the baiting was as primitive, raw, and crude as himself.

"Baracha, eh?" he sneered. "That's where they raise dogs for men. We of the Fellowship spit on 'em—like this!"

He spat in Conan's face and snatched at his own sword. The Barachan's movement was too quick for the eye to follow. His sledge-like fist crunched with a terrible impact against his tormenter's jaw, and the Zingaran catapulted through the air and fell in a crumpled heap by the rail.

Conan turned toward the others. But for a slumbering glitter in his eyes, his bearing was unchanged. But the

195

baiting was over as suddenly as it had begun. The seamen lifted their companion; his broken jaw hung slack, his head lolled unnaturally.

"By Mitra, his neck's broken!" swore a black-bearded sea-rogue.

"You Freebooters are a weak-boned race," laughed the pirate. "On the Barachas we take no account of such taps as that. Will you play at sword-strokes, now, any of you? No? Then all's well, and we're friends, eh?"

There were plenty of tongues to assure him that he spoke truth. Brawny arms swung the dead man over the rail, and a dozen fins cut the water as he sank. Conan laughed and spread his mighty arms as a great cat might stretch itself, and his gaze sought the deck above. Sancha leaned over the rail, red lips parted, dark eyes aglow with interest. The sun behind her outlined her lithe figure through the light kirtle which its glow made transparent. Then across her fell Zaporavo's scowling shadow and a heavy hand fell possessively on her slim shoulder. There were menace and meaning in the glare he bent on the man in the waist; Conan grinned back, as if at a jest none knew but himself.

Zaporavo made the mistake so many autocrats make; alone in somber grandeur on the poop, he underestimated the man below him. He had his opportunity to kill Conan, and he let it pass, engrossed in his own gloomy ruminations. He did not find it easy to think any of the dogs beneath his feet constituted a menace to him. He had stood in the high places so long, and had ground so many foes underfoot, that he unconsciously assumed himself to be above the machinations of inferior rivals.

Conan, indeed, gave him no provocation. He mixed with the crew, lived and made merry as they did. He proved himself a skilled sailor, and by far the strongest man any of them had seen. He did the work of three men, and was always first to spring to any heavy or dangerous task. His mates began to rely upon him. He did not quarrel with them, and they were careful not to quarrel with

196

them. He gambled with them, putting up his girdle and sheath for a stake, won their money and weapons, and gave them back with a laugh. The crew instinctively looked toward him as the leader of the forecastle. He vouchsafed no information as to what had caused him to flee the Barachas, but the knowledge that he was capable of a deed bloody enough to have exiled him from that wild band increased the respect felt toward him by the fierce Freebooters. Toward Zaporavo and the mates he was imperturbably courteous, never insolent or servile.

The dullest was struck by the contrast between the harsh, taciturn, gloomy commander, and the pirate whose laugh was gusty and ready, who roared ribald songs in a dozen languages, guzzled ale like a toper, and—apparently—had no thought for the morrow.

Had Zaporavo known he was being compared, even though unconsciously, with a man before the mast, he would have been speechless with amazed anger. But he was engrossed with his broodings, which had become blacker and grimmer as the years crawled by, and with his vague grandiose dreams; and with the girl whose possession was a bitter pleasure, just as all his pleasures were.

And she looked more and more at the black-maned giant who towered among his mates at work or play. He never spoke to her, but there was no mistaking the candor of his gaze. She did not mistake it, and she wondered if she dared the perilous game of leading him on.

No great length of time lay between her and the palaces of Kordava, but it was as if a world of change separated her from the life she had lived before Zaporavo tore her screaming from the flaming caravel his wolves had plundered. She, who had been the spoiled and petted daughter of the Duke of Kordava, learned what it was to be a buccaneer's plaything, and because she was supple enough to bend without breaking, she lived where other women had died, and because she was young and vibrant with life, she came to find pleasure in the existence.

The life was uncertain, dream-like, with sharp contrasts of battle, pillage, murder, and flight, Zaporavo's red visions made it even more uncertain than that of the average Freebooter. No one knew what he planned next. Now they had left all charted coasts behind and were plunging further and further into that unknown, billowy waste ordinarily shunned by seafarers, and into which, since the beginnings of time, ships had ventured, only to vanish from the sight of man for ever. All known lands lay behind them, and day upon day the blue, surging immensity lay empty to their sight. Here there was no loot—no towns to sack nor ships to burn. The men murmured, though they did not let their murmurings reach the ears of their implacable master, who tramped the poop day and night in gloomy majesty, or pored over ancient charts and time-yellowed maps, reading in tomes that were crumbling masses of worm-eaten parchment. At times he talked to Sancha, wildly it seemed to her, of lost continents, and fabulous isles dreaming unguessed amidst the blue foam of nameless gulfs, where horned dragons guarded treasures gathered by pre-human kings, long, long ago.

Sancha listened, uncomprehending, hugging her slim knees, her thoughts constantly roving away from the words of her grim companion back to a clean-limbed bronze giant whose laughter was gusty and elemental as the sea-wind.

So, after many weary weeks, they raised land to westward, and at dawn dropped anchor in a shallow bay, and saw a beach which was like a white band bordering an expanse of gentle grassy slopes, masked by green trees. The wind brought scents of fresh vegetation and spices, and Sancha clapped her hands with glee at the prospect of adventuring ashore. But her eagerness turned to sulkiness when Zaporavo ordered her to remain aboard until he sent for her. He never gave any explanation for his commands; so she never knew his reason, unless it was the lurking devil in him that frequently made him hurt her without cause.

So she lounged sulkily on the poop and watched the

198

men row ashore through the calm water that sparkled like liquid jade in the morning sunlight. She saw them bunch together on the sands, suspicious, weapons ready, while several scattered out through the trees that fringed the beach. Among these, she noted, was Conan. There was no mistaking that tall brown figure with its springy step. Men said he was no civilized man at all, but a Cimmerian, one of those barbaric tribesmen who dwelt in the gray hills of the far North, and whose raids struck terror in the southern neighbors. At least, she knew that there was something about him, some super-vitality or barbarism that set him apart from his wild mates.

Voices echoed along the shore, as the silence reassured the buccaneers. The clusters broke up, as men scattered along the beach in search of fruit. She saw them climbing and plucking among the trees, and her pretty mouth watered. She stamped a little foot and swore with a proficiency acquired by association with her blasphemous companions.

The men on shore had indeed found fruit, and were gorging on it, finding one unknown golden-skinned variety especially luscious. But Zaporavo did not seek or eat fruit. His scouts having found nothing indicating men or beasts in the neighborhood, he stood staring inland, at the long reaches of grassy slopes melting into one another. Then, with a brief word, he shifted his sword-belt and strode in under the trees. His mate expostulated with him against going alone, and was rewarded by a savage blow in the mouth. Zaporavo had his reasons for wishing to go alone. He desired to learn if this island were indeed that mentioned in the mysterious *Book of Skelos*, whereon, nameless sages aver, strange monsters guard crypts filled with hieroglyph-carven gold. Nor, for murky reasons of his own, did he wish to share his knowledge, if it were true, with any one, much less his own crew.

Sancha, watching eagerly from the poop, saw him vanish into the leafy fastness. Presently she saw Conan, the Barachan, turn, glance briefly at the men scattered up and down the beach; then the pirate went quickly in the direction taken by Zaporavo, and likewise vanished among the trees.

Sancha's curiosity was piqued. She waited for them to reappear, but they did not. The seamen still moved aimlessly up and down the beach, and some had wandered inland. Many had lain down in the shade to sleep. Time passed, and she fidgeted about restlessly. The sun began to beat down hotly, in spite of the canopy above the poop-deck. Here it was warm, silent, draggingly monotonous; a few yards away across a band of blue shallow water, the cool shady mystery of tree-fringed beach and woodland-dotted meadow beckoned her. Moreover, the mystery concerning Zaporavo and Conan tempted her.

She well knew the penalty for disobeying her merciless master, and she sat for some time, squirming with indecision. At last she decided that it was worth even one of Zaporavo's whippings to play truant, and with no more ado she kicked off her soft leather sandals, slipped out of her kirtle and stood up on the deck naked as Eve. Clambering over the rail and down the chains, she slid into the water and swam ashore. She stood on the beach a few moments, squirming as the sands tickled her small toes, while she looked for the crew. She saw only a few, at some distance up or down the beach. Many were fast asleep under the trees, bits of golden fruit still clutched in their fingers. She wondered why they should sleep so soundly, so early in the day.

None hailed her as she crossed the white girdle of sand and entered the shade of the woodland. The trees, she found, grew in irregular clusters, and between these groves stretched rolling expanses of meadow-like slopes. As she progressed inland, in the direction taken by Zaporavo, she was entranced by the green vistas that unfolded gently before her, soft slope beyond slope, carpeted with green sward and dotted with groves. Between the slopes lay gentle declivities, likewise swarded. The scenery seemed to melt into itself, or each scene into the other; the view was singular, at once broad and restricted. Over all a dreamy silence lay like an enchantment.

Then she came suddenly onto the level summit of a slope, circled with tall trees, and the dreamily faery-like sensation vanished abruptly at the sight of what lay on the reddened and trampled grass. Sancha involuntarily cried out and recoiled, then stole forward, wide-eyed, trembling in every limb.

It was Zaporavo who lay there on the sward, staring sightlessly upward, a gaping wound in his breast. His sword lay near his nerveless hand. The Hawk had made his last swoop.

It is not to be said that Sancha gazed on the corpse of her lord without emotion. She had no cause to love him, yet she felt at least the sensation any girl might feel when looking on the body of the man who had been first to possess her. She did not weep or feel any need of weeping, but she was seized by a strong trembling, her blood seemed to congeal briefly, and she resisted a wave of hysteria.

She looked about her for the man she expected to see. Nothing met her eyes but the ring of tall, thickly-leafed forest giants, and the blue slopes beyond them. Had the Freebooter's slayer dragged himself away, mortally wounded? No bloody tracks led away from the body.

Puzzled, she swept the surrounding trees, stiffening as she caught a rustle in the emerald leaves that seemed not to be of the wind. She went toward the trees, staring into the leavy depths.

"Conan?" Her call was inquiring; her voice sounded strange and small in the vastness of silence that had grown suddenly tense.

Her knees began to tremble as a nameless panic swept over her.

"Conan!" she cried desperately. "It is I—Sancha! Where are you? Please, Conan——" Her voice faltered away. Unbelieving horror dilated her brown eyes. Her red lips parted to an inarticulate scream. Paralysis gripped

201

her limbs; where she had such desperate need of swift flight, she could not move. She could only shriek wordlessly.

2.

When Conan saw Zaporavo stalk alone into the woodland, he felt that the chance he had watched for had come. He had eaten no fruit, nor joined in the horseplay of his mates; all his faculties were occupied with watching the buccaneer chief. Accustomed to Zaporavo's moods, his men were not particularly surprised that their captain should choose to explore an unknown and probably hostile isle alone. They turned to their own amusement, and did not notice Conan when he glided like a stalking panther after the chieftain.

Conan did not underrate his dominance of the crew. But he had not gained the right, through battle and foray, to challenge the captain to a duel to the death. In these empty seas there had been no opportunity for him to prove himself according to Freebooter law. The crew would stand solidly against him if he attacked the chieftain openly. But he knew that if he killed Zaporavo without their knowledge, the leaderless crew would not be likely to be swayed by loyalty to a dead man. In such wolfpacks only the living counted.

So he followed Zaporavo with sword in hand and eagerness in his heart, until he came out onto a level summit, circled with tall trees, between whose trunks he saw the green vistas of the slopes melting into the blue distance. In the midst of the glade Zaporavo, sensing pursuit, turned, hand on hilt.

The buccaneer swore.

"Dog, why do you follow me?"

"Are you mad, to ask?" laughed Conan, coming swiftly toward his erstwhile chief. His lips smiled, and in his blue eyes danced a wild gleam.

Zaporavo ripped out his sword with a black curse, and steel clashed against steel as the Barachan came in recklessly and wide open, his blade singing a wheel of blue flame about his head.

Zaporavo was the veteran of a thousand fights by sea and by land. There was no man in the world more deeply and thoroughly versed than he in the lore of swordcraft. But he had never been pitted against a blade wielded by thews bred in the wild lands beyond the borders of civilization. Against his fighting-craft was matched blinding speed and strength impossible to a civilized man. Conan's manner of fighting was unorthodox, but instinctive and natural as that of a timber wolf. The intricacies of the sword were as useless against his primitive fury as a human boxer's skill against the onslaughts of a panther.

Fighting as he had never fought before, straining every last ounce of effort to parry the blade that flickered like lightning about his head, Zaporavo in desperation caught a full stroke near his hilt, and felt his whole arm go numb beneath the terrific impact. That stroke was instantly followed by a thrust with such terrible drive behind it that the sharp point ripped through chain-mail and ribs like paper, to transfix the heart beneath. Zaporavo's lips writhed in brief agony, but, grim to the last, he made no sound. He was dead before his body relaxed on the trampled grass, where blood drops glittered like spilt rubies in the sun.

Conan shook the red drops from his sword, grinned with unaffected pleasure, stretched like a huge cat—and abruptly stiffened, the expression of satisfaction on his face being replaced by a stare of bewilderment. He stood like a statue, his sword trailing in his hand.

As he lifted his eyes from his vanquished foe, they had absently rested on the surrounding trees, and the vistas beyond. And he had seen a fantastic thing—a thing incredible and inexplicable. Over the soft, rounded green shoulder of a distant slope had loped a tall black naked figure, bearing on its shoulder an equally naked white form. The apparition vanished as suddenly as it had appeared, leaving the watcher gasping in surprise.

The pirate stared about him, glanced uncertainly back

the way he had come, and swore. He was nonplussed—a bit upset, if the term might be applied to one of such steely nerves as his. In the midst of realistic, if exotic surroundings, a vagrant image of fantasy and nightmare had been introduced. Conan doubted neither his eyesight nor his sanity. He had seen something alien and uncanny, he knew; the mere fact of a black figure racing across the landscape carrying a white captive was bizarre enough, but this black figure had been unnaturally tall.

Shaking his head doubtfully, Conan started off in the direction in which he had seen the thing. He did not argue the wisdom of his move; with his curiosity so piqued, he had no choice but to follow its promptings.

Slope after slope he traversed, each with its even sward and clustered groves. The general trend was always upward, though he ascended and descended the gentle inclines with monotonous regularity. The array of rounded shoulders and shallow declivities was bewildering and apparently endless. But at last he advanced up what he believed was the highest summit on the island, and halted at the sight of green shining walls and towers, which, until he had reached the spot on which he then stood, had merged so perfectly with the green landscape as to be invisible, even to his keen sight.

He hesitated, fingered his sword, then went forward, bitten by the worm of curiosity. He saw no one as he approached a tall archway in the curving wall, there was no door. Peering warily through, he saw what seemed to be a broad open court, grass-carpeted, surrounded by a circular wall of the green semi-translucent substance. Various arches opened from it. Advancing on the balls of his bare feet, sword ready, he chose one of these arches at random, and passed into another similar court. Over an inner wall he saw the pinnacles of strangely shaped tower-like structures. One of these towers was built in, or projected into the court in which he found himself, and a broad stair led up to it, along the side of the wall. Up this he went, wondering if it were all real, or if he were not in the midst of a black lotus dream.

At the head of the stair he found himself on a walled ledge, or balcony, he was not sure which. He could now make out more details of the towers, but they were meaningless to him. He realized uneasily that no ordinary human beings could have built them. There was symmetry about their architecture, and system, but it was a mad symmetry, a system alien to human sanity. As for the plan of the whole town, castle, or whatever it was intended for, he could see just enough to get the impression of a great number of courts, mostly circular, each surrounded by its own wall, and connected with the others by open arches, and all, apparently, grouped about the cluster of fantastic towers in the center.

Turning in the other direction from these towers, he got a fearful shock, and crouched down suddenly behind the parapet of the balcony, glaring amazedly.

The balcony or ledge was higher than the opposite wall, and he was looking over that wall into another swarded court. The inner curve of the further wall of that court differed from the others he had seen, in that, instead of being smooth, it seemed to be banded with long lines or ledges, crowded with small objects the nature of which he could not determine.

However, he gave little heed to the wall at the time. His attention was centered on the band of beings that squatted about a dark green pool in the midst of the court. These creatures were black and naked, made like men, but the least of them, standing upright, would have towered head and shoulders above the tall pirate. They were rangy rather than massive, but were finely formed, with no suggestion of deformity or abnormality, save as their great height was abnormal. But even at that distance Conan sensed the basic diabolism of their features.

In the midst, cringing and naked, stood a youth that Conan recognized as the youngest sailor aboard the *Wastrel*. He, then, had been the captive the pirate had seen borne across the grass-covered slope. Conan had heard no sound of fighting—saw no bloodstains or wounds on the sleek ebon limbs of the giants. Evidently the lad had wandered inland away from his companions and been snatched up by a black man lurking in ambush. Conan mentally termed the creatures black men, for lack of a better term; instinctively he knew these tall ebony beings were not men, as he understood the term.

No sound came to him. The blacks nodded and gestured to one another, but they did not seem to speak—vocally, at least. One, squatting on his haunches before the cringing boy, held a pipe-like thing in his hand. This he set to his lips, and apparently blew, though Conan heard no sound. But the Zingaran youth heard or felt, and cringed. He quivered and writhed as if in agony; a regularity became evident in the twitching of his limbs, which quickly became rhythmic. The twitching became a violent jerking, the jerking regular movements. The youth began to dance, as cobras dance by compulsion to the tune of the fakir's fife. There was naught of zest or joyful abandon in that dance. There was, indeed, abandon that was awful to see, but it was not joyful. It was as if the mute tune of the pipes grasped the boy's inmost soul with salacious fingers and with brutal torture wrung from it every involuntary expression of secret passion. It was a convulsion of obscenity, a spasm of lasciviousness—an exudation of secret hungers framed by compulsion: desire without pleasure, pain mated awfully to lust. It was like watching a soul stripped naked, and all its dark and unmentionable secrets laid bare.

Conan glared, frozen with repulsion and shaken with nausea. Himself as cleanly elemental as a timber wolf, he was yet not ignorant of the perverse secrets of rotting civilizations. He had roamed the cities of Zamora, and known the women of Shadizar the Wicked. But he sensed here a cosmic vileness transcending mere human degeneracy—a perverse branch on the tree of Life, developed along lines outside human comprehension. It was not at the agonized contortions and posturing of the wretched boy that he was shocked, but at the cosmic obscenity of these beings which could drag to light the abysmal secrets that sleep in the unfathomed darkness of the human soul, and find pleasure in the brazen flaunting of such things as should not be hinted at, even in restless nightmares.

Suddenly the black torturer laid down the pipes and rose, towering over the writhing white figure. Brutally grasping the boy by neck and haunch, the giant up-ended him and thrust him head-first into the green pool. Conan saw the white glimmer of his naked body amid the green water, as the black giant held his captive deep under the surface. Then there was a restless movement among the other blacks, and Conan ducked quickly below the balcony wall, not daring to raise his head lest he be seen.

After a while his curiosity got the better of him, and he cautiously peered out again. The blacks were filing out of an archway into another court. One of them was just placing something on a ledge of the further wall, and Conan saw it was the one who had tortured the boy. He was taller than the others, and wore a jeweled headband. Of the Zingaran boy there was no trace. The giant followed his fellows, and presently Conan saw them emerge from the archway by which he had gained access to the castle of horror, and file away across the green slopes, in the direction from which he had come. They bore no arms, yet he felt that they planned further aggression against the Freebooters.

But before he went to warn the unsuspecting buccaneers, he wished to investigate the fate of the boy. No sound disturbed the quiet. The pirate believed that the towers and courts were deserted save for himself.

He went swiftly down the stair, crossed the court and passed through an arch into the court the blacks had just quitted. Now he saw the nature of the striated wall. It was banded by narrow ledges, apparently cut out of the solid stone, and ranged along these ledges or shelves were thousands of tiny figures, mostly grayish in color. These figures, not much longer than a man's hand, represented men, and so cleverly were they made that Conan recog-

207

nized various racial characteristics in the different idols, features typical of Zingarans, Argosseans, Ophireans, and Kushite corsairs. These last were black in color, just as their models were black in reality. Conan was aware of a vague uneasiness as he stared at the dumb, sightless figures. There was a mimicry of reality about them that was somehow disturbing. He felt of them gingerly and could not decide of what material they were made. It felt like petrified bone; but he could not imagine petrified substance being found in the locality in such abundance as to be used so lavishly.

He noticed that the images representing types with which he was familiar were all on the higher ledges. The lower ledges were occupied by figures the features of which were strange to him. They either embodied merely the artists' imagination, or typified racial types long vanished and forgotten.

Shaking his head impatiently, Conan turned toward the pool. The circular court offered no place of concealment; as the body of the boy was nowhere in sight, it must be lying at the bottom of the pool.

Approaching the placid green disk, he stared into the glimmering surface. It was like looking through a thick green glass, unclouded, yet strangely illusory. Of no great dimensions, the pool was round as a well, bordered by a rim of green jade. Looking down, he could see the rounded bottom—how far below the surface he could not decide. But the pool seemed incredibly deep—he was aware of a dizziness as he looked down, much as if he were looking into an abyss. He was puzzled by his ability to see the bottom; but it lay beneath his gaze, impossibly remote, illusive, shadowy, yet visible. At times he thought a faint luminosity was apparent deep in the jade-colored depth, but he could not be sure. Yet he was sure that the pool was empty except for the shimmering water.

Then where in the name of Crom was the boy whom he had seen brutally drowned in that pool? Rising, Conan fingered his sword, and gazed around the court again. His gaze focussed on a spot on one of the higher ledges.

There he had seen the tall black place something—cold sweat broke suddenly out on Conan's brown hide.

Hesitantly, yet as if drawn by a magnet, the pirate approached the shimmering wall. Dazed by a suspicion too monstrous to voice, he glared up at the last figure on that ledge. A horrible familiarity made itself evident. Stony, immobile, dwarfish, yet unmistakable, the features of of the Zingaran boy stared unseeingly at him. Conan recoiled, shaken to his soul's foundations. His sword trailed in his paralyzed hand as he glared, openmouthed, stunned by the realization which was too abysmal and awful for the mind to grasp.

Yet the fact was indisputable; the secret of the dwarfish images was revealed, though behind that secret lay the darker and more cryptic secret of their being.

3.

How long Conan stood drowned in dizzy cogitation, he never knew. A voice shook him out of his gaze, a feminine voice that shrieked more and more loudly, as if the owner of the voice were being borne nearer. Conan recognized that voice, and his paralysis vanished instantly.

A quick bound carried him high up on the narrow ledges, where he clung, kicking aside the clustering images to obtain room for his feet. Another spring and a scramble, and he was clinging to the rim of the wall, glaring over it. It was an outer wall; he was looking into the green meadow that surrounded the castle.

Across the grassy level a giant black was striding, carrying a squirming captive under one arm as a man might carry a rebellious child. It was Sancha, her black hair falling in disheveled rippling waves, her olive skin contrasting abruptly with the glossy ebony of her captor. He gave no heed to her wrigglings and cries as he made for the outer archway.

As he vanished within, Conan sprang recklessly down the wall and glided into the arch that opened into the further court. Crouching there, he saw the giant enter the court of the pool, carrying his writhing captive. Now he was able to make out the creature's details.

The superb symmetry of body and limbs was more impressive at close range. Under the ebon skin long, rounded muscles rippled, and Conan did not doubt that the monster could rend an ordinary man limb from limb. The nails of the fingers provided further weapons, for they were grown like the talons of a wild beast. The face was a carven ebony mask. The eyes were tawny, a vibrant gold that glowed and glittered. But the face was in-human; each line, each feature was stamped with evil—evil transcending the mere evil of humanity. The thing was not a human—it could not be; it was a growth of life from the pits of blasphemous creation—a perversion of evolutionary development.

The giant cast Sancha down on the sward, where she grovelled, crying with pain and terror. He cast a glance about as if uncertain, and his tawny eyes narrowed as they rested on the images overturned and knocked from the wall. Then he stooped, grasped his captive by her neck and crotch, and strode purposefully toward the green pool. And Conan glided from his archway, and raced like a wind of death across the sward.

The giant wheeled, and his eyes flared as he saw the bronzed avenger rushing toward him. In the instant of surprise his cruel grip relaxed, and Sancha wriggled from his hands and fell to the grass. The taloned hands spread and clutched, but Conan ducked beneath their swoop and drove his sword through the giant's groin. The black went down like a felled tree, gushing blood, and the next instant Conan was seized in a frantic grasp as Sancha sprang up and threw her arms around him in a frenzy of terror and hysterical relief.

He cursed as he disengaged himself, but his foe was already dead; the tawny eyes were glazed, the long ebony limbs had ceased to twitch.

"Oh, Conan," Sancha was sobbing, clinging tenaciously to him, "what will become of us? What are these monsters? Oh, surely this is Hell and that was the Devil——"

"Then Hell needs a new devil," the Barachan grinned fiercely. "But how did he get hold of you? Have they taken the ship?"

"I don't know." She tried to wipe away her tears, fumbled for her skirt, and then remembered that she wore none. "I came ashore. I saw you follow Zaporavo, and I followed you both. I found Zaporavo—was—was it you who——"

"Who else?" he grunted. "What then?"

"I saw a movement in the trees," she shuddered. "I thought it was you. I called—then I saw that—that black *thing* squatting like an ape among the branches, leering down at me. It was like a nightmare; I couldn't run. All I could do was squeal. Then it dropped from the tree and seized me—oh, oh, oh!" She hid her face in her hand, and was shaken anew at the memory of the horror.

"Well, we've got to get out of here," he growled, catching her wrist. "Come on; we've got to get to the crew——"

"Most of them were asleep on the beach as I entered the woods," she said.

"Asleep?" he exclaimed profanely. "What in the seven devils of Hell's fire and damnation——"

"Listen!" She froze, a white quivering image of fright.

"I heard it!" he snapped. "A moaning cry! Wait!"

He bounded up the ledges again and, glaring over the wall, swore with a concentrated fury that made even Sancha gasp. The black men were returning, but they came not alone or empty-handed. Each bore a limp human form; some bore two. Their captives were the Freebooters; they hung slackly in their captor's arms, and but for an occasional vague movement or twitching, Conan would have believed them dead. They had been disarmed but not stripped; one of the blacks bore their sheathed swords, a great armload of bristling steel. From time to time one of the seamen voiced a vague cry, like a drunkard calling out in scottish sleep.

Like a trapped wolf Conan glared about him. Three arches led out of the court of the pool. Through the eastern arch the blacks had left the court, and through it

211

they would presumably return. He had entered by the southern arch. In the western arch he had hidden, and had not had time to notice what lay beyond it. Regardless of his ignorance of the plan of the castle, he was forced to make his decision promptly.

Springing down the wall, he replaced the images with frantic haste, dragged the corpse of his victim to the pool and cast it in. It sank instantly and, as he looked, he distinctly saw an appalling contraction—a shrinking, a hardening. He hastily turned away, shuddering. Then he seized his companion's arm and led her hastily toward the southern archway, while she begged to be told what was happening.

"They've bagged the crew," he answered hastily. "I haven't any plan, but we'll hide somewhere and watch. If they don't look in the pool, they may not suspect our presence."

"But they'll see the blood on the grass!"

"Maybe they'll think one of their own devils spilled it," he answered. "Anyway, we'll have to take the chance."

They were in the court from which he had watched the torture of the boy, and he led her hastily up the stair that mounted the southern wall, and forced her into a crouching position behind the balustrade of the balcony; it was poor concealment, but the best they could do.

Scarcely had they settled themselves, when the blacks filed into the court. There was a resounding clash at the foot of the stairs, and Conan stiffened, grasping his sword. But the blacks passed through an archway on the southwestern side, and they heard a series of thuds and groans. The giants were casting their victims down on the sward. A hysterical giggle rose to Sancha's lips, and Conan quickly clapped his hand over her mouth, stifling the sound before it could betray them.

After awhile they heard the padding of many feet on the sward below, and then silence reigned. Conan peered over the wall. The court was empty. The blacks were once more gathered about the pool in the adjoining court, squatting on their haunches. They seemed to pay no heed to the great smears of blood on the sward and the jade rim of the pool. Evidently bloodstains were nothing unusual. Nor were they looking into the pool. They were engrossed in some inexplicable conclave of their own; the tall black was playing again on his golden pipes, and his companions listened like ebony statues.

Taking Sancha's hand, Conan glided down the stair, stooping so that his head would not be visible above the wall. The cringing girl followed perforce, staring fearfully at the arch that let into the court of the pool, but through which, at that angle, neither the pool nor its grim throng were visible. At the foot of the stair lay the swords of the Zingarans. The clash they had heard had been the casting down of the captured weapons.

Conan drew Sancha toward the southwestern arch, and they silently crossed the sward and entered the court beyond. There the Freebooters lay in careless heaps, mustaches bristling, earrings glinting. Here and there one stirred or groaned restlessly. Conan bent down to them, and Sancha knelt beside him, leaning forward with her hands on her thighs.

"What is that sweet cloying smell?" she asked nervously. "It's on all their breaths."

"It's that damned fruit they were eating," he answered softly. "I remember the smell of it. It must have been like the black lotus, that makes men sleep. By Crom, they are beginning to awake—but they're unarmed, and I have an idea that those black devils won't wait long before they begin their magic on them. What chance will the lads have, unarmed and stupid with slumber?"

He brooded for an instant, scowling with the intentness of his thoughts; then he seized Sancha's olive shoulder in a grip that made her wince.

"Listen! I'll draw those black swine into another part of the castle and keep them busy for awhile. Meanwhile you shake these fools awake, and bring their swords to them—it's a fighting chance. Can you do it?"

"I—I—don't know!" she stammered, shaking with terror, and hardly knowing what she was saying.

With a curse Conan caught her thick tresses near her head and shook her until the walls danced to her dizzy sight.

"You *must* do it!" he hissed. "It's our only chance!"

"I'll do my best!" she gasped, and with a grunt of commendation and an encouraging slap on the back that nearly knocked her down, he glided away.

A few moments later he was crouching at the arch that opened into the court of the pool, glaring upon his enemies. They still sat about the pool, but were beginning to show evidences of an evil impatience. From the court where lay the rousing buccaneers he heard their groans growing louder, beginning to be mingled with incoherent curses. He tensed his muscles and sank into a pantherish crouch, breathing easily between his teeth.

The jeweled giant rose, taking his pipes from his lips —and at that instant Conan was among the startled blacks with a tigerish bound. And as a tiger leaps and strikes among his prey, Conan leaped and struck: thrice his blade flickered before any could life a hand in defense; then he bounded from among them and raced across the sward. Behind him sprawled three black figures, their skulls split.

But though the unexpected fury of his surprise had caught the giants off guard, the survivors recovered quickly enough. They were at his heels as he ran through the western arch, their longs legs sweeping them over the ground at headlong speed. However, he felt confident of his ability to outfoot them at will; but that was not his purpose. He intended leading them on a long chase, in order to give Sancha time to rouse and arm the Zingarans.

And as he raced into the court beyond the western arch, he swore. This court differed from the others he had seen. Instead of being round, it was octagonal and the arch by which he had entered was the only entrance or exit.

Wheeling, he saw that the entire band had followed

him in; a group clustered in the arch, and the rest spread out in a wide line as they approached. He faced them, backing slowly toward the northern wall. The line bent into a semicircle, spreading out to hem him in. He continued to move backward, but more and more slowly, noting the spaces widening between the pursuers. They feared lest he should try to dart around a horn of the crescent, and lengthened their line to prevent it.

He watched with the calm alertness of a wolf, and when he struck it was with the devastating suddenness of a thunderbolt—full at the center of the crescent. The giant who barred his way went down cloven to the middle of the breastbone, and the pirate was outside their closing ring before the blacks to right and left could come to their stricken comrade's aid. The group at the gate prepared to receive his onslaught, but Conan did not charge them. He had turned and was watching his hunters without apparent emotion, and certainly without fear.

This time they did not spread out in a thin line. They had learned that it was fatal to divide their forces against such an incarnation of clawing, rending fury. They bunched up in a compact mass, and advanced on him without undue haste, maintaining their formation.

Conan knew that if he fell foul of that mass of taloned muscle and bone, there could be but one culmination. Once let them drag him down among them where they could reach him with their talons and use their greater body-weight to advantage, even his primitive ferocity would not prevail. He glanced around the wall and saw a ledge-like projection above a corner on the western side. What it was he did not know, but it would serve his purpose. He began backing toward that corner, and the giants advanced more rapidly. They evidently thought that they were herding him into the corner themselves, and Conan found time to reflect that they probably looked on him as a member of a lower order, mentally inferior to themselves. So much the better. Nothing is more disastrous than underrating one's antagonist.

Now he was only a few yards from the wall, and the

blacks were closing in rapidly, evidently thinking to pin him in the corner before he realized his situation. The group at the gate had deserted their post and were hastening to join their fellows. The giants half crouched, eyes blazing like golden hell-fire, teeth glistening whitely, taloned hands lifted as if to fend off attack. They expected an abrupt and violent move on the part of their prey, but when it came, it took them by surprise.

Conan lifted his sword, took a step toward them, then wheeled and raced to the wall. With a fleeting coil and release of steel muscles, he shot high in the air, and his straining arm hooked its fingers over the projection. Instantly there was a rending crash and the jutting ledge gave way, precipitating the pirate back into the court.

He hit on his back, which for all its springy sinews would have broken but for the cushioning of the sward, and rebounding like a great cat, he faced his foes. The dancing recklessness was gone from his eyes. They blazed like blue balefire; his mane bristled, his thin lips snarled. In an instant the affair had changed from a daring game to a battle of life and death, and Conan's savage nature responded with all the fury of the wild.

The blacks, halted an instant by the swiftness of the episode, now made to sweep on him and drag him down. But in that instant a shout broke the stillness. Wheeling, the giants saw a disreputable throng crowding the arch. The buccaneers weaved drunkenly, they swore incoherently; they were addled and bewildered, but they grasped their swords and advanced with a ferocity not dimmed in the slightest by the fact that they did not understand what it was all about.

As the blacks glared in amazement, Conan yelled stridently and struck them like a razor-edged thunderbolt. They fell like ripe grain beneath his blade, and the Zingarans, shouting with muddled fury, ran groggily across the court and fell on their gigantic foes with bloodthirsty zeal. They were still dazed; emerging hazily from drugged slumber, they had felt Sancha frantically shaking them and shoving swords into their fists, and had vaguely heard

216

her urging them to some sort of action. They had not understood all she said, but the sight of strangers, and blood streaming, was enough for them.

In an instant the court was turned into a battleground which soon resembled a slaughterhouse. The Zingarans weaved and rocked on their feet, but they wielded their swords with power and effect, swearing prodigiously, and quite oblivious to all wounds except those instantly fatal. They far outnumbered the blacks, but these proved themselves no mean antagonists. Towering above their assailants, the giants wrought havoc with talons and teeth, tearing out men's throats, and dealing blows with clenched fists that crushed in skulls. Mixed and mingled in that mêlée, the buccaneers could not use their superior agility to the best advantage, and many were too stupid from their drugged sleep to avoid blows aimed at them. They fought with a blind wild-beast ferocity, too intent on dealing death to evade it. The sound of the hacking swords was like that of butchers' cleavers, and the shrieks, yells and curses were appalling.

Sancha, shrinking in the archway, was stunned by the noise and fury; she got a dazed impression of a whirling chaos in which steel flashed and hacked, arms tossed, snarling faces appeared and vanished, and straining bodies collided, rebounded, locked and mingled in a devil's dance of madness.

Details stood out briefly, like black etchings on a background of blood. She saw a Zingaran sailor, blinded by a great flap of scalp torn loose and hanging over his eyes, brace his straddling legs and drive his sword to the hilt in a black belly. She distinctly heard the buccaneer grunt as he struck, and saw the victim's tawny eyes roll up in sudden agony as blood and entrails gushed out over the driven blade. The dying black caught the blade with his naked hands, and the sailor tugged blindly and stupidly; then a black arm hooked about the Zingaran's head, a black knee was planted with cruel force in the middle of his back. His head was jerked back at a terrible angle, and something cracked above the noise of the fray, like the breaking of a thick branch. The conqueror dashed his victim's body to the earth—and as he did, something like a beam of blue light flashed across his shoulders from behind, from right to left. He staggered, his head toppled forward on his breast, and thence, hideously, to the earth.

Sancha turned sick. She gagged and wished to vomit. She made abortive efforts to turn and flee from the spectacle, but her legs would not work. Nor could she close her eyes. In fact, she opened them wider. Revolted, repelled, nauseated, yet she felt the awful fascination she had always experienced at sight of blood. Yet this battle transcended anything she had ever seen fought out between human beings in port raids or sea battles. Then she saw Conan.

Separated from his mates by the whole mass of the enemy, Conan had been enveloped in a black wave of arms and bodies, and dragged down. Then they would quickly have stamped the life out of him, but he had pulled down one of them with him, and the black's body protected that of the pirate beneath him. They kicked and tore at the Barachan and dragged at their writhing comrade, but Conan's teeth were set desperately in his throat, and the pirate clung tenaciously to his dying shield.

An onslaught of Zingarans caused a slackening of the press, and Conan threw aside the corpse and rose, bloodsmeared and terrible. The giants towered above him like great black shadows, clutching, buffeting the air with terrible blows. But he was as hard to hit or grapple as a blood-mad panther, and at every turn or flash of his blade, blood jetted. He had already taken punishment enough to kill three ordinary men, but his bull-like vitality was undiminished.

His war cry rose above the medley of the carnage, and the bewildered but furious Zingarans took fresh heart and redoubled their strokes, until the rending of flesh and the crunching of bone beneath the swords almost drowned the howls of pain and wrath.

218

The blacks wavered, and broke for the gate, and Sancha squealed at their coming and scurried out of the way. They jammed in the narrow archway, and the Zingarans stabbed and hacked at their straining backs with strident yelps of glee. The gate was a shambles before the survivors broke through and scattered, each for himself.

The battle became a chase. Across grassy courts, up shimmering stairs, over the slanting roofs of fantastic towers, even along the broad coping of the walls, the giants fled, dripping blood at each step, harried by their merciless pursuers as by wolves. Cornered, some of them turned at bay and men died. But the ultimate result was always the same—a mangled black body twitching on the sward, or hurled writhing and twisting from parapet or tower roof.

Sancha had taken refuge in the court of the pool, where she crouched, shaking with terror. Outside rose a fierce yelling, feet pounded the sward, and through the arch burst a red-stained black figure. It was the giant who wore the gemmed headband. A squat pursuer was close behind, and the black turned, at the very brink of the pool. In his extremity he had picked up a sword dropped by a dying sailor, and as the Zingaran rushed recklessly at him, he struck with the unfamiliar weapon. The buccaneer dropped with his skull crushed, but so awkwardly the blow was dealt, the blade shivered in this last surviving giant's hand.

He hurled the hilt at the figures which thronged the arch, and bounded toward the pool, his face a convulsed mask of hate. Conan burst through the men at the gate, and his feet spurned the sward in his headlong charge.

But the giant threw his great arms wide and from his lips rang an inhuman cry—the only sound made by a black during the entire fight. It screamed to the sky its awful hate; it was like a voice howling from the pits. At the sound the Zingarans faltered and hesitated. But Conan did not pause. Silently and murderously he drove at the ebon figure poised on the brink of the pool.

But even as his dripping sword gleamed in the air,

the black wheeled and bounded high. For a flash of an instant they saw him poised in midair above the pool; then with an earth-shaking roar, the green waters rose and rushed up to meet him, enveloping him in a green volcano.

Conan checked his headlong rush just in time to keep from toppling into the pool, and he sprang back, thrusting his men behind him with mighty swings of his arms. The green pool was like a geyser now, the noise rising to deafening volume as the great column of water reared and reared, blossoming at the crest with a great crown of foam.

Conan was driving his men to the gate, herding them ahead of him, beating them with the flat of his sword; the roar of the water-spout seemed to have robbed them of their faculties. Seeing Sancha standing paralyzed, staring with wide-eyed terror at the seething pillar, he accosted her with a bellow that cut through the thunder of the water and made her jump out of her daze. She ran to him, arms outstretched, and he caught her up under one arm and raced out of the court.

In the court which opened on the outer world, the survivors had gathered, weary, tattered, wounded, and blood-stained, and stood gaping dumbly at the great unstable pillar that towered momentarily nearer the blue vault of the sky. Its green trunk was laced with white; its foaming crown was thrice the circumference of its base. Momentarily it threatened to burst and fall in an engulfing torrent, yet it continued to jet skyward.

Conan's eyes swept the bloody, tattered group, and he cursed to see only a score. In the stress of the moment he grasped a corsair by the neck and shook him so violently that blood from the man's wounds spattered all near them.

"Where are the rest?" he bellowed in his victim's ear.

"That's all!" the other yelled back, above the roar of the geyser. "The others were all killed by those black——"

"Well, get out of here!" roared Conan, giving him a thrust that sent him staggering headlong toward the outer archway. "That fountain is going to burst in a moment——"

"We'll all be drowned!" squawked a Freebooter, limping toward the arch.

"Drowned, Hell!" yelled Conan. "We'll be turned to pieces of petrified bone! Get out, blast you!"

He ran to the outer archway, one eye on the green roaring tower that loomed so awfully above him, the other on stragglers. Dazed with blood-lust, fighting, and the thunderous noise, some of the Zingarans moved like men in a trance. Conan hurried them up; his method was simple. He grasped loiterers by the scruff of the neck, impelled them violently through the gate, added impetus with a lusty kick in the rear, spicing his urgings for haste with pungent comments on the victim's ancestry. Sancha showed an inclination to remain with him, but he jerked away her twining arms, blaspheming luridly, and accelerated her movements with a tremendous slap on the posterior that sent her scurrying across the plateau.

Conan did not leave the gate until he was sure all his men who yet lived were out of the castle and started across the level meadow. Then he glanced again at the roaring pillar looming against the sky, dwarfing the towers, and he too fled that castle of nameless horrors.

The Zingarans had already crossed the rim of the plateau and were fleeing down the slopes. Sancha waited for him at the crest of the first slope beyond the rim, and there he paused for an instant to look back at the castle. It was as if a gigantic green-stemmed and white-blossomed flower swayed above the towers, the roar filled the sky. Then the jade-green and snowy pillar broke with a noise like the rending of the skies, and walls and towers were blotted out in a thunderous torrent.

Conan caught the girl's hand, and fled. Slope after slope rose and fell before them, and behind sounded the rushing of a river. A glance over his straining shoulder showed a broad green ribbon rising and falling as it swept over the slopes. The torrent had not spread out and dissipated; like a giant serpent it flowed over the

221

depressions and the rounded crests. It held a consistent course—*it was following them.*

The realization roused Conan to a greater pitch of endurance. Sancha stumbled and went to her knees with a moaning cry of despair and exhaustion. Catching her up, Conan tossed her over his giant shoulder and ran on. His breast heaved, his knees trembled; his breath tore in great gasps through his teeth. He reeled in his gait. Ahead of him he saw the sailors toiling, spurred on by the terror that gripped him.

The ocean burst suddenly on his view, and in his swimming gaze floated the *Wastrel,* unharmed. Men tumbled into the boats helter-skelter. Sancha fell into the bottom and lay there in a crumpled heap. Conan, though the blood thundered in his ears and the world swam red to his gaze, took an oar with the panting sailors.

With hearts ready to burst from exhaustion, they pulled for the ship. The green river burst through the fringe of trees. Those trees fell as if their stems had been cut away, and as they sank into the jade-colored flood, they vanished. The tide flowed out over the beach, lapped at the ocean, and the waves turned a deeper, more sinister green.

Unreasoning, instinctive fear held the buccaneers, making them urge their agonized bodies and reeling brains to greater effort; what they feared they knew not, but they did know that in that abominable smooth green ribbon was a menace to body and to soul. Conan knew, and as he saw the broad line slip into the waves and stream through the water toward them, without altering its shape or course, he called up his last ounce of reserve strength so fiercely that the oar snapped in his hands.

But their prows bumped against the timbers of the *Wastrel,* and the sailors staggered up the chains, leaving the boats to drift as they would. Sancha went up on Conan's broad shoulder, hanging limp as a corpse, to be dumped unceremoniously on to the deck as the Barachan took the wheel, gasping orders to his skeleton of a crew.

Throughout the affair, he had taken the lead without question, and they had instinctively followed him. They reeled about like drunken men, fumbling mechanically at ropes and braces. The anchor chain, unshackled, splashed into the water, the sails unfurled and bellied in a rising wind. The *Wastrel* quivered and shook herself, and swung majestically seaward. Conan glared shoreward; like a tongue of emerald flame, a ribbon licked out on the water futilely, an oar's length from the *Wastrel*'s keel. It advanced no further. From that end of the tongue, his gaze followed an unbroken stream of lambent green across the white beach, and over the slopes, until it faded in the blue distance.

The Barachan, regaining his wind, grinned at the panting crew. Sancha was standing near him, hysterical tears coursing down her cheeks. Conan's breeks hung in bloodstained tatters; his girdle and sheath were gone, his sword, driven upright into the deck beside him, was notched and crusted with red. Blood thickly clotted his black mane, and one ear had been half torn from his head. His arms, legs, breast and shoulders were bitten and clawed as if by panthers. But he grinned as he braced his powerful legs, and swung on the wheel in sheer exuberance of muscular might.

"What now?" faltered the girl.

"The plunder of the seas!" he laughed. "A paltry crew, and that chewed and clawed to pieces, but they can work the ship, and crews can always be found. Come here, girl, and give me a kiss."

"A kiss?" she cried hysterically. "You think of kisses at a time like this?"

His laughter boomed above the snap and thunder of the sails, as he caught her up off her feet in the crook of one mighty arm, and smacked her red lips with resounding relish.

"I think of Life!" he roared. "The dead are dead, and what has passed is done! I have a ship and a fighting crew and a girl with lips like wine, and that's all I ever asked.

Lick your wounds, bullies, and break out a cask of ale. You're going to work ship as she never was worked before. Dance and sing while you buckle to it, damn you! To the Devil with empty seas! We're bound for waters where the seaports are fat, and the merchant ships are crammed with plunder!"